SNOW ANGELS AT GOLDEN SANDS BAY

THE GOLDEN SANDS BAY SERIES - BOOK FIVE

GEORGINA TROY

Boldwood

First published in Great Britain in 2023 by Boldwood Books Ltd.

Copyright © Georgina Troy, 2023

Cover Design by Alexandra Allden

Cover Illustration: Shutterstock

A CIP catalogue record for this book is available from the British Library.

Paperback ISBN 978-1-80426-097-5

Large Print ISBN 978-1-80426-098-2

Hardback ISBN 978-1-80426-099-9

Ebook ISBN 978-1-80426-096-8

Kindle ISBN 978-1-80426-095-1

Audio CD ISBN 978-1-80426-104-0

MP3 CD ISBN 978-1-80426-103-3

Digital audio download ISBN 978-1-80426-102-6

Boldwood Books Ltd
23 Bowerdean Street
London SW6 3TN
www.boldwoodbooks.com

To my dearest cousin Peter James Le Lievre, who is always in our hearts, our minds and our conversations. X

1

LONDON

Portia

Portia leant against her white quartz kitchen worktop as she took a sip from her steaming coffee. Even with Charlie's back to her she couldn't miss the tension in his shoulders as he gathered up his laptop and pushed it into his rucksack.

'Are you sure you're all right, Charlie?' she asked for the second time that morning. 'If only you'd confide in me about what's bothering you, I'm sure we could find a way to work things out.'

He closed the zip on the top of the bag and leaving it on the table turned to her. 'I'm fine, honestly.'

Portia wished he was being truthful but noticed that the smile he now gave her as he took her in his arms didn't quite reach his beautiful blue eyes. Suspecting he was concerned about upsetting her, Portia held her coffee cup to one side as she returned his kiss. 'Are you unhappy living in London?'

'Please stop worrying about me.' He kissed the tip of her nose.

'I'd better get a move on or I'll be late and we have a couple of early bookings at the restaurant. I'll see you later.' He stepped away and lifting his bag, hung one of the straps over his right shoulder. 'Would you like me to fetch anything special for supper tonight?'

Portia shook her head, swallowing a mouthful of coffee to be able to speak without crying. Ever since their first kiss at the Burns Night party at the hotel where Charlie used to work in Jersey, the pair of them had been inseparable. For the past few months though she had felt him becoming more distant even though he tried hard to hide it. She loved Charlie so much but sensed he was becoming more miserable each day. 'We could go out somewhere to eat, if you'd rather?'

It was a pathetic attempt to cheer him up and Portia suspected she needed to do much better if she wasn't going to lose him completely. The thought terrified her.

Ever since she and Charlie had come together the speed and intensity of their relationship had surprised them both, but especially Portia. She had been struggling to come to terms with losing her fiancé, Alistair, two years before and never imagined she would fall in love with anyone again. Let alone feel as if she had been slammed by a thunderbolt when she and Charlie noticed each other at the party that first night.

'If you like.'

Portia took a moment to recall her question. 'Charlie?'

He turned to face her, an expectant look on his handsome face. 'Yes?'

'We are OK, aren't we?'

His shoulders drooped slightly and her heart dipped. 'Of course we are.'

She was losing him. She just knew it. Not wishing to ever be that needy girlfriend, she forced a smile. 'You'd better get going. I'll see you later.'

Portia watched him leave and as he closed the front door to the flat, she sighed. How was she going to resolve what had gone wrong between them? She still loved him as fiercely as she had ever done, but Charlie clearly wasn't happy – not that he would ever admit it. How could she make things better with him if she didn't have any idea what was wrong?

She thought back to how exciting life had been when she and Charlie were first together. He loved his job working as an assistant hotel manager near the boardwalk in Jersey but gave it up willingly to follow her to London, she recalled wistfully. Maybe he simply hated managing the restaurant in London, or was it more than that? A terrible thought occurred to her. Maybe it was their relationship making him miserable?

She finished her drink and then, trying to avert her thoughts to more cheerful matters, decided she had better hurry if she wasn't going to be late to her stint at one of the two charities where she was a committee member helping to arrange fundraising events. Portia loved living in Chelsea and had desperately wanted to believe Charlie when he assured her several days ago that he was happy there. Although they had met in Jersey, he had grown up in New Zealand after his parents moved there when he was small, but only the previous week he had promised her he didn't feel the need to return there for a while.

How was it already eleven months since he had moved from Jersey to live with her in London? The time had flown by and Portia knew the first five of those months had been the happiest in her life. His too, he had said and she believed him.

As she checked her make-up in her compact mirror, she tried to recall any subtle changes between them and when they had appeared.

'Towards the end of summer,' she reminded herself, applying her favourite lipstick carefully. Yes, that was when it had become increasingly clear to her that Charlie was becoming despondent. Maybe it was the heat of living in a city at the height of summer he hadn't liked.

'There's no sea breeze here,' she recalled him complaining one sultry July night when she had woken to find his side of the bed empty and Charlie sitting silently on the rooftop terrace staring out over the London skyline.

'There won't be.' She had been momentarily confused by his comment, then recalled how Charlie's summers had been spent near the seafront either in New Zealand or Jersey. 'We're nowhere near the sea here in London.'

'I understand that,' he had replied thoughtfully. 'I suppose I just hadn't expected it to feel so airless here at times.'

'Isn't it like that in the summer on the island though?' she had asked, confused.

'Not really. Even during heatwaves, there's always a freshness to the air especially where I lived near the beach.'

Something seemed to shift in him then, she was certain of it. 'He's missing Jersey,' Portia murmured, surprised not to have worked out the reason before. 'Of course, that's it.'

City life wasn't for everyone, but when Charlie had first moved to London to live with her he had seemed entranced to discover the lively nightclubs, attend opening nights at theatres, go to concerts at the Royal Albert Hall and accompany Portia as her plus one at charity events she had helped arrange. She smiled, remembering how he especially enjoyed going with her to smaller, more intimate clubs Portia had introduced him to. Was she wrong to have believed him to be as happy as her back then?

Satisfied to have resolved the mystery, she pulled on her new camel coat and, picking up her favourite handbag, left the flat.

After her meeting she returned home, choosing to walk instead of taking a cab. She wanted time to think things through properly and chatting to a cabbie wasn't going to offer her the solitude she desperately needed. She supposed Charlie hadn't wanted to upset her by admitting anything was wrong.

How typical of her darling Charlie to be more concerned by her happiness than his own. But if he wouldn't tell her what was wrong, how could she possibly help put things right? And, she pondered as she entered the building and went to press the button for the lift, even if he did talk openly to her about his feelings was she ready to do whatever it took to see him truly smiling again? Yes, she decided, of course she was. She needed to think about what to do next.

She covered her mouth as she yawned, annoyed after another night when she had quickly fallen asleep only to wake at three in the morning, her mind racing, after a nightmare where first Alistair vanished, then Charlie. Her heart raced as she recalled her desperate attempts to reach them both. She folded her arms across her chest willing her breathing to calm, aware she didn't have the strength to face the acute pain of loss again in her life. She had barely survived it the first time and the fear that it could happen again with Charlie threatened to overwhelm her.

The lift stopped two floors down from hers. The doors opened and a smart blonde woman around her age stepped inside. Portia fixed a smile onto her face, not wishing anyone to see her distress.

The woman checked the lift was going to the ground floor, and not wishing to correct her, Portia nodded.

'Portia?' The woman beamed at her. 'It is you, isn't it?'

Wondering how much worse her day was going to get, Portia struggled to place the woman for a moment before realising that they had attended the same boarding school. The woman's hair was much lighter than it had been when they were pupils together and she was several sizes slimmer, but her enthusiastic manner hadn't changed. 'Venetia Adams?'

'It's Knight now,' Venetia beamed at Portia, clearly delighted to have been recognised. 'You don't live here, do you?'

Portia nodded. It embarrassed her to meet ex-pupils who remembered her from those miserable days when her parents went through their acrimonious divorce, even leaving her at boarding school at times during the holidays unless friends invited her to stay with them. Had Venetia been one of those people whose parents had taken pity on her? No, they weren't, she concluded with relief. 'I do, as a matter of fact. You?'

Venetia shook her head, looking frustrated. 'I wish. I've just been to a viewing for one of the flats.' She pointed upwards. 'The agent told me as soon as I arrived that an offer had been accepted only ten minutes before.'

'Oh, that's a shame.' Portia was sorry to hear of her disappointment. 'Couldn't they have called to save you the trouble of coming, especially on such a cold day?'

'You would think so, but he seemed more interested in showing me details of two other flats nearby I imagine he hoped to show me instead. It's here that I'd set my heart on living though.' Venetia pursed her lips. 'Toby, my husband, has always wanted a flat here ever since he stayed with one of his friends years ago. I had every intention of making an offer today. I was hoping to surprise him.'

Portia didn't have the heart to leave her disappointed friend without at least trying to help cheer her up. She considered inviting Venetia to her penthouse for coffee, changing her mind almost immediately in case she added further disappointment to her.

Portia reconsidered her options. 'If you've got time we could always go for a coffee. You can tell me all about your husband and how your life has been since we were at school?'

The other woman smiled. 'I'd love that. I need to come to terms with losing the flat before I go home anyway. Toby is working from his home office most of the time now and I need to at least try and appear positive about our flat hunting before seeing him. And,' she said, placing her hand on Portia's forearm, 'it will be wonderful to catch up with you after all this time.'

Several minutes later, they settled down in the warm, cosy coffee shop Portia liked to visit several times each week, and gave their orders.

'So you mentioned that you're married,' Portia said, hoping to turn the conversation to something more cheery. 'Recently?'

She listened as Venetia told her about meeting her husband and knowing within moments that he was *The One*. The wedding sounded magical, as did their life together and Portia realised that the only thing marring Venetia's happiness was not living in their chosen building.

'If you ever decide to move, you will give me first refusal,' Venetia said, leaning closer, her piercing eyes boring into Portia's.

'Yes,' Portia agreed. 'But I can't see that happening anytime soon. I love living there and don't see me wanting to move.'

'But you never know.'

Portia laughed, reminding herself that she was aiming to cheer her friend and not dash yet another hope. 'Of course.'

'In fact, let's swap numbers now so that you have mine just in case.'

Portia struggled not to smile, remembering Venetia's determination, which clearly hadn't lessened with age.

Having done as Venetia asked, Portia sat back to drink her coffee, listening as the other woman chatted on and on about her life, her wonderful husband, and giving up work because she was reaching burnout.

'I'm lucky Toby has done so well for himself,' she confided. 'Thankfully there's no need for me to earn a living any more.' She glanced around, then lowering her voice, added, 'I hated working in finance, although it probably didn't help that I wasn't very good at it.'

Portia seemed to recall Venetia struggling during maths lessons at school and barely hid her surprise to learn that she had held any job in the finance industry. 'Was it very stressful?'

Venetia's face clouded over for a second before she regained her composure. 'I was losing sleep and weight and it must have been about eighteen months ago when Toby caught me sobbing in our room.'

'That's horrible.'

'I was at my wits' end, but the darling man comforted me and insisted I give notice straight away and take off for a while until I felt strong enough to return. Thankfully, since then he has begun to do incredibly well and there's been no need for me to find another job.'

Portia couldn't miss the relief on Venetia's face. 'I'm glad.'

'So am I. It's why I've been able to look for somewhere new for us.' She sighed. 'I had imagined I'd be arranging decorators in the next couple of months but now someone else's offer was accepted that clearly won't be happening.'

They talked for a bit longer until Venetia's phone pinged. She picked it up and studied the screen. 'Damn, it's Toby. He wants to know whether our offer was accepted. I suppose I can't put off going home and telling him what's happened any longer.'

Portia pulled a sympathetic face. 'Good luck. And you never know, another one of the flats might come up for sale soon.' She doubted it. The residents mostly seemed to have lived there for years as far as she was aware. Portia noticed Venetia's uncertain expression. 'I promise I'll let you know if I do hear anything.'

'Thank you.' Venetia finished her coffee and pulled on her coat. 'It was good to see you again. If I didn't say so before, you're looking amazing. But then you always did. It was girls like me who took years to work out how to make the best of themselves.'

Portia wasn't sure what to say to that comment so simply smiled. 'It's been great catching up with you.'

She watched Venetia leave. As Portia was alone again her thoughts returned to Charlie and her mood plummeted. She loved him so much and couldn't bear for him to be miserable. But what could she do to change things? She finished her drink and left to walk the short way home.

What was the point of only one of them being happy? And how could she possibly enjoy life if her sweet Charlie didn't share that happiness? The light had disappeared from his beautiful blue eyes and as much as he insisted everything was all right, Portia knew it wasn't. He had given their life in London his best shot but it was clear to her that the place was too noisy and hectic for an islander like Charlie. She hated to think of him yearning for the tranquillity of his old life back in Jersey.

As she stood in the lift going up to her flat, she thought of Venetia. Maybe bumping into her had been a sign? Portia tried to work out how exactly, but couldn't come up with anything.

She unlocked her front door and stepped inside. Closing it, Portia remembered the first time she had stepped into Oliver's fishermen's cottage in Jersey and how safe and protected being there had made her feel. It was the second anniversary of her late fiancé's death and, having lost contact with many friends and even to a lesser extent, her parents, she knew the only person who could offer her the support she craved was Alistair's brother, Oliver.

She had flown to Jersey desperate to be with another person who would understand the heartache of her reality. Portia thought back to how friendly the locals had been, welcoming her into their group of friends, their kindness acting like a salve for the loss that was still so raw. And then she had met her darling Charlie and been overwhelmed by their instant mutual attraction.

Portia gasped. Why hadn't she thought of this before? If going to the island had been the balm her spirit had needed the previous year, then surely it would be the perfect way to perk Charlie up now. Wouldn't it?

She placed her bag on the hall table, accidentally knocking over a silver-framed photo of her and her friend, Cressida. They had been very close once, she mused. She picked up the photo and thought back to when it had been taken years before on the night she met Alastair. Staring at it, Portia couldn't help reminiscing how life had seemed more carefree back then. How lousy of a friend was she, she thought, realising she hadn't spent any time with Cressida since Charlie had moved in with her.

Putting the photo back onto the table, her thoughts returned to Charlie. She might have lost touch with her friend – all of her friends, in fact, she thought guiltily – but Charlie's happiness and their relationship was her priority now and she needed to think how best to help him.

A bird fluttered before settling on the windowsill, drawing her attention to the deep blue of the sky, and it dawned on her exactly what she needed to do.

Taking her mobile from her pocket, she scrolled down to find Lexi's number.

'Lexi?' she said as soon as her friend answered, her mind whirring in excitement as she made plans for Charlie's surprise.

'Portia, how are you?'

'I need to ask a favour of you.'

'Anything. Ask away.'

2

PORTIA

'That was a bumpier flight than I would have liked,' Portia admitted as they sat in Oliver's car on their way towards the board-walk several days later. 'But it's good to be back, don't you think, Charlie?'

'Amazing.' He turned his gaze from staring out of the window to face her, leaning closer and kissing her. 'I still can't believe we're here again.'

Portia gave his hand a gentle squeeze. She was beginning to realise that Charlie wasn't the only one excited by some time away from London. Now she thought about it, life there hadn't seemed nearly as exciting as when she initially moved there with Alastair several years before. Had she been pretending to herself about loving life in the city because Charlie had given up so much to be with her? Was all this mess her fault, after all?

'You all right?' he whispered.

Portia nodded. She had no idea why she hadn't thought of suggesting this trip sooner. It had taken very little persuasion for Charlie to request a week off from his job managing the plush restaurant in the city where he had been earning a living for the past few months.

Charlie hadn't been the only one acting differently, she realised. Could all those sleepless nights, the occasional headaches she had been suffering from and lack of appetite been because she was burning herself out with the effort of trying to make everything seem perfect in their lives?

Portia pushed the thought away, determined to be present and make the most of being back on the island where they had fallen in love. This trip was important and she needed to ensure both she and Charlie found their way back to how they had once been together. She watched as he lowered the back window fully before taking a deep breath of the fresh sea air.

'You can't beat that smell,' he said wistfully. 'This was a brilliant idea of yours. Thank you.'

Her heart contracted on hearing the joy in his voice. The light had returned to his eyes the moment she had told him about the booked flights and that Lexi and Oliver had invited the pair of them to stay in the end cottage for their stay.

'You're both welcome to come over any time. The cottage is yours until the season starts at the end of March,' Oliver said, smiling at them both through his rearview mirror.

Lexi twisted around in the passenger seat. 'We've both been incredibly excited to see you again. I hadn't expected you to come over for a while yet, especially now winter is setting in and the weather's that much colder. I thought you'd be enjoying the Christmas lights in London and all those magical window displays I recall seeing years ago.'

'We'll still see those,' Charlie said. 'We're only here for a few days.'

'But we'll be able to come again very soon,' Portia reminded him, aware it might be exactly what they both needed. 'For week-

ends and don't forget the Christmas holidays will soon be here.'
And yet another anniversary of Alastair's death to get through.

'I thought you wanted to spend Christmas in London?' Charlie
asked, giving her a surprised look. 'You also mentioned something
about travelling to stay with friends of yours in the Cotswolds.'

Portia remembered being invited to stay at a friend's for the
holidays earlier in the year, but she had forgotten all about it. At
the time it had seemed like a perfect way to show Charlie an
English country Christmas in a characterful home. Now though, as
she looked out of the car window at the sea down the hill, she
realised that a country Christmas wasn't what Charlie would enjoy
most.

'No,' she said, determined to make sure their first Christmas
together was one he remembered fondly. 'You don't need to spend
Christmas with people you don't know. Anyway, I think that now
we have use of the cottage maybe we should consider spending our
Christmas here on the island with our mutual friends.' As she
spoke she realised he wasn't the only one to miss the tranquillity of
the island where the only noise disturbing them at night was the
sound of waves crashing against the rocks on the beach below the
boardwalk.

'You'd really prefer being here?' Charlie's wide-eyed surprise
warmed her.

'I can't think of a better way for us to celebrate together, can
you?'

Charlie gazed at her in silence for a few seconds before his
mouth drew back in a wide smile. 'No.'

Oliver drove slowly down the hill, indicating before turning
towards their parking area at the side of the cottages where he and
Lexi lived. 'Here we are,' he said, switching off the car and stepping
out. Portia took Charlie's hand in hers as soon as they were
standing outside and closed her eyes, drawing in a deep breath.

'Bliss.' It wasn't just the sea air filling her nostrils, or the sound of the seagulls squawking at each other nearby – it wasn't even hearing their friends' voices as they spoke about whether to take the cases directly to their cottage – but the happiness exuding from her darling Charlie that made this moment completely perfect.

Portia opened her eyes and smiled at him. 'Happy?'

'Very,' he whispered before pressing his lips against hers in a kiss. 'I couldn't be any happier.'

Charlie noticed Oliver carrying both cases and withdrew his hand from hers to go and take them from him. 'Let me take those,' Portia heard him say as she spotted Lexi lifting bags of shopping from the boot of the car.

'Give me some of those bags,' Portia said, taking two from Lexi's hands. She waited for her friend to empty the boot and close the door, then walked with her along the pathway to the first cottage where Oliver and Lexi lived.

'No,' Lexi said. 'These are for you two.'

Portia was a little taken aback. 'But you needn't have gone to the trouble,' she said, trying to work out what might be in the four completely full shopping bags.

'Not at all. Anyway, you can't come here and have nothing to eat.'

'But we could have gone shopping for ourselves,' Portia argued, feeling guilty to have put her friend to so much trouble. She knew before entering the cottage that Lexi and Oliver would have spent time ensuring the cottage was freshly vacuumed, floors washed and everything wiped down and beds made but hadn't expected them to buy all their food too. 'You've gone to so much trouble for us already.'

Lexi followed Oliver and Charlie into the cottage and didn't stop until she had placed the bags she was carrying onto the floor next to the kitchen cupboards. 'No, we haven't. You're the ones who've caught a plane and flown over here to see us. It's the very least we can do for two of our dearest friends.'

Portia didn't like to correct Lexi but as far as she was concerned it was Oliver and Lexi who had come to her rescue and she was very grateful to them. 'It's fabulous being back here again,' she admitted. She lowered her voice and added, 'I don't think I've seen Charlie this happy for months.'

Lexi stilled and glanced at Oliver, alerting Portia to the fact that she had said more than she meant to. Portia glanced at the small living area near the kitchen, relieved that it was only the three of them in the room. Oliver stared at her, a surprised look on his face as he knelt in front of the log burner, his hand in mid-air as he had been about to add another log into the fire.

He sat back on his heels. 'Is everything all right between the pair of you?'

Horrified Charlie might be coming back downstairs after taking the cases to their bedroom, Portia shushed them both, raising a finger to her lips. 'Please, don't say anything to him.'

'Don't say anything about what?' Charlie asked, cheerfully coming up behind her.

Portia had no intention of letting her careless chatter ruin their trip. She forced a smile before turning to him and slipped her arms around his waist.

'I was talking about Christmas presents,' she fibbed. 'Now, let's change the subject and open one of these bottles of red wine I've spotted in the bag over there.'

'You guys sit down. Portia and I will get the drinks,' Lexi said, walking to the bag and lifting one of the bottles of red wine from it and placing it onto the worktop. 'The corkscrew is in that drawer there,' she said, indicating one to their left.

Portia was grateful Charlie appeared to believe her and gave Lexi an appreciative smile. 'Thank you,' she whispered, opening the drawer and taking the corkscrew from it. 'I seem to recall the glasses are up in this cupboard.' She reached up, opened the door and took out four, setting them down next to the bottle.

The groceries put away and wine poured, Lexi put crisps and nuts into two bowls and took everything through to the living area where the women settled down onto the comfy sofa.

'Here's to a relaxing few days on the island,' Portia said, raising her glass in a toast.

'Hear, hear,' Charlie said, blowing her a kiss. 'This place is really cosy.'

'We're glad you think so,' Lexi said. 'We want your stay here to be perfect.'

'If it carries on this way,' Charlie laughed, 'then it's sure to be. Don't you think, Portia?'

'Absolutely.' She took a sip of the rich liquid and sat back into the deep cushions, letting the concern about Charlie's recent quietness melt away. She watched him speaking to her friends, relieved she had come up with the idea to visit them and spend time near the sea again.

She listened to Charlie talking animatedly about what it meant to him to be back on the island and couldn't help thinking how much at home he seemed in this pretty cottage.

'What are your plans for tomorrow?' Oliver asked eventually.

Charlie gave Portia a questioning look. 'I don't think we've thought that far yet. I was so taken aback by Portia booking the flights that all I could think of was how happy I was to be coming home again.'

Portia suspected the first thing he would hope to do was visit friends down on the boardwalk. 'I have an idea,' she said.

'Great.' Charlie grinned. 'What is it?'

'I thought we could start the day by walking down the hill to

Summer Sundaes Café for one of Sacha's delicious full English breakfasts.'

'I like that idea,' Charlie nodded. 'Go on, what's next?'

'We could take a stroll to Boardwalk Books maybe and see what Jools has been getting up to before walking to Bella's cottage and having a look at what antiques she's got on display in her little front-room shop.'

'Sounds good to me.' He narrowed his eyes thoughtfully. 'We could finish off our morning by taking off our shoes and walking barefoot on the beach. How does that sound?'

Charlie gazed at her with so much love in his eyes that for a moment Portia almost agreed. 'I like the idea of the beach walk,' she admitted, laughing. 'Although I can't commit to taking off my shoes, not when it's this cold.'

Charlie smiled. 'All right. We'll keep our shoes on then.'

He really was incredibly happy being here, she thought, hating the idea that they were only on the island for a few days before she would be taking him back to city life.

'I think it sounds exactly like what I would have chosen to do,' Oliver agreed.

Portia took a sip of her drink. 'Then that's what we'll do.'

'There's an autumn market down at Greve de Lecq Barracks,' Oliver added. 'You could pop in there before walking back up to the cottage. You might find a few bits you like.'

'Great idea,' Charlie agreed. 'I'll have a look to see if the cider maker is there with his stall. That's delicious stuff I seem to recall.'

'And don't miss the artisan baker, Remi,' Lexi added. 'Oliver loves his sourdough loaves, but if you're not a sourdough fan Remi sells loads of other types of bread.'

'That sounds like my thing,' Portia said, deciding that was where she would be heading to.

Charlie sighed happily and Portia watched as he sat quietly, lost in his own thoughts. 'This is the perfect treat,' he said eventually. 'I know we're going to have a wonderful few days.'

'I think so too,' Portia said, closing her eyes and relishing the relaxed atmosphere between them as he pulled her into his arms for a hug. 'It's good to be back here again.'

It really was, she thought, glad that she had no charity commitments that weekend and was able to act upon her instinct to book the flights to the island. Charlie hadn't been the only one needing a break from the tension of their London lives.

3

CHARLIE

Charlie opened his eyes, confused for a moment when he heard the sound of the sea. A seagull squawked somewhere outside and he sighed happily, remembering they were back in Jersey.

Portia's soft breathing interrupted his thoughts. He turned on his side, careful not to wake her, wanting to watch her angelic face as she slept peacefully next to him. He noted the time on his watch and realised he had slept for over eight hours without waking once during the night. Charlie didn't think he had slept so deeply or for so long the entire time he had been living in London. Returning to the tranquillity of his adopted coastal village surrounded by the fresh sea air was clearly what he needed.

Portia stirred and he lay on his side watching her, his head resting on his arm. She really was the most exquisite woman and it still surprised him that she loved him so much. It was strange to think that three years earlier Portia had faced the loss of her fiancé, Alistair, when he had been killed in an accident. Charlie knew she had only come to the island for the first time the previous Christmas to find solace with Oliver as she was unable to face the second anniversary of Alistair's death alone. Oliver missed his brother as much as Portia did and Charlie knew their bond was very deep.

He thought of his own brother and the distance between them since he had left New Zealand to move back to Jersey nine years ago leaving his mother heartbroken. Charlie still felt guilty about emigrating but maybe if his parents hadn't sent him to stay for an entire summer with his great aunt in Jersey when he was sixteen he might not have fallen in love with the place and decided to live there as soon as he was old enough to leave home. At the time he had resented his brother being allowed to remain in New Zealand. But since spending that idyllic summer in Jersey it had been his brother's envy of him that had continued the discord between them.

He glanced at his bedside table drawer inside which he had placed the solicitor's letter that had come for him two days earlier. He knew Portia had picked up that something was wrong and felt guilty for not sharing his news with her yet, but he still needed a little more time to process what this unexpected bequest meant for him.

Portia murmured Charlie's name in her sleep. He stroked her temple lightly with the tip of his finger. 'It's all right, sweetheart,' he soothed. 'I'm right here.'

Charlie was glad she had Oliver to turn to over the past few years. She could be very independent and self-sufficient, but there was something broken about her that compelled him to want to protect her. Not that he ever let her know that, he thought, smiling to himself. Portia would hate for him to think she wasn't perfectly capable of looking after herself.

Charlie also knew Portia had not expected to make such close friends when she came to Jersey that first time, or fall in love again. He hadn't ever imagined someone glamorous and sophisticated like Portia could possibly fall for someone as ordinary as him. He was a very lucky man, and he knew it.

Why then did life in London seem so difficult to navigate? He desperately wanted his new life with her to work out, but despite his, and, he realised, her best efforts, living where everyone seemed to be a stranger focusing only on reaching whatever destination they were heading for, proved more of a struggle than he had expected. In Jersey it didn't matter how long his shifts at the hotel were, he could always take a moment to look outside at the waves lapping at the water's edge on the beach below, or open a window to hear the sea, watch the many birds on the cliffs to the right of the bay. In London the only sounds were of tense voices and traffic. In Jersey, his commute had been a short, peaceful stroll along the boardwalk, stopping several times to chat to one of the other locals, whereas in London he was one of thousands of anonymous people making their way along the Underground passageways to crowded platforms, rushing to catch the train that would take each of them to work.

And now there this new turn of events and it made him feel even more unsettled than before.

Portia stirred and took a slow, deep breath before stretching as she slowly opened her eyes. Charlie watched as she stared up at the ceiling for a few seconds, probably listening to the sound of the waves and trying to work out where she was, as he had done. He saw her mouth slowly draw back into a smile before she closed her eyes again.

Charlie felt his heart contract with emotion as he witnessed her reaction to waking up on the island. She probably assumed he was still sleeping and he decided to wait patiently to see what she did next.

Her hand found his thigh making him hold his breath. Portia smiled, then opened her eyes and looked at him.

'Good morning. Have you been staring at me for long?'

'Not very. You seemed content and I didn't want to disturb you.'

'I slept so well.' She stretched languorously.

'Me too. Then again, I always sleep better when I'm near the sea,' he said, gazing at her. 'But mostly I'm happiest waking up next to you.' He saw something flash across her face; doubt maybe? Not wanting her to worry, he settled back down next to her, happy when Portia snuggled up closer to him. Her hand moved higher up his thigh and Charlie pulled her to him, kissing her.

* * *

An hour later, showered and dressed for the cold weather they knew would greet them outside, Charlie took Portia's gloved hand in his as they began their walk down to Summer Sundaes Café.

'I'm looking forward to my breakfast,' she said, her stomach rumbling in protest. 'How about you?'

'Definitely. I think I might have even dreamed about eating there last night.'

He enjoyed being with someone who loved her food as much as he did. He gazed at her, knowing he needed to tell her about the solicitor's letter he had received, especially now they were in Jersey and he had little time to make an appointment to visit the law office before they left to return to London.

Hearing voices, Charlie noticed a few locals already chatting on the boardwalk, despite it still being fairly early. He wasn't surprised; this might be a holiday destination in the summer but it was still a working village the rest of the year.

'Charlie? Is that you?' Tony, a fisherman friend he knew well, waved at them.

'That's the man who married Bella's mother the previous spring, isn't it?'

'Yes, that's Tony.' Charlie waved back at the well-built man with a hand on each of his children's shoulders. The little boy and girl seemed happy and had grown since he had last seen them at Tony and Claire's beach wedding. 'Back for good, I hope?'

He felt Portia's hand tense briefly in his own. He hated to think she was unsettled by Tony's question, but it was a natural thing for anyone to ask him. He hesitated slightly before answering, not wishing to upset her by saying the wrong thing. 'No, we're just here for a brief visit this time.'

'That's a shame. Hopefully we'll have time for a catch-up before you leave again.'

'I'd like that.'

Portia gave a friendly wave. Charlie knew she liked most of the residents she'd met here. Then again, they were a friendly, close-knit bunch of people and, unlike where she lived in London, seemed to look out for and knew each other's names.

'I might see you both in the café, if you're still there when I've dropped the kids off at their sports club.'

'That would be lovely,' Charlie said.

'Bring Claire if you can,' Portia suggested. 'I'd love to catch up with her while we're here.'

'She's in town for the day, visiting a friend.'

'Bella still hand modelling?' Portia asked, picturing the bubbly girl who was one of Lexi's closest friends and her mother, Claire, who, she recalled, had only returned to Jersey the previous year having spent most of her daughter's life away trying to *find herself* in various far-flung locations across the globe while Bella was being brought up by her grandmother.

'She is, but hasn't done much these past few months. Been focusing on sorting out her antiques to give a bit more space in the living room for when the baby arrives.'

Portia thought of the pretty blue cottage halfway along the

boardwalk where Bella lived with Jack and sold antiques from her small front room to earn extra money when she wasn't hand modelling.

'I'd better get going. Don't want these two to be late for training.'

Charlie and Portia walked on again towards the café, stopping at the iron railings in front of the beach to take in the breathtaking view.

Charlie took a slow, deep breath and sighed happily. 'Nothing beats the smell of the sea.'

Portia did the same. 'I have to agree with you. It certainly beats the smell of the exhaust fumes on our street at home.' Her stomach rumbled noisily making Charlie laugh.

'Come on, let's get some food into us.'

They entered the warm, bright café and he immediately felt like he hadn't been away. The scent of breakfasts, toast and ground coffee filled the air. Charlie spotted a vacant table and led her over to it.

'That was lucky,' Portia said, sitting opposite him. 'I hadn't expected it to be this busy yet and certainly not in November.'

'Portia? Charlie? What are you two doing here?' Sacha beamed at them. She grabbed two menus and hurried to them, turning her notepad onto a fresh page. Charlie liked how delighted the café owner was to see them again. They didn't have a chance to answer the question before Sacha shouted over her shoulder for her brother. 'Jack, look who's here.'

'Hey, mate.' Charlie stood and turned towards the kitchen as Jack came over to join them.

Jack hugged Charlie, patting his back before going to Portia and bending to kiss her cheek. 'I hope you've both seen the error of your ways and are back for good,' he said, looking from one of them to the other.

Charlie winced. It was the second time in less than five minutes that someone had made such a comment. He noticed Portia smile tightly as she took the menu from Sacha.

'Just ignore him,' Sacha said, shooting a glare at her twin. 'He's got the tact of a... I'm not sure what.'

'It's fine,' Portia insisted. 'It's lovely to know we've been missed.'

'Sorry, Jack,' Charlie apologised, sitting down again. 'We're only back for a few days, but hopefully we'll be able to meet up for a chat. I'd love to know what's been going on since we were last here.'

Jack raised a finger. 'I'll keep you to that.' Two more people entered the café. 'I'd better look after these two. It's great to see you though. Both of you.'

'Good to see you too,' Charlie and Portia replied in unison.

Sacha pointed to a blackboard on the wall to Portia's side. 'We've got everything on the menu and those specials up there. Give me a wave when you've had a chance to make up your minds.'

As Sacha walked away, Portia reached out and took Charlie's right hand in hers. 'I'm sorry, Charlie.'

'What for?'

'Your friends have obviously missed you very much.'

'They've missed you too.'

Portia looked at him doubtfully. 'Maybe a bit, but not like they have you. I feel bad that you left all this behind for me.'

He took her hands across the table, determined to reassure her. 'Listen, I left here to be with the woman I love. I'm happy wherever you are, I hope you know that.'

'I do,' she said, a catch in her voice. 'But I know that ideally you'd rather be here near the sea, not in some noisy city where everything is chaotic.' She grinned. 'And you can't go swimming whenever you wish in London either.'

'I could find somewhere,' he argued. 'But maybe not in the sea.'

He frowned. 'Anyway, there's much more to life than that. I'm fine. You do believe me when I say that, I hope?'

She stared at him for a moment and he wondered what was going through her mind. 'I do, but we both know you'd be happier living back on the island.'

'I'm happy being wherever you are,' he insisted, wishing he didn't have to tell her about the letter. If she was unsettled now, how was she going to feel when he told her his news?

'Let's order, shall we?' he said, wanting to change the subject and lifting one of her hands to his mouth before kissing it. 'I'm starving and you haven't had your first cup of tea yet.'

Portia raised his hand to her lips. 'You're the loveliest man, do you know that?'

'I'm glad you think so,' he said, teasing her and hoping that she'd let the matter drop.

'I do. Right, let's order.'

As they ate he could tell she was trying her best to be cheerful. Charlie focused on enjoying his full English breakfast and coffee, but although Portia looked as if she was enjoying her pancakes with blueberries and maple syrup, which he knew from experience were delicious, somehow today she didn't seem as enthused as usual and appeared to be having to force herself to finish them.

He couldn't remain quiet a moment longer. Charlie lowered his cutlery to his plate. 'Sweetheart, I know you're determined to give me a perfect few days here, but I need to know you're enjoying yourself too and not spending your time worrying about me.'

Portia stared to her right out of the large window where locals walked between them and the rough jade sea below the promenade. 'I just can't help feeling guilty that you've given all this up to be with me.' She looked into his eyes and Charlie knew she was about to bring up the one thing he tried to avoid discussing with her. 'Regardless of how you insist otherwise,

Charlie, I know you've become increasingly miserable living in London.'

Charlie gritted his teeth. Damn, he had tried so hard to hide his feelings and had presumed he was doing a reasonable job. Obviously, he had failed spectacularly.

'Charlie? I know something's wrong. What I don't understand is why you won't share your concerns with me.'

She looked hurt and Charlie hated that he was the cause. He was going to have to tell her about the solicitor's letter. There was nothing else for it. But then, knowing Portia, she would insist they returned to live on the island, and he couldn't let her leave her beloved home just because of his circumstances. He still needed to tell her though, and sooner rather than later.

'Charlie? Please tell me what's wrong.'

He took her hands in each of his. 'Fine. But I want you to let me tell you everything before you react. Promise?'

She nodded slowly, looking pale. 'Go on then.'

He cleared his throat. 'Firstly, I think you'll agree it takes time to get used to living somewhere new. Anyway,' he added, aware she didn't seem convinced. 'I don't mind living in London.'

'Charlie, we both know that's not true.' Portia stared at him for a moment.

This wasn't going to be as easy as he had hoped. 'I admit I prefer living here, but London has its bonuses.'

Portia laughed. 'Go on then, tell me some of them.'

He shrugged. 'Theatres, nightclubs, um, lots of parks.'

'Fair enough.' She smiled. 'Sorry, I interrupted. Carry on.'

He withdrew the letter from his solicitor from his coat pocket and handed it to her to read.

'What's this?' She glanced from him to the letter.

'I received it in the post a couple of days ago.'

She took the letter and glanced up at him questioningly before studying the envelope. 'Why haven't you told me about it sooner? What is it about?'

'Read it and you'll see,' he replied softly.

As she read, Charlie thought of his mother never missing an opportunity to take a snipe at his dad for insisting they left Jersey to emigrate to New Zealand when his business went bust. Charlie and his older brother had only been young, but he had grown up aware of his father's mortification and regret at letting his family down so badly that he felt the need to take them to the other side of the world, far from everything he and his mother knew, and where no one would know their circumstances.

He realised Portia was staring at him. 'You've inherited a chateau? Here?'

Charlie nodded. 'It's more of a manor house, I think, but yes, that's right.'

'You've never mentioned a great aunt before, have you?'

He wasn't sure. 'She was a recluse. I visited her occasionally but not for a few years now.'

'But what will you do with it?'

Charlie sighed. 'I've no idea,' he said honestly. 'It's very run down now, I imagine.' He laughed. 'It was in a bad shape when my parents sent me here for the summer when I was sixteen.'

Portia looked stunned. 'Was that when you first came back to the island after your parents emigrated when you were seven?'

'That's right. I fell in love with the place and was heartbroken when they insisted I return to them.'

She reached out and took his hand in hers. 'But you came back as soon as you left uni, didn't you?'

He had. It had been the longest six years of his life, but he knew he needed to attend university in New Zealand because his parents hadn't had enough money to send him to a British university.

Portia stared at him thoughtfully for a moment. 'Do you think your father would have ever returned here if he'd lived longer?'

Charlie had often wondered the same thing, but not for long. 'No. He was too ashamed about going broke to ever want to face people who knew him back then. My mother always insisted she would come back as soon as possible but when Dad had his heart attack and died, she remarried months later and now I can't see her ever coming back.'

'What do you think you'll do with the chateau?'

He had no idea. All Charlie did know for certain was that had no intention of repeating his father's mistakes. He couldn't bear to be the cause of any resentment between himself and Portia. She loved her life in London and if he was to ensure she remained happy, then he needed to find a way to settle there happily too.

'I'm not sure what I'll do with it yet,' he replied, wanting time to figure out how best to deal with this unexpected gift.

4

PORTIA

'You are both still here,' Oliver said, joining them at the table with Lexi by his side.

'I didn't see you come in.' Portia wasn't sure if she was relieved or disappointed for her and Charlie's conversation to be cut short. She needed time to mull over his news. No wonder she hadn't been able to shift the sense that something had been bothering Charlie for the past couple of days.

'We thought we'd pop in to see if you were here.'

She smiled, happy to see her dear Oliver. He always ended up being there when she needed him most.

'You seemed lost in thought just then.'

'Did I?' Oliver knew her far too well to misread her mood. 'I was just thinking how beautiful the sea is when it's this stormy. I love it this dramatic and wild.'

'It is rather impressive, isn't it?' Oliver said, glancing over his shoulder for a quick look out of the window. 'No wonder you didn't see us.'

'You joining us?' Charlie asked, pulling out the seat next to him for Lexi to take.

'We've eaten already but Oliver wondered if you might like to go with him and meet up with Tony and Jack for a coffee and a catch up. I was hoping to take Portia to the artisan market just over the road from where you'll be.'

'Portia?' Charlie's eyebrows raised in question. 'Would that be OK with you?'

'Of course.' She smiled at Lexi gratefully. 'I was also hoping to pop in to see Jools, and then Bella, sometime this morning and say hello.'

'Jools is away with Marius in London,' Sacha said, arriving next to their table holding two plates of food. 'They're meeting someone about a proposed exhibition in the spring.'

'How typical that they're there when we've come here,' Portia shrugged, disappointed at the timing. 'Will they be back in the next couple of days, do you know?'

'Unfortunately not,' Jack said. 'They're having a mini break afterwards at some Airbnb. I think they needed a little time, just the two of them, before the run up to Christmas gets going.'

'I see.' Portia hoped her disappointment didn't show on her face. 'We'll just have to make a plan to visit again soon then so we can catch up with them then.'

'Bella said she'll try and join us in a bit,' Lexi said.

Oliver pointed at Charlie's shoulder. 'You still OK to come with Tony and me for a bit though? I thought we could take you to sample some of the local cider. We can find Lexi and Portia afterwards. It's also at the Artisan Market.'

Portia watched as Charlie gave her a questioning look. She couldn't miss the hope in his eyes that he might go with his friends and wanting to do whatever made him happiest, Portia nodded. 'You go and enjoy yourselves. I'm looking forward to spending some time with Lexi. We'll see you all a bit later.'

'Great. Well, if you're both finished here,' Sacha said, returning to stand near their table. She picked up their plates and cups and handed them to Jack. 'If you could take these, I'll give the table a wipe.'

'We just need to settle our bill,' Charlie said, standing.

'No need,' Jack said. 'All taken care of.'

'What?' Portia didn't want them to think that she and Charlie were expecting a free meal.

Lexi must have seen the concern on her face because she cocked her head to one side. 'Oliver treated you, so if you want to argue about it, he's the one to do it with.' She gave Portia a wink.

How typical of him, Portia mused, leaning forward and kissing his left cheek. 'Thanks, Oliver.'

'My pleasure. Now, Charlie, let's get going before the ladies here find jobs for us to do.'

Portia watched, amused, as Oliver and Charlie left the café. She wasn't sure why Oliver was rushing Charlie away but had her suspicions. Pulling on her coat, she fastened it and accompanied Lexi outside back into the cold.

'I'm excited to finally spend some time with you,' Portia confided as she pulled on her hat. 'Even if it's just a short while.'

'Yes, I was hoping we'd be able to finish our conversation from yesterday.'

Portia suspected that Oliver taking Charlie out with Tony was a way to give her and Lexi a chance to speak openly without any fear that Charlie might overhear what Portia needed to tell them. 'Were you the one to instigate Oliver taking Charlie out for a while?'

Lexi nodded, confirming her suspicions. 'He knew it was probably the only way the two of us could speak openly.'

Portia wondered how Oliver always seemed to find ways to help others. 'He's such a darling, isn't he?'

Lexi sighed. 'He really is. So perceptive. I adore how he looks out for those he cares about.'

'He's always been there for me,' Portia said, thinking back to how Oliver's kindness towards her after Alistair's death had helped her keep going when she believed her life wasn't worth continuing.

They crossed the road and she noticed Charlie, Tony and Oliver disappearing into one of the small rooms at the barracks where she presumed the cider maker had his stall set up out of the worst of the cold weather.

'So, where shall we go first?' Portia asked aware that Lexi would have something planned.

'This way.' Lexi led her to the end of the barracks past stalls selling handmade crafts, small paintings, charity Christmas cards and wrapping paper and various other items. They reached the end entrance and Lexi led the way inside. Portia knew they had walked into a baker's area as soon as the smell of delicious bread and cakes filled her nose.

'A baker's?'

'Not any old baker's,' Lexi said, indicating for her to take a seat at one of the vacant tables in the corner. 'This is Remi's Bakery. He's the artisan baker I mentioned earlier.' Portia followed Lexi's smile as she waved at a dark-haired man returning her acknowledgement behind the makeshift counter as he served the first woman in a queue of others. 'He's a great guy,' Lexi said. 'I met him last year at the autumn fayre.'

'But if we're here to buy bread, don't you think we should get into the queue?'

Lexi shook her head. 'No, we can buy some later but I know that Remi won't mind us sitting here in the corner. I thought we could chat here.'

'Ah, I see.' Not wishing to waste any time they might have together, Portia told Lexi all about her concerns for Charlie and his happiness. 'So, I thought I'd bring him home for a few days and hope it cheered him up.'

'I sense a *but* coming,' Lexi said, narrowing her eyes.

Portia sighed. 'It's dawned on me how much happier he is when he's on the island and I'm not sure the odd weekend here is enough to make him happy. I'm beginning to think too, that Charlie won't ever truly settle in London and that I'm being selfish wanting him to try and fit in with my lifestyle.'

Lexi didn't respond immediately and Portia tensed, aware Lexi was trying to find a way to reassure her without lying. She reached out and rested a hand on Lexi's forearm. 'It's all right,' she said quietly. 'You don't have to comment.' They talked for a bit longer.

'I wonder if you could help me,' a voice with an obvious French accent said, making Portia jump. 'Sorry, I did not mean to startle you.'

'It's fine,' she replied, a little embarrassed to have reacted in such a way. She turned and saw that she and Lexi were alone in the room. 'You've served all those customers already?'

Lexi shook her head. 'We were chatting for longer than you probably realise.' She looked up at Remi. 'How can we help?'

He tapped the phone in his hand that until then Portia hadn't noticed him holding. 'Would you look after the stall for a short time while I make a private phone call?'

'Of course we will,' Portia said, happy to help out.

'Hi girls,' Bella waved from the door, hurrying over to give Portia a hug. 'I'm so excited to see you again.'

'Likewise.' Portia hugged her friend carefully not wishing to squash her pregnant stomach at all. She stepped back and studied her. 'You look radiant.'

Bella scoffed and waved the comment away. 'Rubbish, I look exhausted.' She lowered her voice and laughed. 'Which I am. Going away for the day for work and taking my mother with me is fun but incredibly tiring.'

'I suppose we should go and stand behind the stall,' Lexi

suggested after Remi left to walk outside. 'I've helped out a couple of times in the past, so we should be fine.'

'This is fun,' Bella said.

Portia loved being with her friends again, remembering how comforting it felt to be with women who cared for her. 'I'm so excited to be with the pair of you again.'

'Me, too.' Bella smiled.

It was fun serving the customers over the next few minutes and Portia only made one mistake undercharging one of them. Thankfully the woman was honest and told her what she had done, so Remi wasn't out of pocket.

Remi returned looking concerned. 'Thank you.'

'Is something wrong?' Lexi asked.

'You may as well confide in us,' Bella said softly. 'We love helping people and if you need us to do anything for you, you only need to ask.'

'That's very kind of you.' After serving another customer he showed them over to a corner table and when they were all sitting explained what his call had been about. 'You see, I have only a few weeks until I need to move out from my small cottage.'

'We can ask around and try to find you another place to live,' Bella suggested.

He sighed. 'That is kind, but unfortunately I will also be losing my small bakery and if I can't bake my loaves I will lose my livelihood.'

He looked devastated and Portia wished there was something she could do to help the poor man.

He stood suddenly. 'I must not trouble you after you've all been so kind,' he said, raising a finger. 'One moment before you go.'

They watched as he hurried to the counter and, taking three brown paper carrier bags, placed a freshly baked loaf in each followed by a smaller bag containing three doughnuts. He held out each bag for Lexi, Bella and Portia to take.

'To say thank you for listening to me when I needed a friend.'

Portia took her bag and thanked him, hating to go and leave the poor man with his worries. 'I wish there was something we could do to help him,' she admitted as they moved on.

'We can ask around and try to find him somewhere new to live and a place where he can run his business,' Lexi said.

'Yes, don't worry. We'll do our best for him.'

Portia linked arms with her two friends and couldn't help thinking how lucky she was to have met these wonderfully kind women.

5

PORTIA

'I hope you don't mind me saying something,' Lexi said as they began walking again.

Portia swallowed anxiously. 'Go ahead.'

Lexi gave Portia a thoughtful stare. 'You mentioned you wanted to find a way to make Charlie happy.'

Portia struggled over whether to share Charlie's news with her friends. She knew Lexi and Bella were discreet and only wanted the best for her and Charlie, but it wasn't her news to tell. 'Go on.'

Bella's phone made a buzzing sound. 'That's my alarm, sorry.' She took her phone from her bag and switched off the alarm. 'That's reminding me I have a doctor's appointment.'

'Everything's all right, I hope.' Portia waited anxiously for Bella's reply as her friend returned her phone to her bag.

'Yes, all fine. It's just a check-up to make sure everything stays that way.' She kissed them on the cheek. 'I'd better rush, I don't want to be late and parking near the surgery can be a nightmare.'

'Good luck,' Portia called as they both waved Bella off.

'Where were we?' Lexi wondered. 'Oh, yes. I can tell there's something troubling you deeply. I hope you know you can confide in me about anything and I would keep it between us.'

Portia did. She was also relieved it was just the two of them now. She was close to Bella but preferred to keep things to between Lexi and herself. 'I know you would,' Portia said gratefully. 'But what's troubling me isn't my thing to share.'

'Ah, so it is about Charlie. I thought I sensed a little tension when we collected you from the airport. To be honest, Oliver did too.'

Portia groaned inwardly. If she kept this to herself how could she expect Lexi to be any help?

'Portia? I promise I won't tell anyone, not even Oliver, if that's what you want.'

Portia felt her friend's hand rest on her forearm and stopped walking. She closed her eyes as if not looking at her friend might help her open up to her. 'Charlie has inherited a chateau from his great aunt.' When Lexi didn't reply, she opened her eyes. 'Lexi?'

Lexi still didn't speak. 'I don't understand.'

Portia wasn't sure what there was to be confused about. 'He's inherited—'

'I heard that, but I thought he was from New Zealand. I didn't realise he had relatives on the island.'

Portia explained about the family emigrating when Charlie was small, leaving out the details about why his father had wanted to go – not that Charlie had told her much, but he had said that his father had gone broke for some reason and it had damaged all their lives.

'Wow, so this great aunt...' her voice trailed off. 'I've only ever seen one chateau over here and it wasn't very chateau-like.' Lexi's mouth dropped open. 'You don't think it could be the one up the hill from the boardwalk, do you?'

'I didn't know there was one up there.'

'Not many people are aware of it. I presumed the place was abandoned. It's been closed off for as long as I can remember.' She stamped her feet and slapped her gloved hands together. 'Let's get walking again,' Lexi added, shivering. 'It's too cold to be standing about in this weather.'

They continued on their way, each lost in thought until Lexi grabbed Portia's arm and stopped her again. 'Why don't you ask Charlie to take you there.'

'I was going to,' Portia agreed. 'I've never visited a chateau before and would want to have a look around so that I might be able to help him decide what to do with it.'

'Would you consider living there?'

'What?' What a strange question, Portia thought, staring at Lexi in confusion.

Lexi shrugged. 'Why not? You tell me you want to make Charlie happy. Maybe this is one way of doing it?'

Portia thought of her pristine penthouse, with its chic interior and minimalist décor. Could she leave it for a rundown building that had been lived in by a recluse for decades? Would that even be something Charlie might consider?

'If you don't fancy living there, then maybe you could renovate it, or at least do it up to sell it. Then you could find somewhere new for the pair of you to live in with the proceeds.'

Portia struggled to imagine them doing such a thing. 'Do you mean so we could end up somewhere that's both of ours equally?'

'Well, yes. I mean it must be unsettling for him to know he's living somewhere that's very much your place.' Lexi's face reddened slightly. 'I don't mean to infer anything, it's just a thought.'

'I appreciate you being direct.' Portia couldn't deny that Lexi had a point. She thought through her suggestion. It was a good idea, but she couldn't imagine how it might work. 'I'm not sure we could manage though.'

'You told me only recently how clever Charlie was fixing that door of yours when the contractor didn't do a good enough job. I know he's done various odd carpentry jobs at the hotel when they needed him to, so he does have some idea about it.'

She was right. 'Charlie told me a few stories about working with his dad during school holidays. I gather he was made to help out with some of the properties his dad worked on.' Could they make this work? she wondered.

Lexi clasped her hands together. 'I don't know if it does make sense, Portia, but if you could manage to make it happen, would you?'

Portia considered Lexi's question and realised she would. 'Yes, I think so.' She was as surprised as Lexi clearly was to think she might even consider something like this. Leaving her flat and moving to the island to renovate an old building wasn't like her at all. Then again, Portia decided, she had recently begun to see London through Charlie's eyes and was becoming increasingly aware how tired she was of her life there. Maybe this was what she needed to revive her spirits, not just Charlie's? Thinking of Charlie, Portia wondered how she would go about broaching the suggestion to him.

'It's kind of you to try and help me, but I can't let Charlie know you suggested this. He'd be furious that I broke a confidence.'

'Then don't tell him it was my idea,' Lexi said just before they reached the cider stall where Charlie, Oliver and Tony were raising a toast to something.

'Good idea, I won't.'

The men appeared to be in high spirits, Portia noticed, cheered slightly to see Charlie relaxed and upbeat. In fact, she realised, he seemed happier than he had done at any time in London. She thought through Lexi's idea again, trying to work out the practicalities. All her money was tied up in her flat and unless Charlie's great aunt had left any money for the renovations, she was going to have to sell it to finance them. Yes, she thought, if they were to move into the chateau, she would want to do it as an equal partner. Would Charlie agree to that?

'What are you thinking?' Lexi asked, quietly nudging her. 'Look, I don't want you to stress about this, it was only a suggestion and probably a ridiculous one. This is none of my business and I would hate to think I'd had a hand in you making a decision that was wrong for you or,' she said, grimacing, 'encouraging you to do something that lost you money, or made either of you unhappy.' She shuddered. 'Why don't we forget I said anything and go and have some fun with the guys.'

'It is a good idea,' Portia whispered as they neared the cider stall. 'I just need time to mull it over before mentioning anything to Charlie.'

They joined the men at the stall and Portia was relieved to push the notion to the back of her mind. She caught Charlie's eye as he noticed her and her stomach gave a little flip when he smiled, clearly delighted to see her. He was the most important thing in her life. The thought caused her to panic. Was she really going to give herself up to another man and risk losing love a second time in her life if it all went wrong? She forced the thought away, unable to consider facing life without Charlie.

'Hey, there you are,' he said, reaching out to her. She stepped into his embrace. 'Have you had as much fun as we have this morning?'

Portia gave his glass of cider a pointed smile and shrugged. 'Probably not, but we did have a good time.' She kissed him and wrapped her arms around his waist cuddling him and enjoying standing next to him and warming up slightly. 'That taste good?'

He held the glass to her lips for her to take a sip. 'It's warm. Try some, you're frozen.'

She hadn't expected the sweet drink to warm her up and, taking the glass from him, took another sip before handing it back. 'It's delicious.'

'Would you both like a glass each?' Oliver asked.

Portia shook her head. 'Not for me, thanks.' She relaxed against him, relishing the pressure of his arm around her waist. It was fun being with their friends again. The camaraderie as they joked and teased each other made her wonder again how it might be if this could be a regular occurrence. She imagined it would suit Charlie very much.

She watched Charlie's smiling face as he spoked animatedly about having fun with Oliver and Tony, and knew that if she wanted what was best for him then she needed to consider Lexi's suggestion seriously. They didn't have long on the island and the last thing she wanted was to hesitate for too long and miss the opportunity. There were enough people with money here, Portia knew, who might be only too happy for the chance to support a renovation like the one she had in mind.

'You're very quiet,' Charlie whispered, interrupting her thoughts. 'Is everything all right?'

She nodded. 'Perfectly. I'm just enjoying being here and listening to everyone's chatter. We bumped into Bella earlier, which was lovely.'

'That's nice. How is she?' Charlie asked.

Jack arrived at the table. 'Sorry I'm later than I expected, guys.'

'We were wondering how Bella is?'

'She's doing well. I wanted to take her to the doctor's this morning because I usually go with her but she had promised her mum that she could go this time, which is fair.' He glanced in the direction of the boardwalk about a hundred metres down the hill from them. 'Claire is over the moon at the thought of becoming a grandmother.'

'She is?' Lexi asked, before covering her mouth. 'Sorry, I didn't mean to sound rude then.'

'You're not,' Tony said, shaking his head, clearly also amused that his new wife was turning out to be more maternal than any of them had expected. 'I was surprised, too. In fact I think her excitement at the thought of her own daughter having a baby has taken her a little off guard but the closer we get to Bella's due date the more Claire shops for the baby. She even mentioned plans about babysitting to give Bella time to return to selling her antiques, or even going to London for modelling jobs if she's offered them.'

Portia didn't know Claire all that well but recalled someone saying how she had been an absent mother for most of Bella's life, having left her as a baby with her own mother so that she could go travelling. It was only recently that she had returned to the island, surprising everyone by settling down and marrying Tony.

'I never asked Bella how her job in London went yesterday.'

Tony took a sip from his cider. 'By the amount of shopping she brought back she enjoyed using my credit card.'

Portia winced.

Jack laughed. 'You must have known it was asking for trouble lending it to her?'

Tony nodded. 'I did, and I don't really mind. I wanted Claire to treat herself and Bella to something, but I think she might have forgotten that I'm only a poor fisherman and got a bit carried away.'

Lexi smiled at Portia. 'Hopefully Bella made sure her mother didn't get too carried away.'

Tony visibly relaxed at the reminder. 'I hope you're right. I didn't dare ask how much she spent.'

The conversation went on to the state of fishing during the

winter months and Portia's mind wandered back to Charlie's situation and Lexi's suggestion. She wanted more days like this one. She certainly liked the thought of seeing Charlie this happy. He was always sociable and friendly whenever they were in company but she knew nothing could ever replicate how he felt with his friends back on his beloved island. She needed her old Charlie back. She also needed to find something to make her whole again. Was moving here and taking on an enormous renovation the best way to do that though?

She glanced up at him and catching his eye, smiled. Portia realised she would certainly do it for Charlie's sake. She also suspected that no matter how miserable Charlie might be on the inside he would insist they remain in London if he believed that's what she would prefer. The only way she was going to persuade him that selling her flat was a good idea would be if he believed that investing in the chateau was something she wanted to do for them as a couple and not something she was doing for his sake.

She saw Lexi watching her. 'You all right?' Lexi mouthed.

Portia nodded and gave her a reassuring smile, realising that she was feeling happier and more relaxed than she had in months.

6

CHARLIE

Charlie sat in confused silence.

'Well, say something.' Portia stopped her pacing and turned to face him, her hands clasped tightly together in front of her.

He leant forward, took her hands in his and pulled her gently to sit next to him on the sofa. 'I just need to try and absorb what you've just told me.'

'You don't like the idea?'

Did he? He wasn't sure. He shook his head. 'It's not that I don't like it, it's just that it's unexpected.' Keeping hold of one of her hands, he leant back in the seat. 'Why don't you go over your plan for the chateau again.'

She looked tense and he wasn't surprised. He would be too if he was broaching such a life-changing suggestion. He loved that she never failed to surprise him. 'Go on.'

She took a deep breath and crossed one long leg over the other, turning to face him.

'I've seen how happy you are here. I am too,' she said, though he wasn't sure if she intended making him feel less like this was about him and more something to suit the pair of them.

'I admit I do love it here.'

'I thought we should arrange to visit the property. Have a good look at the state it's in and if we think we can take it on as a project, then I—'

He saw her expression change slightly and instinctively knew she was about to add something she hadn't mentioned earlier. 'What could you do, Portia?' he asked warily.

'I could sell my flat.'

'No.'

She tensed. 'You haven't listened to what I was going to suggest yet.'

He shook his head. 'No. I'll not let you give up your flat for me.' It was the one thing he insisted upon. He had seen only too painfully how lives disintegrated when one person selflessly agreed to change their life on another's whim. Portia's penthouse was all she had left of her life with Alastair, and as much as Charlie wished he had been the one to provide her with such a home, he had no intention of being the reason she parted with it.

'Listen, Charlie.'

He pulled her into a hug, hating to think he was upsetting her. Portia was fiercely independent and he loved her for it, but also couldn't let her do anything that might de-stabilise her future. 'Please don't be cross with me, darling,' he said, kissing her hair. 'I love that you want to help me, but I can't let you lose your beautiful home.'

She pushed him away and he saw her anger immediately. 'Hasn't it occurred to you that you might not be the only one needing a fresh start?'

Shocked by her comment, he took a moment to speak. 'What do you mean?'

'Not from you, Charlie.' She rested her free hand lightly on his cheek, calming him. 'I need something new to focus on and I thought maybe this might be the answer.'

He tried to unscramble his thoughts. 'Sorry, I hadn't realised. Carry on, I'll promise not to interrupt you again.' He needed time to think and letting her explain her idea more fully would hopefully give him that.

'I thought that if we both believe we can cope with the renovations, then I can put my penthouse on the market to help fund them.' She narrowed her eyes. 'I'm presuming your great aunt didn't leave you any money for the work. I suppose that if she had any money she would have used it to do the place up for herself.'

He didn't say anything but having never seen any signs of his great aunt having money, presumed Portia was correct in her assumptions.

'I thought that once we had done up a couple of living areas and one or two bedrooms, that we might be able to rent out rooms, with the plan eventually to host events there.' She smiled, clearly feeling encouraged by his silence. 'As you know, I have experience planning and hosting events and you've carried out DIY jobs throughout your life working for your dad and helping at the Seabreeze Hotel when they needed things fixed.'

He waited for a few seconds and assuming she had finished, smiled. He needed to be positive about what she had said. Portia might appear confident on the outside but he knew from experience how sensitive she could be and lacking in the self-confidence people assumed she had.

'It's a very good idea.' Her shoulders relaxed and she opened her mouth to speak, but he raised a finger to stop her. 'However, we need see the place first. Find out exactly what we would be letting ourselves in for. And, if we think we can cope, we'll take it from there. Agreed?' Unwilling to commit to anything without being certain, especially when she was offering to sell her home, he wanted to be clear about their options. 'If I think there's too much work for us to do, then I'll do one of two things.'

'And they are?'

'Either put the place on the market as it is and try to get whatever I can for it.'

'I can't imagine you'll really be happy doing that. Option B?'

'Slowly do the work, then sell it in a slightly better state.'

'I want to finance the project if we do go ahead though.'

He took both her hands in his, raising them to his lips. 'I don't want you to do that though, Portia. I won't put your home at risk. You love it there so much.'

'I told you, I'm tired of my life in London.'

'Are you though?' he asked doubtfully. She always seemed perfectly happy. Had she really been hiding her dissatisfaction there, or was it, he thought guiltily, that he had been so wrapped up in his own inability to settle that he hadn't noticed how she was feeling?

'I wouldn't say it if it wasn't true.'

He studied her face looking for any hint that she wasn't being completely honest with him. Not finding any reason to doubt her he shrugged.

'I don't want your misguided protectiveness towards me to ruin this for us, Charlie.'

'Portia. The penthouse is your only security. If you sold it you'd probably never get another chance to buy it back again.'

He felt her hands grabbing his shoulders. 'Charlie, I loved Alastair as you know, but I'm with you now. You're my priority now.' He went to argue but she shook her head. 'I should have said *our* relationship is my priority. I admit, the penthouse is beautiful and I've loved living there, but this could be a new start for us. One that we both venture into equally. That is, if you agree to me investing the money from the sale of my flat.'

He wanted to argue with her, to tell her about his parents and how their lives, and his, had been upended by trying to restore his father's pride. 'Portia, it's not that I don't want to do this, or that I'm ungrateful, but if this went wrong we could end up losing everything. What if the strain of us taking on a project like this tears us apart? What then? Are you really happy to risk that happening?'

She frowned and he watched as she mulled over his words.

'We need to be sensible, because if this doesn't work out it could ruin our lives.'

Still she said nothing for a while. 'Hug me, Charlie,' she said eventually.

He pulled her into his arms and held her tightly against him. 'I love you, sweetheart, so much, and I couldn't bear it if I was the cause of you losing your home.'

He loved her more than he had ever done before. To know that she was willing to risk her own security for a future with him meant more than he could say. However, Portia selling her beloved home was a step too far. He realised she had finished speaking and took a moment to gather himself, not wishing to upset her when clearly she believed this was a feasible idea.

'Well?' she asked, her pale blue eyes peering at him with an intensity that told him she was aware how big a deal this suggestion was for them both.

'No.' He swallowed, aware that his refusal wasn't what she was expecting to hear.

'But, Charlie, I've just explained.'

'You thought you would give up everything you've built for yourself, for me.'

'I explained, it's not like that.'

He stared at her and shook his head slowly. 'That is exactly what you're suggesting, Portia, and I won't let you do it.'

'Let me?' she scoffed and he knew he had gone too far. Her cheeks reddened.

'I don't mean to upset you,' he said, reaching to take her hands in his. He watched her lower her gaze to their hands. 'Portia, please look at me.' He waited for her to do as he asked. 'I am grateful to you for being willing to give up everything you have in London to make me happy.'

'I'm not.'

'You are,' he said quietly, emotion catching in his throat. 'And I love you even more than I already did for being so unselfish, but surely you can understand why I couldn't possibly agree to you doing this for me.'

'I want to though, Charlie.'

He knew she did but that didn't soften his stance on the issue. 'I know. And that's incredibly generous of you, but I already feel our relationship is more one-sided than it should be.'

He saw her stiffen. 'What do you mean by that?'

'I know you understand what I mean.' Why did this have to happen now? 'I can't give you all the things Alastair was able to. All I can offer is my love and I won't let you sell your place in London for a rundown pile of stone up the hill from here.' When she didn't react, he added, 'You're always saying how long it took you to find the perfect place and do it up, and now you're willing to sell it for a... a renovation project? It's madness.'

'But Charlie.' Her eyes hardened. 'What's your real reason for being against this idea?'

He sighed heavily. 'I couldn't bear it if you ended up resenting me for giving up a life that you love.' There, he'd said it. He hoped it was enough to persuade her not to keep pushing for them to take such an enormous chance.

Portia didn't speak. He waited anxiously for her to respond.

Then, when her eyes darkened, Charlie braced himself for what she was about to say hoping he hadn't pushed her too far.

'This isn't all about you, Charlie,' she said quietly, her voice tight and barely above a whisper. 'Didn't I say I've tired of life in London?'

'Yes, but—'

'I know this suggestion is out of the blue, but the thought of starting a new life here with you, working towards something next to you, has made me very excited.' She didn't speak for a moment. 'Don't you want to at least try to see if we've got what it takes to build something this amazing together?'

Did he? He thought of the last time he had visited the chateau when he was sixteen. 'I haven't been there for over twelve years,' he said, aware it wasn't the reply she wanted. 'It was in a terrible state even then.'

She frowned thoughtfully. 'If you're so worried about me losing my money, then why don't we ask Oliver to draw up a contract between us, with a clause stating that if the business doesn't work within a certain amount of time that the chateau be sold? At least that way we would both be protected in some way.'

Charlie knew what she said made sense. He sighed, feeling his resolve weakening; it was clear she had made up her mind.

'Do I sense your resistance waning?' she asked, her eyes twinkling.

He nodded. 'If you mean do I know when to give up, then yes.'

'So you'll do it?'

He looked at the woman he loved and seeing the excitement in her eyes realised she was more fearless than anyone he had ever known before.

'What?' she laughed.

'You're a brave woman, Portia.'

'Brave?'

'Brave, beautiful and,' he said, pulling her into his arms and kissing her, 'very, very persuasive.'

'Is that a yes?'

He groaned, aware that he had lost the argument. 'It is.'

Portia squealed. 'Great. But I want to hear you say it.'

'Yes, Portia. I'll join you in this chateau venture.'

'You mustn't worry, Charlie,' she said, kissing him enthusiastically. We'll save a fortune with you doing a lot of the physical work and the money will go three times as far than if we were paying contractors.'

'You do realise I don't have any experience renovating properties, especially big ones like this one?'

She hugged him tightly to her and kissed his neck. 'Maybe not, but neither do I. And at least you do have some DIY experience. Anyway, you can learn anything from videos online.'

'Are you sure about that?' he laughed, incredulous at her lack of fear.

'Stop finding problems before we begin. I know that together we can achieve anything.'

He only hoped she was right. A thought occurred to him. 'And where will we live while all this is taking place?'

'Lexi said we can stay in the end cottage until the season begins and they need it for holidaymakers.'

'You've mentioned this to Lexi already?' He stiffened, unhappy to think he wasn't the first to know about her idea.

Portia gave him a teasing smile. 'You wouldn't want me to present this idea to you without first thinking things through, would you?'

Aware she was right, he sighed. 'Of course not.' Remembering they only had a few months until the holiday season began again, he asked, 'Where will we stay when the season starts and Lexi needs the cottage back?' He didn't fancy the pair of them having to sleep on friends' sofas for months at a time.

'If we get a move on we'll have a couple of bedrooms renovated by then,' she said with the assurance of someone who wasn't used to failing. 'Then we will have somewhere to sleep and a place to store our things.' He listened while she spoke. 'We'll renovate the rooms we need for events first, then continue with guest bedrooms and other areas of the chateau and as soon as it's up and running you can do what you do best and manage the business. That's when you'll come into your own. Think about it, Charlie. You're going to have your very own hotel to run when the chateau renovations are complete.'

She had thought things through, he realised, unsurprised. 'It does sound exciting,' he admitted. 'What do you suggest we do after that?'

'I was hoping you'd give my idea a chance,' she said. 'So I phoned the lawyer who kindly arranged for us to visit the chateau first thing in the morning.'

Charlie laughed. 'Of course you've already arranged the next step in the process.' He looked down at her and shook his head. 'I don't think I've ever met anyone more persuasive or determined than you.'

'We've already ascertained that. Now, kiss me and tell me how much you love me.'

He did as she asked, hoping the pair of them weren't about to make the biggest mistake of their lives.

7

PORTIA

Portia parked Lexi's car at the rusted chateau gates and switched off the ignition. Charlie had persuaded the lawyer that he knew the place well and didn't need anyone to show them around. As soon as he had the keys in his possession, they had left for the short drive up the hill to Chateau de Caesarea with Charlie making small talk on the short drive from the cottage.

She couldn't miss the tension he was giving off each time he clasped his hands together only to release them again and rest his palms on his knees, and wished he wasn't quite so anxious about this idea of hers.

Portia stared at a weather-worn painted sign hanging across the entranceway from a chain someone had strung from one side to the other. *Danger! Keep out!*

'Not exactly welcoming,' Charlie said, getting out to unhook one end of the chain and carrying it to the other side to allow them access to the driveway.

'I imagined we would see the property from the road,' Portia admitted, getting out to join him and locking the car.

'You want to walk up the driveway? Won't it be quicker to drive so we can see the place quicker?'

'I thought that by parking here and walking we'd get a better first impression.' Was she trying to persuade herself or him? No, doing it this way was right, she was certain of it. 'People's arrival will be vitally important when we do open this place.' She felt Charlie turn to look at her. 'What?'

'Nothing.' He turned away.

Portia sensed she had said something wrong. Then it dawned on her that maybe she should have said *if*, rather than *when* they open. She was going to need to be a little more thoughtful about what she said if she was to persuade him that this was a good idea.

She took Charlie's hand, hoping to reassure him before they set off along the driveway.

'Don't worry. I'm aware I'm getting a little ahead of myself.' She gave his hand a gentle squeeze to emphasise her words. 'I've always believed in being positive about something. It's the best way to broach opportunities.'

'I suppose you're right.' He leant forward and kissed her. 'Unfortunately, my way of looking at things is to try to imagine the worst happening and then working out if I can handle that scenario.'

'I know, and that makes good business sense.'

'Shall we get going now then?' he asked, looking slightly more at ease.

Portia tugged his hand and led him through the gates. As they walked in silence along the grassy driveway, each lost in their own thoughts, she tried to take in everything around her and was saddened to presume that this place hadn't looked pristine for many decades. Portia made a mental note to suggest one of the first things they needed to do when working on the gardens was to pay for a tree surgeon to sort out the trees leaning at varying angles over the only route to the chateau.

'It'll only take one storm and half of these could crash down,' Charlie said, stopping to study them.

'I was thinking something along those lines, too. Anyway, how long do you think this driveway might be?' she asked, almost to herself.

'Long enough to take a lot of work to keep it looking good,' Charlie joked. 'It's curving to the left a little way ahead so hopefully we're almost there.'

As they passed the bend Portia saw that it then curved to the right before straightening up again. A couple of minutes later she spotted a turret through the branches as the place slowly began to reveal itself to them.

Portia gasped and pointed. 'Look Charlie, can you see that?'

He peered through the leafless branches and drew in a deep breath. He had forgotten how impressive this place was after all these years.

'You never told me it looked like a castle from a fantasy movie.' She wondered if seeing the pretty masonry was making the experience much more real for him now. 'I can't wait to see more.'

'Let's hurry up and explore then.' Charlie broke into a run, pulling her along next to him, both of them laughing like excited teenagers. If this is how working on the chateau is going to make him feel, Portia thought, then she had been right to go with her gut instinct and suggest the idea to him.

They reached the large circular carriage driveway in front of the building and Portia pulled Charlie's hand to stop him. He looked up and she followed his gaze.

'There are two. Look.' She turned to him. 'Why didn't you tell me this place was so pretty?'

'It is?' he teased. 'Fine. I wanted it to be a surprise.' Charlie pointed up at the second turret on the opposite end of the building. 'Although by the looks of things these turrets might not last much longer in their present state.'

She stared at the second turret, disappointed to note that this one only had a partial roof and ivy growing through cracks in crumbling areas near the windows. 'It's a shame. It looks so unloved in its current state.'

He didn't reply immediately and Portia presumed he was trying to find the words to say something positive about the rest of the front aspect of the chateau. Her heart plummeted when she saw how many windows were broken, the spaces where they should have been now replaced with water-stained cardboard, and in some places strips of wood stuck in between the stone. The windows that were still intact were on the side of the building where the better turret stood but even they were mostly covered with ivy and she doubted much light entered the rooms inside.

'The roof doesn't look too good either, does it?' she grumbled. There were missing slates where the timbers appeared to be rotten or at least on their way to some sort of decay; surely this sight would be a dealbreaker for Charlie? She hoped not. Despite what she had told him she had already set her heart on committing to this venture with him.

'It's larger than I expected,' she admitted, not wanting him to know that she was dead set on doing this.

'It is?'

She wished she was able to read something in Charlie's non-committal response.

'Yes, quite a bit.'

'Is it in a worse state than you expected too?' Charlie asked, not hiding the concern in his voice.

'It's a little sadder than I had imagined it to be,' Portia admitted.

His frown deepened. 'I hope I didn't give you a false impression of this place?' he said, shaking his head. 'Maybe I should have described it better to you.'

'Not at all,' Portia replied, wanting to reassure him. 'I think maybe I was being too optimistic when I envisaged it.' She shivered and rubbed her arm with her free hand. 'It's chilly out here. Shall we go inside, then you can show me around the rest of the place and we can see what we're taking on.'

Charlie let go of Portia's hand and withdrew the larger key from his pocket and held it up.

She stared at the impressive key. 'I love that it's exactly the sort of chunky, elaborate key I imagined a chateau door to have.'

'I was thinking the same thing.' Slotting the key into the keyhole with a little difficulty, Charlie looked uncertain. 'It's probably no warmer inside.'

'I suppose that's only to be expected with all these broken windows.'

He turned the key and pushed the door open. When he didn't immediately step inside, Portia looked at him. 'Is something the matter?'

'It feels a bit strange being back here after all this time,' he answered his voice quiet. 'It feels odd to think that this place is mine now.'

Not wanting Charlie to overthink what he was about to do, Portia decided to take matters into her own hands, and strode into the hallway determined to find something to raise their spirits.

'Come along. Let's go and explore.'

After a moment's hesitation, Charlie followed her. 'Yes, I suppose we should find out what we're letting ourselves in for.'

She needed to see what was left of the character in the rooms, determined to replicate any pieces of cornicing still there, or copy wallpapers, floor tiles, anything.

Portia stopped and looked down, unsure whether there might

still be decent tiles or floorboards under their feet. At the moment all they appeared to be standing on was a muddy mess. She wondered if it was some sort of carpeting but doubted it. Looking around her, she noticed a large, dusty light fitting and realised that at some point in the building's past it might have been an elaborate chandelier. All that was left now though were clusters of dull stones hanging on cobwebbed chains she hoped might be washed to reveal crystals. There weren't enough to make the chandelier perfect again but she was sure she could source similar ones online to bring it back to some sort of glory.

Aware she was being fanciful and had far bigger issues to deal with than a damaged light fitting, Portia decided that there was little else of note in the hallway to excite her.

'The cantilevered staircase is incredible,' Charlie said, walking forward to stand underneath where the staircase curved around the outside of the room and upwards to the next floor. 'I'd forgotten how impressive it was.' He laughed. 'I probably never noticed it when I was sixteen.'

Portia's mood lifted slightly. Charlie had found something worth loving and she could see the delight on his face. She wasn't sure why the staircase was so impressive, until she studied it and noticed the sleek wooden handrail and intricately carved rods connecting it to the base.

'I'm trying to picture the well-dressed guests and beautiful brides descending the staircase in a few months' time,' Portia said thoughtfully, imagining herself gliding down dressed in an exquisite handmade dress covered in intricate lace as she slowly made her way to join Charlie. She shook her head. Now wasn't the time for daydreams. She had her work cut out if she was to persuade him that this was the best way forward for the pair of them.

'It is rather lovely,' she agreed. 'Shall we go through to this room over here?' Without waiting for him to agree Portia turned to her right and opened one of the double doors, having to push hard to get them to move. This was another room that must have been impressive at some point with its floor-to-ceiling windows and huge white marble fire surround.

'I'd have loved to visit the chateau in its heyday.'

'Me, too,' Charlie agreed.

She walked further into the room, touching the peeling paint on the shutters folded back against the wall on either side of the windows. Some moved when she tried to ease them forward, others were painted in place. At least they were still there though, Portia thought.

She heard Charlie walk to the other end of the room but wanted to make up her own mind about the chateau as she tried to imagine it after they had finished working their magic. The last thing she intended to do was allow his fears to dampen what was left of her spirits.

She went to the next room and found another large reception room only this one was slightly narrower. Eventually Portia reached a smaller staircase that led down into what she presumed to have been a kitchen.

'Another enormous room,' she said to herself, looking at the old-fashioned range that couldn't have been used in years. How on earth had Charlie's great aunt survived to be over a hundred in this stale, rotting place? Although, she had to admit, it did hold a certain charm. There was a smaller room off the kitchen at the back where Portia was surprised to see stainless steel work surfaces and what looked like a very up-to-date oven. She thought of Remi, upset to be losing his bakery, and wondered if once they no longer needed this room, they could rent it out to him? It would help to bring in some money and, she thought, gazing around the large, echoey space, be nice to have an extra person working at the chateau.

Portia looked back at the old kitchen through the doorway. It was a mess, but there was something rather romantic about this building in all its crumbling glory. She realised she was smitten, despite her determination to see all its faults, and hoped desperately that Charlie could find it in his heart to at least want to try and put their mark on this place.

If they could fix it up and make a business out of it, then surely it would set them up for a future where Charlie would feel on an equal footing to her. She knew that nothing less was going to be needed if they were to be truly happy together.

Portia closed her eyes and willed Charlie to agree her plans.

Hearing footsteps, she braced herself for Charlie's reaction and turned to face him, aware that whether she liked it or not, this was his chateau and she was bound by his final decision.

'So? she asked, taking a deep breath. 'What do you think of it so far?'

8

CHARLIE

'I'm already intimidated by the amount of obvious work I've spotted so far and we haven't taken a step upstairs yet,' Charlie grumbled, his stomach in knots at the prospect of taking on such a daunting project.

'You are?'

She seemed surprised. Had Portia fallen for the beauty of what this place might look like if they somehow found a way to achieve all they hoped? If she had, surely she was ignoring the rotting floorboards, dodgy-looking ceilings and crumbling stonework, and that was just for starters.

'Portia, if you're not going to be realistic about what renovation will entail, then I'm not sure we should carry on even looking,' he said warily, unsure if Portia was simply saying all the things she thought he hoped to hear to get her own way. 'Portia?'

She frowned. 'Stop worrying so much, Charlie. I know this place is a mess, I'm not completely blind to it, but I can't help loving it already. Don't you?' She walked up to him and he felt her hands slip around his waist before she kissed him. 'Even a little bit?'

He knew when he was being played and this was one of those times. Charlie sighed. If anyone else acted this way with him he would have no problem rebuffing them, but this was Portia, and much as he was concerned about taking on a project he had little experience for he also couldn't help wanting to do whatever it took to make her happy.

'Don't you think it's going to be fun for the two of us to live in this amazing place?' she continued. Then after a brief hesitation, added. 'And what about us being able to work side by side each day while we drag this place back to its former glory?'

Charlie's mood dipped further. Portia hadn't only fallen in love with the chateau, she had romanticised their future here as well.

His heart lurched as she pulled a pleading expression. 'Charlie? What do you think?'

He saw the hope on her face and hated the thought of disappointing her, especially when, thanks to his inability to settle fully in London, she was opting to completely change her own lifestyle hoping to make him happy. 'I suppose it will be exciting working with you,' he admitted. He laughed as a thought occurred to him.

'What's so funny?' she asked, narrowing her eyes.

'I'm not sure *exciting* is the correct word to describe it though.' He smiled to soften his words. 'I'm probably too startled right now with how run-down this place is to think of a better description.'

She grinned. 'Maybe *interesting* is more fitting.'

'Yes, probably.'

'We'll take things one step at a time,' Portia said, her voice soothing him slightly. 'I can help you whenever you need me to and when each room is finished I'll be able to design the layout. I'll make every room plush and perfect for our guests.' She rested her head on his shoulder. 'We could go to auctions to find the right pieces of furniture.'

Not ready to think that far ahead, Charlie shook his head.

'Shall we stick to the most important bits right now and carry on looking through this enormous building with its many, many rooms?'

She hugged him tightly against her. 'We can do this, Charlie, and we will. You just need to trust me.'

What choice did he have, Charlie wondered as they found their way back to the beautiful staircase and walked upstairs to the next floor hand in hand. Portia insisted she was doing this because she wanted to find a way for them both to move to Jersey and try something new. But was that really all there was to it? He still wasn't sure he had the courage to take on this project and allow Portia to invest her life savings in it.

'Charlie,' she said, interrupting his thoughts. 'Tell me you're happy to agree to this. I know it's the perfect next step for us to take.'

He wished he had her confidence. He stared into her eyes, searching for any doubts, but either she was completely convinced, or she was brilliant at hiding them. If she was willing to do this for their relationship, then didn't she deserve him putting his trust in her instincts?

'But what if we fail?' he asked, unable to ignore the childhood trauma of losing his own family home thanks to his father's well-meant decisions.

She stepped closer to him and, resting her palms on his chest, whispered, 'Have you considered how life will be for us if we succeed though?'

He hadn't. 'No, but—'

'Charlie? You can do this. We can both do this.'

'We can?' He wanted her to be right more than anything.

She nodded. 'Abso-flippin-lutely.' Portia slipped her arms around his neck and Charlie let her pull him down so that their lips met in a kiss.

'All right then,' he said, pushing away his doubts. 'But only after we've looked through the rest of the house. Then we'll go away, crunch some numbers and see if we can realistically make this work.'

Portia squealed and took his face in her hands, pressing her lips firmly against his again. 'I just know we'll be brilliant at this, Charlie.'

He wished he shared her belief in their abilities, but thought it best not to say so.

9

PORTIA

The following week, as Portia carefully packed her precious handbags while the rest of the flat was being done up by a removal firm, she hoped that she was doing the right thing having everything stored in a safe unit until she and Charlie had completed the work on the chateau and were ready to move in. She stroked the dust cover of her favourite bag and knew there was no going back now that the flat had been sold to Venetia and her husband, and Oliver's lawyer had drawn up the contract between her and Charlie that they had each signed a few days earlier.

She looked at her watch and saw that they only had two hours before they needed to leave for the airport to fly back to Jersey. It wasn't easy to leave her flat behind forever, but it was too late to do anything about it now. She was determined not to regret this decision.

Apart from her friendship with Oliver, selling her flat would mean one less connection to Alastair. He had been her entire life until his death, but spending time with Charlie had shown her more as time passed that maybe Alastair hadn't been the perfect man she had committed to her memory. Even so, she mused as she swallowed the lump in her throat, if it hadn't been for Alastair leaving her money in his will she never would have had the funds to buy her flat in the first place. And, apart from when she was with Oliver, for those first two years her flat had been where she felt safest and closest to Alastair as she struggled to survive those first dark months without him.

Was it right to use that money to invest in a future with Charlie? Of course it was. Hadn't Oliver assured her many times that his brother would have wanted her to be happy, to move on with her life and not spend the rest of it mourning him? Yes, Alistair might have had his faults but she couldn't deny that he had loved her deeply and wouldn't want his death to define her future.

'I hope I have your blessing about this next stage in my life, Alastair,' she whispered.

He had wanted the best for her, she knew Oliver was right about that, and this opportunity with Charlie surely was exactly that.

She took a deep breath to try and calm her emotions. As much as she had encouraged Charlie to agree to do this, now she had had time to stop and think about their move in detail, her nerves had kicked in.

'Don't overthink this, Portia,' she mumbled. Charlie deserved this fresh start and she needed to keep his enthusiasm going for the project if it was to be a success. This wasn't the time for doubts. Portia reminded herself that she had insisted they could do this and she had meant it at the time. All she needed to do now was focus on the end result.

She could hear Charlie answering questions from the removal staff, then his footsteps as he came into the bedroom.

'How are you getting on?' He sat on the end of the stripped bed mattress and watched her. 'Do you need me to help you with anything?'

He was so thoughtful, Portia thought smiling up at him, loving how much he adored her. She couldn't want for more.

'No, thanks' she said, getting to her feet. 'I'm pretty much done in here.'

'If your case is ready to be closed I can take it and your hand luggage through to the living room with mine. The guys are almost done in there and all they need to do is come and take these boxes, then we'll be ready to hand the keys over to Venetia and leave.'

Not wishing to let Charlie notice her doubts, Portia forced a smile and sealed the final box with a roll of package tape.

'Right, let's get a wriggle on,' she joked. 'I'll carry my hand luggage, if you carry through my suitcase.' She closed it and laughed when Charlie grimaced as he lifted it from the bed onto the floor.

'What on earth have you packed in here?' he asked through gritted teeth.

'Nothing I won't need.' She suspected she was taking far too much with her to Jersey but the thought of leaving her favourite boots and coats behind was too much. She didn't like to admit it but she was surprised she had managed to fit as much as she had into one case. 'I don't think I've ever travelled this light,' she teased.

Charlie puffed out his cheeks. 'I don't own enough to fill half of this, let alone pack it fit to bursting.'

She followed Charlie out of the room, turning to give her bedroom one last look. With all her possessions either already gone or packed in boxes it didn't have the same familiarity as it once had. She had loved living here both before Charlie had moved in and especially afterwards but, wanting to make today a positive one, forced her memories to the back of her mind. Dwelling on the past was not the way to move into this new phase in her life. This future was hers and Charlie's and she was determined that together they would achieve even more than they hoped.

* * *

As their plane neared the coast, Charlie pointed to the view from the seat next to hers. 'Look at the sea. Doesn't St Ouen's bay look stunning? I can't wait to get down there and take my first walk.' He kissed her shoulder. 'It's good to be back, isn't it?'

She gazed past the plane's wings at the long stretch of pale golden sand running from one end of the beach at L'Etacq to the other end at La Pulente. Charlie was right, it was good to be back. She reached for his hand without taking her eyes from the beautiful sight beneath them, glad for the reminder that where she was going was incredibly beautiful and welcoming.

'This is an exciting time for us, Charlie. I just know we're going to make this work.'

The plane veered left to line up with the runway and Portia settled back into her seat and turned to Charlie, wanting to take her mind off the landing. 'The first thing we need to do is find a way to bring in deposits from people wanting to hold their events at the chateau,' she said, soothed by the thought of making more plans. 'It'll be a good way to boost our funds so that we have more for the renovations.'

Charlie smiled and kissed her. 'You must think about this venture all the time. I hope you're going to be able to switch off at the end of each day.'

She doubted she would, or if she really wanted to. Portia pictured her life savings now sitting in her bank account waiting to be poured into the chateau. No, she didn't *want* to make this work, she *needed* to, and as quickly as possible. She wouldn't be able to relax fully until they had enough of the work completed to be able to start holding events and bring in much-needed funds. Picturing the state of the chateau when she and Charlie had visited it, Portia knew, regardless of her assurances to Charlie and their friends, that they had an enormous amount of work to get through before they could even hope to achieve that.

10

CHARLIE

Charlie wasn't surprised to see Oliver waiting for them in the arrivals hall. He watched Portia race ahead to greet their friend with their hand luggage as he followed behind pulling their larger cases.

'I can't tell you how excited Lexi and I are to have the pair of you living back here full-time,' he said, smiling at Charlie over Portia's shoulder as he hugged her. 'I think you're both very brave but I'm also certain you'll be brilliant and will soon have the chateau running as a viable business.'

'Thanks, Oliver,' Portia said. 'But you're always certain I can succeed at whatever I put my mind towards.'

'That's because he's right,' Charlie said, unsurprised that Oliver believed in her so completely. 'Portia has to be the most determined person I've ever met.'

Oliver gave him a knowing look. 'She's been that way for as long as I've known her and I can't see her changing any time soon.'

'You'd want me to?' Portia grinned as the doors from the hall automatically opened and they stepped out into the bright wintery sunshine.

'Never.'

Charlie helped Oliver load their cases into his Range Rover and then got into the passenger seat next to him looking over his shoulder at Portia, happy to see her finally looking relaxed. He suspected that leaving the flat had been far harder for her than she had let on and loved her all the more for her insistence that they move to the island. He reached back and smiled at her as she took his hand briefly in hers.

'I always forget how it's warmer in the city than here on the island,' Portia grumbled, pulling the collar of her puffy coat closer around her neck. She shivered. 'I'll be glad to get to the cottage and settle in. I'm exhausted after all the packing and planning we've done recently.'

'You both look very well for all of that though,' Oliver said as they drove away from the airport car park. 'I expected to be greeting two haggard people, not the glamorous pair that walked through from the baggage hall.'

Charlie couldn't hide his amusement. 'I'm not sure you could honestly describe me as being remotely glamorous.'

Oliver glanced at him and pulled a face. 'Maybe you're not in Portia's league, but then who is?' He looked at her in his rearview mirror. 'Your boyfriend is always immaculately turned out though, isn't he?'

'Yes, you are, Charlie. I think it's having to always be presentable working front of house in hotels.'

Charlie supposed they were right. He always liked to have his hair neatly cut each month and rarely went unshaved. 'Probably.' He doubted either of them would be looking nearly as tidy once they started work.

'You are right though, Oliver,' Portia said from the back seat. 'It has been rather exhausting, but more emotionally than physically. I only packed up my most precious things, and the flat was easy enough to sign over to my friend, Venetia. She was thrilled when I called her offering to sell it to her and more than happy to pay the going rate for the place, so at least there wasn't any haggling.'

'Well, you're here now,' Oliver said. 'I know you're going to want to get going as soon as possible, but tonight you must come to our cottage for supper. Lexi is at home cooking something comforting for you both and she won't listen to any excuses.'

'Dear Lexi, she's always so thoughtful.' Portia sighed.

Charlie was relieved he and Portia wouldn't have to think about making food. Lexi and Oliver were always great company and he looked forward to a quiet evening with them. He suspected they would have been shopping for groceries for their cottage too like they always did for their guests.

'It's very kind of you both to look after us so well,' Charlie said. 'And I'll certainly look forward to sitting still for a while this evening.'

He felt Portia's hand on his arm. 'Only for this evening,' she teased. 'Tomorrow, first thing, you and I will need to start getting on with things.'

'I can tell she's going to be a right bossy boots to work with,' Charlie joked.

Oliver gave him a wry smile before nodding. 'Rather you than me, mate.'

Portia frowned. 'Actually, I've been thinking, Oliver...'

Charlie wondered what Portia was about to suggest. He could tell by the tone of her voice that it was something serious.

'Here goes,' Oliver groaned. 'Go on then, what's on your mind?'

'Well, now you and Lexi are engaged, I thought the pair of you might enjoy being the first couple to have your wedding at the chateau.'

Charlie expected Oliver to agree simply because he always

seemed to whenever Portia wanted something, so was surprised when Oliver shook his head.

'Sorry, Portia,' he said, pulling an apologetic face at Charlie.

'No?' Portia seemed surprised too, Charlie noted. 'You *are* getting married, aren't you?' she asked, leaning forward in her seat.

'We are. But Lexi doesn't want a big deal made of it.'

'She doesn't?'

Charlie heard Portia's disbelief and it dawned on him that when they married she would want a lavish wedding with all the trimmings. He supposed that at least they would have their own special venue where they could hold the event.

'No,' Oliver said. 'I know she's made it up with her father after he went behind her back and sold her fishermen's cottages to me, and is even on much better terms with her dad's girlfriend, Gloria, after her underhand part in encouraging him to sell, but Lexi insists she doesn't want any fuss. I have to agree with her when she told me that if she can't have her late mother there, then she really doesn't relish planning a big wedding, as she would only miss her more if we did that. Also, my father is increasingly poorly and my mother won't leave him in Scotland to come here, which is understandable. The two of us have decided that we'd far rather go away somewhere quiet and get married, just the two of us.'

Charlie understood the reasons for them making their decision. 'I don't blame you.'

'Darling Oliver,' Portia said, placing her hand on his shoulder. 'I completely understand. Anyway, a wedding should be special to the people getting married. It infuriates me when couples are cajoled to do what others want rather than be allowed to make their own choices for their wedding day. Good for you two. I'm sure wherever you decide to marry it will be very special.'

He raised his hand and rested it on top of Portia's. 'Thanks, you sweet girl. I told Lexi you'd understand.'

Charlie smiled inwardly at the thought that Lexi and Oliver knew Portia well enough to be prepared for her approaching them about holding their wedding at the chateau.

'Portia's right,' Charlie said, wanting to let her know he supported her. 'You must do whatever's best for the pair of you.'

'Maybe we can hold a party for you after the wedding?' Portia suggested.

Charlie swapped glances with Oliver, smiling when his friend rolled his eyes heavenward. 'We both know she's not one to give up too easily.'

'She isn't. Which is why I'm glad you're the one going into business with her and not me.'

'Charming! I am still here you know.'

11

PORTIA

Oliver drew up into his parking space at the end of the row of fishermen's cottages. 'Portia, why don't you go and say hello to Lexi while I help Charlie take these cases to your cottage?'

'I like that you're calling it our cottage already,' she teased. 'I'll take my handbag with me. My phone is in there and I want to be sure I don't miss any calls if Venetia or the removal people need me.'

She left the two of them moaning about the weight of her case. 'Lexi?' she called as she opened the first front door and went inside.

'Through here.'

Portia took off her coat and hung it from one of the hooks by the front door and hurried through to join her in the living room. 'Oh, this is bliss.' She walked up to the multi-fuel fire and rubbed her cold hands together in an attempt to warm them. 'It's such a relief to finally be in a warm room again. The plane was freezing and not much warmer than outside.'

'Where are the guys?'

Portia explained about the cases. 'They shouldn't be long.'

'I'm not sure I could have done all that you have and go straight from packing to the airport,' Lexi said, carrying a tray with a cafetière and several mugs over to place it on the coffee table. 'I had imagined you might stay in a hotel for one night to rest before flying over.'

'In hindsight it would have been a good idea but we were both anxious to get here and start this new phase in our lives.'

'You must be shattered.' Lexi lifted the cafetière and asked whether Portia wanted a cup.

'Yes please, I'm terribly thirsty.'

'Well, we've stocked up the cupboards and fridge for you in your cottage, but if we've forgotten anything you must let one of us know.'

'Thanks, but we'll need to start looking after ourselves now we're here for good.' She took the mug of coffee from Lexi and poured in a little milk, cupping the mug in her hands to help warm them. 'I'll be honest with you,' she said, lowering her voice in case Charlie and Oliver came back. 'I'm a little nervous about this renovation work. All of this is very new to me. To both of us.'

Lexi poured herself a drink and sat down next to her. 'The two of you will be fine. You get along well and you'll be learning together. I think that as long as you keep communication open between the pair of you, everything should be fine.' She took a sip of her drink and set the mug down onto a place mat on the table. 'I can't wait to see the chateau. I never knew it existed until you told Oliver and me about it.'

'As soon as we get going, we'll invite you both up to show you around.'

Lexi moved on the seat to face Portia. 'It's exciting that you and Charlie have your own place together now.'

Lexi was right. It was exciting and she must take care not to lose sight of that. 'We need to start as we mean to go on. This is such an amazing opportunity for us and I hope we remember that when we get tired and irritable.'

'Yes. Resentment is a dangerous thing.'

'Who's resenting whom?' Oliver asked, walking into the living room with Charlie following him.

'Only that Charlie and I need to remember not to hide any concerns we might have about the work.'

'That's right,' Lexi smiled at Charlie. 'Is it wonderful being back here for good?'

He sighed happily, causing Portia's heart to sing. 'I have the most generous girlfriend anyone could ever hope for,' he said, reaching out and taking her hand in his. 'I still can't believe Portia has financed this by selling her precious flat.'

Not wishing Charlie's concerns to get the better of him, Portia decided to stop any further conversation on the matter. 'We wouldn't have anywhere to live in or renovate if it wasn't for your chateau, Charlie, don't forget that. Anyway, as I've told you before, I'm not just doing this for you,' she said, giving him what she hoped was a convincing look. 'I'm doing it because it's an amazing, once-in-a-lifetime opportunity for the pair of us.'

'It's certainly going to test you both,' Oliver said, then catching Portia's glare, added. 'But it'll probably be the most gratifying thing either of you ever do.'

'Maybe that's a bit of an exaggeration, Oliver.' Portia smiled, grateful to him for trying to help.

'You never know though,' Charlie said. 'He could be right. Maybe this will be the best thing we ever do.' He pulled a face. 'It's certainly going to be the most testing at times, I imagine.'

'But you're still willing to give it a go?' Portia asked, hoping he wasn't having doubts now that they were about to start work.

'Absolutely. We've come here to make this work, and I'll give it my best shot, as I know you will.'

'I'm sure you both will,' Lexi said, picking up her cup and drinking.

'In fact,' Charlie said. 'I've been thinking that it's never too early to start working on a social media presence for the chateau.'

Portia was surprised to hear him say so, but also reassured to learn that Charlie had spent time thinking about it. 'Talk about starting as you mean to go on?'

'Well, you don't want to waste any time.'

'True.' Charlie smiled at her.

'We need to set up social media accounts,' Oliver continued. 'I thought that if we shared photos of the progression on one site and short videos of what work we're doing, our plans for each room, that sort of thing, then it might spark interest.'

'Great idea,' Lexi agreed. 'The more people start following you the more word will get out about the chateau, then by the time you're ready to take bookings hopefully that awareness will alert people looking for somewhere to hold events, or stay, and they'll contact you.'

'But how can we do that when the place is such a wreck and there's nothing to show off?'

'We'll think of something,' Charlie said. 'There will be parts that we can make look better for photos maybe?'

Maybe Charlie wasn't as anxious about the venture as she had supposed. 'I think that's a great idea,' Portia said, feeling a little reassured.

'You'll need a website, too,' Oliver added. 'That way prospective customers will know how best to contact you and how things are coming along.'

'I've only ever used websites that have already been set up by someone else,' Charlie admitted.

'Don't worry about it,' Oliver said. 'There's no rush and I can help you with the site when you want me to. I think for now you just need to decide what exactly you want to achieve at the end and write down the different stages. One step at a time.'

Portia finished her coffee as she thought about what lay ahead of them. 'I suppose if we want to take photos for a website or social media account then we must first concentrate on making the front drive up to the chateau and one of the formal rooms perfect so they can be styled somehow and photographed.

'Ooh, I have an idea.' Lexi clapped her hands together.

'What is it?' Portia asked, her friend's excitement surprising her and making her hand shake. Thank heavens she had finished her drink otherwise she might have spilt coffee onto the immaculate rug at their feet.

'Go on,' Oliver urged.

'We should ask Megan Knight if she would be free to pop over to the island.'

Portia wasn't sure why. She pictured the beautiful woman whose face seemed to grace most of the magazines she saw on shelves in her local shop in Chelsea. 'What will we need her for?'

'To come and open the chateau to the public, of course.'

'Why would she agree to do that?' Portia asked, confused at the unrealistic suggestion. 'I mean, do we even know how to get hold of her? Would we have to pay her an appearance fee?' She wasn't sure they could afford to spend money on luxuries such as booking celebrities.

'That's true,' Charlie agreed. 'Surely it would cost a fortune asking someone like her to travel to Jersey?'

Lexi shrugged. 'I'm not sure about cost, but Bella, Sacha and her partner Alessandro, Jack and I met her when she came to the island last year. We helped her with a couple of things and got to know her quite well.'

'You did?' Portia was surprised. 'Was she nicer than she sometimes comes across in interviews?'

'She was,' Lexi smiled. 'I think coming here changed ⬛ little, or at least brought out a nicer side to her. I'll speak to Bella and see what she thinks about the idea.'

'We would certainly get a lot of attention if she did agree to come,' Portia said, sitting back in her seat trying to picture her friends being friendly with the current media golden girl. By the sounds of things they seemed to know her rather well.

12

PORTIA

Portia wished the takeaway coffee cup in her hands had stayed warm for longer. They had spent the past hour walking through each room of the chateau with Charlie taking notes and her drawing little sketches so they could sit down afterwards and talk through what they planned on doing and in what order.

He opened a door on the second floor. 'This is the room where my great aunt's carer was living,' he said, standing to one side to let her have a look.

Portia withheld a groan. The room was dark and smelt of damp. There were wooden shutters folded to the side which added character but not the warmth curtains might have done. The single bed had an ottoman at the end of it but apart from a chair there was very little else. Thank heavens she and Charlie had the luxury of Lexi and Oliver's cottage for the worst of the winter.

'The poor thing,' she said, unable to help herself. 'She must have been freezing in here during the colder weather. I wonder how she managed to keep warm?'

Charlie indicated the window. 'She must have chosen this room because it was close to my great aunt's but also because it

was one of the few rooms with unbroken glass in the windows.'
Charlie studied the room silently. 'When I stayed here I remember
wearing lots of clothes during cooler evenings and each of us
always made up fires in the small fireplaces in our rooms. It was
the only heating, I seem to recall.'

'We'll need to find somewhere to cook? And wash.'

Charlie waved for her to follow. 'The bathroom is down there,'
he said, pointing to the end of a long corridor. He led the way,
opening the door. 'It has a bath, although it's a little rusty.' He
turned on both taps and Portia waited a few seconds, unsure if any
water would appear. When it did, she cringed on seeing the
orangey-brown colour.

'It still works,' Charlie cheered. 'There's a lavatory next door.'
His smile slipped when he caught her eye and Portia wished she
had thought to hide her reaction.

Charlie smiled. 'Don't worry, we'll renovate at least one bathroom before the spring for us to use when we move in.'

'That's a relief. I was getting a little worried.'

'Let's go down to the kitchen,' Charlie suggested. 'There's a
large one that even when I stayed here was unusable, but the
smaller kitchen at the back of the main kitchen should be func-
tional for the time being. You might remember it from when we
came here before.'

She did. Hopefully the cooker still works,' she said, trying to
sound positive. 'At least there's a work surface and sink.'

Charlie hugged her tightly. 'We'll make this work, don't
worry.'

She knew they would. 'I suppose the smaller kitchen was
updated for your great aunt.'

'I imagine it was.' Charlie flicked the old Bakelite light switch
and a bare bulb lit the room. 'At least we know the electricity
works,' he said, looking relieved.

Portia realised it hadn't occurred to her that it had been switched on. 'What about hot water?'

'The boiler needs replacing,' Charlie explained. 'I asked my lawyer to arrange for someone to come and put on the electricity while checking a few basics for us, like water in the cisterns for the sink and the boiler. All of them will need attention before the spring but at least we'll have something to work with.'

Another thing that would cost money, she realised. And lots of it. 'Definitely.' She focused on the current state of things, deciding she had no intention of moving in somewhere and having to take a cold bath. Portia shivered at the thought. 'Roll on summer,' she laughed, hoping to take the anxious look from his face.

'We'll probably be grateful for cold water when we're working here at the height of the summer.'

* * *

Her feet ached from the cold despite wearing her warmest cashmere socks. She looked down at her expensive wellington boots, aware now that although they were fine when walking in wet places, they did little to keep her feet warm.

'What's the matter?' Charlie asked, stopping her from going down the stairs from the attic. 'You seem...' He looked her up and down as if trying to decide how best to describe her.

Not wanting to delay ending their tour, she thought it best to help him rather than have to wait for him to guess. 'I'm frozen,' she moaned.

Charlie immediately went to remove his thick jacket.

Portia held up her hand. 'Please, don't. You need that as much as me. Anyway, it's my feet bothering me most of all.'

'Ahh. I didn't like to say anything when I saw what you were wearing.'

'Thanks.' So he had known she wasn't wearing the right clothes. 'Why didn't you say something before we left the cottage?'

'We were already running late and I presumed that if you were wearing these then you wouldn't have brought work boots.'

He was right. Portia felt foolish not to have known better.

'You weren't to know,' he said, stroking her arm. 'Tell you what, why don't we go and find somewhere that sells the right boots for you, then you'll be properly kitted out for tomorrow. I think you'd be better off having steel-capped ones, just in case anything ever falls on your feet. Wellies won't protect you from anything heavy.'

'Fine.' She turned from him. Their first day and already she had shown how little she understood about what they had taken on. She couldn't help feeling foolish and just like the city girl she truly was.

'Hey,' Charlie said, taking hold of her hand. 'Don't feel bad. I'm bound to make mistakes along the way too. This will be a learning curve for us both, Portia, not just you.'

She loved him for trying to make her feel better, but he had some experience at DIY and this really was all very new to her. She indicated his footwear, noticing for the first time that he was wearing hardy leather boots. 'At least you know what to wear on your feet.'

He moved closer to her and whispered in her ear. 'Only because I looked it up on the internet first.'

Feeling her sense of humour returning, Portia laughed. 'That's all right then.'

He put his arm around her waist and they began descending the main staircase.

'I'm going to make sure I have the right clothes for tomorrow,' she said, determined this would be the last day she would arrive on site looking like someone playing dress-up. She was a business-woman and had no intention of letting anyone think she wasn't serious about their project. No, she was going to show everyone, including herself, that she had what it took to work as hard as Charlie. They were equal partners now and she had every intention of proving that she would be a valuable asset to him where this chateau was concerned.

They went to what they presumed had been the dining room and as there were no chairs they sat on the floor with three A3 sheets of white paper that Oliver had given to them the previous night for their plans. He spread each one out in front of them and she saw that two were blank and Charlie had started drawing what Portia presumed to be an outline of each of the three floors on the other.

'That looks impressive.' She leant forward and studied the page on which Charlie had drawn an outline. 'The ground floor, I presume?'

'It is. I tried to do it from memory when I woke early this morning and will need to amend a few areas, but it's mostly right.' He indicated a black marker lying on the floor. 'Maybe you're more artistic than me. You were the one drawing bits from each room on a notepad.' He slid the large sheet of paper he was working on over towards her.

Portia was eager to add her touch to the plan and withdrew her small notepad from her jacket pocket, flicking through pages until she found the one she wanted. Picking up the marker, she pulled the lid off with her teeth and began making additions to the rough outline.

He pulled a blank piece of paper towards him and, taking another marker from his pocket, began making thick dots on the paper one under the other until he had ten of them.

'For our bullet points for the first floor?' she asked, excitement racing through her.

'Yup.'

Portia grinned. 'This is getting exciting now, don't you think?'

Charlie laughed. 'I imagine our enthusiasm might wane a bit when we begin the physical, mucky jobs.'

She agreed. 'Well, let's make the most of this stage then.'

'What do you think I should put first?' Charlie asked.

'Maybe we should start with the roof.'

Charlie grimaced. 'Good point. We need to have the roof looked at urgently. Hopefully we'll be able to have areas repaired because it's going to cost a fortune to replace a roof of this size.'

Portia sighed, picturing her bank balance diminishing rapidly. 'And we will have little choice to replace windows and some of those are huge. Should I put the roof and windows on the list for the ground floor?' They hadn't even begun and already the work ahead was seeming almost insurmountable.

'I suppose so.' Charlie stared at her before laughing. 'We really are starting at the beginning with this, aren't we?'

'So it seems.' She checked her sketches and changed one of the areas on the plan he'd already drawn. 'Just put what you think we need on that floor. Things like, update the bathrooms, or one of them. Then, remove plaster. Re-plaster, paint skirting boards and picture rails; ceilings; walls. I can't think what else.'

'We mustn't worry too much if we think of other things as we go on,' he said after writing the first few bullet points. 'We can always add them to the list, or rewrite it if it gets too messy. Or if we change our minds about what we see as priorities,' Charlie added.

Portia stopped what she was doing and read the list as he wrote. 'We should be fairly set on what order we intend our first stage of the renovations to be though, I think. We don't want to over-order things like cement, nails.' She tried to think of other items they might use. 'Glass for windows, that sort of thing. We'll want to have them to hand when we need them, but it would be silly to buy them too early and have to store them here for long.'

They sat in companionable silence as they worked until Portia sensed him watching her.

'What is it?'

'I think the most important thing we need to do before anything else is make this place wind- and water-tight.'

'I agree.' She was frozen and didn't want to have to work without there being some protection from the winter weather.

'Although, to help save us time when we're removing old plaster, baths and anything we want to remove, we could take advantage of the missing windows from each room by using one of those chutes and attach it to the windowless frame. It would be much quicker to drop any rubbish down those plastic bottomless bucket things held together with chains into a skip. I don't fancy carrying loads of heavy masonry through the building to the outside if I don't have to.'

'That makes sense,' Portia said, imagining how much time it would also save them. She made a note to find out what they were called and hire one.

'I think we're going to work well together,' Charlie said. 'We'll both discover what our strengths are in different areas. I know we can do this.'

By the time Charlie had finished working on his three plans and Portia had added everything they could think of to their lists, her bottom was almost numb from sitting on the cold oak floor.

Portia got to her feet after a bit of effort because her legs were stiff from sitting cross-legged for so long. She stretched her arms and flexed her fingers, then her toes, trying to get some feeling back into them.

'What do you suggest we do with these now?' she asked, indicating the plans and lists.

Charlie stood, groaning. 'One moment. I'll be back.'

She watched him run from the room, returning soon after with a roll of masking tape. 'We'll use this to stick what we've done already to one of the walls in here. This way we'll know where to look to check what needs doing next.'

'Great idea.' Portia stood behind Charlie and, slipping her hands around his waist, enjoyed the feel of his firm stomach muscles against her palms. She felt his stomach contract on her touch and smiled to herself, loving the effect she had on him. She kissed the back of his shoulder, then peered around him at the plans.

'We have so little time to make this place presentable I'm concerned we might waste some of it doing jobs twice, or forgetting to order something because of lack of experience.'

'We'll do our best not to,' he said, his hand resting lightly on hers.

She knew their plans didn't remotely depict all the hard work they had ahead of them, but it was a start and she decided that rather than fret about it she would focus on the end result and the day when each room would be ready for her to start styling it in preparation for their opening.

Charlie turned to face her and kissed the tip of her nose. 'Much as I'm enjoying standing here with you, I think we should get started on the first room.'

Eager to please him, she nodded. 'Where do you think we should go first?'

'On the room that no one is likely to see.'

'To get in a bit of practice, you mean?' She liked the idea, it made a lot of sense and at least she might have more confidence in her abilities by the time they moved on to more important rooms.

'We need to think about making this place watertight as a priority though.' He rubbed his unshaven chin. 'We're going to have to get some quotes as soon as possible. Firstly from a roofer and someone for the windows. As far as we're concerned, I believe the kitchen should be the first room we get ready for fitting up.'

She nodded her agreement.

'I have more contacts on the island than you,' Charlie said. 'So, why don't I get on my phone while you make a start on the kitchen.'

'Let's get going then,' Portia sighed.

A few hours later her phone buzzed, and pulling it from her pocket she noticed Lexi was calling her. 'Lexi, hi,' she said, brushing plaster dust from her hands onto the legs of her jeans.

'Sorry to interrupt you,' Lexi said. 'But do you remember Remi, that artisan baker guy?'

'Yes?'

'I was chatting to him earlier when I saw him delivering bread at the café and he reminded me that he desperately needs somewhere to bake his bread. I was wondering if maybe you had a spare room he could set up in at the chateau.'

Recalling her thoughts about Remi renting the smaller kitchen and how it might be a way to bring in a bit of income, Portia smiled. 'I had a similar thought myself,' Portia admitted. 'If you send me his number, I'll chat to Charlie and as soon as we've decided if it's something we can do, we'll let him know.'

'Great. I'll send it to you now.'

Portia ended the call and slipped the phone back into her pocket. It wasn't much, but the thought of having some money coming into their coffers to help with the work excited her. She looked around and, wondering where Charlie had got to, ran off to find him.

'There you are.'

Charlie looked up from the store room at the back of the house where he seemed to be rearranging furniture. 'I've found these in here,' he said, pointing to a wicker table and lifting one of the chairs. 'I thought they'd do for the dining room. At least that way we won't have to keep sitting on the cold floor when we're in there.'

'Thank heavens for that,' she said, walking into the room and taking one of the light chairs from him. 'Bring a couple of those and we'll start taking them through while I tell you what's just happened.'

As they walked she told him about Lexi's call and her idea.

'Rent out the small kitchen?' It was in a decent state, but was it good enough for a baker? 'I thought we were going to use it until we sorted the larger kitchen out?'

'It was just a thought, but I think it's a good one.' Portia linked arms with him as they returned to fetch the table and rest of the chairs. 'Imagine, money coming in instead of pouring out, and hopefully he'll give us some of his tasty bread at a hefty discount.'

'Hmm, I like the sound of that.'

'Me, too. Right, I'll give him a call and suggest he comes here to have a look. If it's not suitable then we've at least made the offer.'

She left him making the dining room more comfortable and dialled Remi's number that Lexi had texted to her.

13
———

CHARLIE

'Hellooooo.'

'Did you hear that?' Portia asked, when they were busy working on one of the rooms a week later.

Charlie lowered his hammer and chisel and went to see who it was. 'I think that's Sacha?' Charlie lowered his tools. 'I'll bring her through.'

'Portia? Charlie?'

Charlie hurried through to the front hall and saw Alessandro standing with her in the open doorway.

'Hey, good to see you both.' Charlie opened his arms in welcome. 'Come to see our building site for yourselves?'

Sacha held up two bags which seemed to contain food from her café. He watched her gaze around the room before looking into the living room on the right. 'Wow, it's um...

'In a state?' Charlie joked.

'I was going to say *enormous*.'

Alessandro stared wide-eyed. 'It has some work needed but it is an impressive building.' He looked at the ceiling, the walls and the tiled floor. 'I did not know this place was here and I have driven past the entrance many times since I came to the island last year.'

'I didn't know it was here either,' Sacha admitted. 'I can't get over that it's been hidden from view all this time.'

'I stayed here with my great aunt about twelve years ago, so I knew it wouldn't be in the best condition, but even I was shocked when we came up the drive for the first time.' Charlie didn't like to add that his stunned reaction was probably heightened by the notion that he and Portia were to move in at some point, and the thought that clearly the pair of them hadn't understood the enormity of the work they would need to carry out to put the place right. 'Come through,' he said, not wanting to think about it. 'I'll take you to Portia. We've been in the kitchen all morning chipping off the old plaster where it hasn't already fallen off.'

'We aren't interrupting you?' Sacha asked.

'We're happy to take a break, don't worry – especially if those drinks in Alessandro's hands are for us.' He nodded at the two trays his friend was carrying. Then smiling at Sacha added, 'Please tell me those are pastries from your café?'

Sacha held up a bag in each hand. She raised one slightly higher. 'These are pain au chocolat and pain au raisin. Five of them. I gather from Lexi that Remi is here today.'

Charlie had been surprised when Portia mentioned the previous week about offering a baker their smaller kitchen at some point in the future. He had been even more amazed when the man had asked to move in to one of the rooms in the chateau and offered to help pay his way by helping with renovations.

Sacha raised the other bag. 'These are sandwiches. I've made a selection because I wasn't sure what everyone would prefer.'

'Our very first guests.' Charlie went to take the bags from her, but she shook her head.

'Just lead the way. I'm looking forward to seeing what you've been up to.'

'Then let's go through to the kitchen.' Charlie waved for them to follow him. 'Portia will be delighted to see you, as am I. We've barely begun the work and I think the two of us are only now beginning to realise the enormity of what we've taken on.'

'You two?' Alessandro asked. 'Or just you?'

Charlie stopped and smiled at his friend. 'Me definitely, but I sense by Portia's thoughtful mood that the same thing has occurred to her this morning.' He hoped that with Remi's help things might get a little easier.

Alessandro patted his back. 'Sacha has an idea. It is why we have come here to interrupt you.'

Charlie was intrigued but was happy to wait until he was with the other two before hearing what she had to suggest.

As they neared the back of the house Charlie heard a hammer banging and knew that Portia and Remi were still hard at work trying to get the kitchen up and ready. He led the way into the large room.

'Hey Portia,' he called, 'look who's come to see us.'

Portia turned, delight registering on her face when she saw who it was. Placing her tools on the floor, she brushed the worst of the dust from her hands and walked up to Sacha and Alessandro. 'I'm filthy, I'm afraid, but it is wonderful to see you both here.'

'We've brought treats,' Sacha explained.

'And cappuccinos,' Alessandro added, nodding a hello to Remi as he laid down his tools and joined them.

'Why don't we go through to the old dining room,' Charlie suggested, not expecting anyone to eat or drink in the dusty room. 'We found an old wicker table and chairs in one of the back rooms a while ago. I imagine they could have originally been in the old summer house.'

'Yes, let's do that,' Portia agreed. 'Charlie can show you where to go while Remi and I wash our hands. We won't be long.'

Charlie took one tray of drinks from Alessandro and led them back to the front of the house. 'In here,' he said, opening the door and indicating the table. 'You two take a seat and I'll quickly wash. Won't be long.'

By the time the five of them were seated at the table, Sacha produced paper napkins from her coat pocket which they used instead of plates.

'Alessandro and I were looking at your plans on the wall there,' she said. 'This is a big old place, isn't it?'

Charlie took a bite of his sandwich and listened while Portia shared some of their ideas.

'Lexi suggested asking Bella to contact Megan Knight about maybe popping over to open the chateau to the public when we've got far enough with the renovations to have a few rooms to show off.'

Alessandro nudged Sacha. 'Tell them your idea.'

'What is it?' Portia asked, glancing at Charlie, an excited look on her face.

'Alessandro and I were chatting with Lexi and Oliver over breakfast at the café this morning. They mentioned how you hoped to garner interest in the place but weren't sure how to because there's nowhere ready yet to be photographed.'

'That's right,' Charlie said, loving their friends for being thoughtful and trying to come up with ways to support him and Portia.

'What's your idea?' Portia asked, before popping the last piece of her sandwich in her mouth.

'It's Christmas in a couple of weeks.'

Charlie realised he and Portia had given the festivities little thought since starting work. 'I'd forgotten.'

'We're too busy to stop for Christmas,' Portia said. 'Remi will be flat out baking for the Christmas markets and his clients leaving Charlie and I to focus on the place, otherwise we'll fall behind with our plans.'

'Not necessarily.' Sacha rested her elbows on the table and smiled mysteriously as she steepled her fingers.

Intrigued, Charlie waited for her to continue.

She took a sip of her coffee. 'Firstly, I think it's important you celebrate your first Christmas here. And how better than to hold a party for everyone from the boardwalk.'

'What?' Charlie and Portia asked the question at the same time. Charlie laughed at the ridiculous notion. 'We can't expect people to come here, not like it is now.'

Portia seemed bemused. 'Charlie's right, Sacha. It's kind of you to want to help us, but I can't imagine why anyone would want to come to a party here. It's in such a state.'

'I agree,' Remi said quietly.

Portia said. 'Anyway, we wouldn't have the time to prepare for it, even if there was a room ready for us to hold it in.'

Sacha swapped glances with Alessandro who motioned for her to continue. 'I know it sounds odd, but just hear me out.' She took a deep breath. 'I remembered Alessandro telling me about the time his aunt inherited an old farmhouse in Tuscany. She held a huge party there before having any work done on the place.'

Charlie didn't understand how that situation might relate to them. 'But look at the state of this place,' he said, shaking his head. 'I doubt his aunt's home was open to the elements in most rooms.'

'Exactly,' Portia said taking Charlie's hand in hers. 'Why would anyone want to come to somewhere where there's no heating, or a working kitchen to make food?' She shook her head. 'It's very sweet of you to try and help, Sacha, but I think it would be better if we just got on with the work and had a quiet Christmas together in the cottage.'

Alessandro said. 'Tell them the rest, Sacha.'

'Sorry, I'll get to the point. Alessandro, Jack and I will bring all the food and drink you need.'

Charlie didn't think he could take on anything else and doubted Portia had the energy for a party. 'No, I—'

'We will, Charlie.' She stared into his eyes and Charlie realised there was something more to Sacha's suggestion, so kept quiet.

'The party at Alessandro's aunt's place was in the summer but didn't even have a roof. She brought large tubs with small trees into the room.' She looked at Alessandro. 'You said it was magical, didn't you?'

'It was,' he confirmed. 'I still remember it well, not because of the house, but the atmosphere and being at a party very different to any other I had attended.'

'You could hold the party in this room,' Sacha suggested. 'Or maybe this one, the hall and the other large room across the hall that I noticed when we arrived. Bring in more old furniture for people who need to sit. This sort of thing.' She rested her hand on the table. 'Nothing fancy and certainly no antiques. Deckchairs even, if you have any.'

Charlie laughed. 'We haven't come across any of those yet.' He was surprised to realise he was beginning to warm to the idea. Then it hit him what Sacha was hoping to achieve from the event. 'Are you trying to tell us it would be a good way for other locals to see this place, feel involved in some way in our venture and plans for the chateau's future?'

'Yes,' Portia said quietly. 'Then they could go and tell all their friends?'

He swapped a stunned glance at Portia. Maybe Sacha's idea had come just at the right time.

Portia clasped her hands together. 'We could use any photos on our social media accounts to get attention for the project.'

'Exactly!' Sacha sat back in her chair and brushed her palms together. 'Tell everyone to share their photos, also their experience coming to this unique place. Word of mouth is the best way to succeed with something new. They can share how, even in the depths of winter, this place has a magical atmosphere, how they can see your vision for the place and how incredibly amazing it's going to be by the time the renovations are done.'

A huge grin spread across Charlie's face as his mind sped ahead with a hundred and one ideas that Sacha's proposition had sparked.

'So?' Sacha asked, looking across the table at each of them. 'What do you think?'

After a brief hesitation, Portia laughed. 'I think it's perfect. And I, for one, believe we should definitely do this.' She turned to Charlie, then Remi. 'What do you both think?'

Charlie couldn't agree more. 'I think we should definitely do this. In fact, I'm already looking forward to the party. Imagine, not having to worry about spillages, or anything being damaged.'

'Not that the people we know from the boardwalk would damage anything intentionally, but these things do happen,' Portia said thoughtfully.

'I love the idea,' Charlie admitted, holding his coffee in the air for a toast. 'To Chateau de Cesarea's Inaugural Christmas Party.'

'The chateau's Inaugural Christmas Party,' the rest of them cheered.

14

PORTIA

Portia opened her eyes and closed them immediately after shading her face with her forearm against the glare of the early morning sun. It might seem romantic waking up with the natural light each morning, but as far as she was concerned curtainless windows were not ideal. She felt Charlie stir next to her in the small double bed, his body warm against hers as he instinctively turned on his side and spooned her. He slipped his arm around her, holding her close against him.

Portia sighed contentedly. They had been living at the chateau for the past two days and nights since Lexi admitted she had forgotten to diarise a booking over Christmas for a family of six. Both the middle cottage where she and Charlie had been staying, together with the one at the end were needed for her guests, and as the pair of them had somewhere else to go, Portia reassured Lexi that moving to the chateau would be fun.

'It'll be fun,' she recalled saying, determined to stop Lexi from feeling guilty. 'Just like camping. We don't mind at all.' What she had omitted to add was that she had no experience of camping. She expected their stay to be a little uncomfortable and rather cold, but when Charlie didn't seem to mind, she had forced herself not to mind either. Besides, Lexi and Oliver had been very generous to them since their arrival on the island and both had promised they could move back to their end cottage as soon as the guests left in the New Year. Portia wriggled her toes in her thick bed socks and had to admit she couldn't wait to be back in the warm cottage again.

Charlie's breathing was deep once more and she wished she could fall asleep as effortlessly as he managed to. He somehow switched off his worries as soon as his head touched the pillow and fell into a deep sleep, snoring gently within minutes. Not that he had slept this soundly in London, she reminded herself. She, on the other hand, had spent the past two nights lying awake listening to unknown creaks and sounds emanating from the building, or from outside. All with her worries jumbled in her head as she struggled to push them away to lose herself to sleep. At least she was warm sleeping next to him though, that was something to be grateful for.

Unlike poor Remi, she mused. He had pleaded with them to let him rent one of the rooms so he could be on-site to get up early and bake. He also helped them prepare the smallest room upstairs as his bedroom before moving in. Portia hadn't minded him being there. In fact it was pleasant having another person living in the vast property and made the whole experience a little less overwhelming.

It must be freezing sleeping alone though, she thought, glad she didn't have to do it. There were so many nooks and crannies in this place and she certainly felt safer lying next to Charlie. Not that she didn't feel secure on the island, but in a place this enormous, with rooms they hadn't had time to inspect yet, Portia knew it was going to take time to get used to living there. Night-time was the worst, especially when she needed to use the bathroom and had to run along the corridor with the glow from the one working light casting spooky shadows.

She felt Charlie's lips on her neck and snuggled back into his embrace. For all the oddness of living in this place, Portia was happy. Even before she had inherited money from Alistair, she had been used to a fairly luxurious lifestyle and not only because her father had earned well and had investments, but also thanks to her own years modelling in several upmarket campaigns. If anyone would have told her six months ago that she would be happier than ever before living in a freezing, run-down building site, with manicures a thing of the past and her hands roughened by manual labour, she would have told them they were delusional. Here she was though, lying in an uncomfortable bed with her boyfriend and apart from the odd hiccup, settling into her new life.

'How early is it?' Charlie murmured.

She looked at her watch. Even that was an old one she had retrieved from her jewellery box. She hadn't worn it since she was a teenager. Her expensive watch and jewellery were all stored away at Oliver and Lexi's cottage being kept safe until they were ready to move in to the chateau full time.

'It's ten past seven,' she replied, pulling the cover over their shoulders from where it had slipped down the bed when Charlie had moved during the night. Resting her hands on his, lying against her stomach, she said, 'I suppose we should get up soon.'

'Not yet,' he groaned. 'I'm enjoying lying here with you far too much.'

So was she. But they had a lot to do. 'Five minutes but no more,' she soothed, determined to keep up with their work. 'It's the party in a few days and we have so much to do before then.'

'Make it ten,' he murmured, kissing her neck, his hand slipping down to the top of her thighs. 'Or maybe fifteen, and I'll walk down to the café and buy our breakfast.'

Portia was happy to stay where she was and needed little persuading. Anyway, she thought dreamily as Charlie kissed her and rain began falling against the window, she had no place she would rather be right now. 'That's a deal.'

* * *

As she finished her croissant and swallowed the last of her coffee, Portia rubbed her hands together wishing she could wear proper thermal gloves to keep her hands warm instead of the fingerless ones she needed for working. She was wearing her ski top and thermal leggings with three layers of sweaters of various thicknesses under her oldest padded jacket.

It was proving harder today to motivate herself than on the previous two days but Portia had no intention of letting the guys know how she was feeling. No doubt they had the same thoughts about having to work another day in the cold, but what choice did they have?

She watched Charlie frowning as he read something on his phone and hoped it wasn't bad news.

'What time is the roof chap coming to start replacing the missing timbers and tiles in those areas that need replacing?' Remi asked, snapping her out of her thoughts.

Charlie gathered up their rubbish and pushed it into the paper bag he had brought into the room with breakfast. 'He should be here just after nine, and I've just received an email with the quote for the first lot of windows the chap measured up for the other day.'

'I can tell by your face that it's not good news,' Portia said, feeling uneasy at the thought of how much it was going to cost them to replace the front windows alone. They had agreed to leave the ones at the sides and rear until spring, but had little option about replacing the larger ones at the front. They let in the most light and cold and she and Charlie had reasoned that if they were to start taking photos of the property for promotion then having boarded-up windows was simply not an option.

'It's about 35 per cent on top of what we had expected,' Charlie grumbled.

Determined not to let this news dampen their spirits, she focused on staying positive. 'Then that's what we'll have to pay.'

'I suppose you're right,' Charlie said thoughtfully. 'Maybe I could learn how to replace the smaller windows he hasn't quoted for. It would save a lot in labour.' He lifted up his phone showing the quote. 'And the vast majority of this seems to be for the work his men will need to carry out.'

'Good idea,' Remi said. 'If we watch them working I'm sure we'll be able to pick up some tips on how to do it and I'm happy to help you both where I can. After all, you've been very kind letting me move in here since I lost my home.'

'That's kind of you, Remi.' Portia gave him a grateful smile. 'Then that's what we'll do.'

She wondered if the new windows would be fitted as soon as the chap had expected. Late February was the rough date he had given. That was two months away but maybe they might be lucky and have them fitted by the time the coldest part of the winter descended. She certainly hoped that would happen, she didn't like to think about having to work in even colder conditions than what they were already dealing with.

'All right then.' Charlie stood and pushed his phone into his back pocket.

'That was delicious,' Remi said, having eaten his bacon and egg roll. 'I'll make an extra batch of sourdough today for us to eat at breakfast tomorrow. I can make scrambled eggs in the microwave to go with toasted slices of it.'

Charlie grimaced as he wiped his mouth on the napkin making Remi laugh.

'It is not as bad as it sounds,' Remi said. 'I have been eating this for a lot of meals since I moved in here.'

'That and baked beans,' Portia said. 'I can't wait to have a proper kitchen where we can cook decent meals.'

'Where I can cook them, you mean,' Charlie teased.

She was relieved to see Charlie cheer up slightly. She was finding it harder being at the chateau than she had expected and harder still to pretend she wasn't struggling so that Charlie didn't fret about her.

'I've missed your meals,' she said, her mouth watering at the memory of his perfect roast dinners. Charlie enjoyed cooking and she knew he must be missing making their meals since they moved from the cottage. Hopefully, though, he wouldn't have to wait too much longer now until the kitchen was finished. She hoped not. She was looking forward to sitting down to tasty meals herself.

'Right,' she said, standing. 'Enough sitting around chatting. We'd better get to work if we're going to make any headway today.'

Every minute counted with the work they had to do, especially now that they had committed themselves to holding a party for the locals.

15

CHARLIE

Charlie returned to the kitchen carrying two heavy tubs of plaster he'd collected from one of the outhouses. He noticed the area Remi had been working on before leaving to go and check on his baking was rather messy.

Charlie's mood dived. He liked Remi very much but he wasn't very good at plastering. Maybe Remi's creativity was at its best when he was baking. He was a sweet man though and Charlie didn't want to offend him by saying anything, especially as he was only trying to help them.

'Oh dear. You're staring at the bit of plastering Remi attempted earlier, aren't you?' Portia grinned, coming up to him in the kitchen.

'You've seen it already then?'

'I have. I knew you'd be unhappy with it.'

'It's not good, but I'm not sure what to do. I don't want to upset him by saying anything, or going over his work as that might be even more offensive. This is an area that needs to be perfect as we won't be covering it with tiles, or even furniture, so it'll be on display.'

Portia stared at the area thoughtfully. 'Hmm. I was thinking the same thing.' She rubbed the worst area with the tips of her fingers. 'Maybe we could place the large dresser in front of it though? We were going to bring one in here and that would hide it.'

Charlie wanted to agree. 'But it would look odd there.' He preferred the furniture to be symmetrical in the room. 'And anyway, I'd still know it was a mess behind it.'

'What do you suggest?' Charlie heard the amusement in Portia's voice. 'It's not as if we can afford to redo plastering, or have the time to do it either.'

She was right. Charlie rubbed his chin searching for a quick solution. 'I think I'll just have to sand it down and redo it as best I can, but I can't do that each time he plasters.' Charlie groaned. 'I'm going to have to speak with him about this, aren't I?'

'I think you will. But what are you going to say?'

He wished he knew. 'I suppose I'll explain that plastering is clearly not his forte and that he should leave it to us. We're not perfect at it by any means, but we are pretty good, if I do say so myself. He can find other jobs to tackle that don't need quite so much precision.'

Portia smiled and Charlie relaxed slightly, grateful they had come to a conclusion that both of them were happy with. He realised she was staring at him. 'What?'

'I'm worried you're pushing yourself too far, Charlie.'

'Rubbish. I'm fine. In fact,' he said, patting his flat stomach, 'I feel better than I have for ages. Working on this site is far better for me than it was when I was going to the gym several times a week when we lived in London.' He thought back to the plush state-of-the-art gym that Portia had paid an annual membership for on his behalf and how it had taken him time to fit in with the bespoke-suited men and women he came across there.

He saw Portia look him up and down.

'What?' he asked, returning her amused smile.

'I always thought you looked super sexy in your smart work suits but now I see you here, all dishevelled and unshaven, I find I'm liking it. Very much.'

He laughed, enjoying her reaction to his messy state. 'If I'd known all I had to do was get all sweaty and mucky, then I might have suggested we do something like this months ago.' He opened his arms for her to step into them.

Portia moved slightly then stopped and shook her head. 'Maybe when you're not covered in plaster dust,' she laughed.

Amused by her reaction and loving that Portia never seemed to do anything just because it was expected of her, he grinned.

'What?' She moved her hand to her hair tucking a loose strand behind her ear.

'I don't know how you do it but you always seem well turned out.'

She grimaced and looked down at her clothes. 'I'm in a state,' she argued, raising her hands and wriggling her fingers about. 'These nails are ruined and I doubt they'll ever recover.'

He hadn't noticed her hands but remembering the shiny varnishes that her fingernails usually displayed couldn't hide his surprise. 'You really have gone into this head on,' he said in admiration. 'I never imagined you could do it to this extent.'

'You doubted me?'

Charlie tried to gauge if she was annoyed. 'I'd never do that. On the contrary, I think you're amazing.'

Seemingly forgetting her wish to not hug him while he was so dirty, Portia stepped into his arms. 'You really are adorable, do you know that?'

'What makes you say that?'

'Because you see the real me, like Alistair did,' she added quietly. 'And I love you for it even more than I already did.' She rested her head on his chest. 'And I like that you're more muscly now, too.'

He heard the teasing in her voice. 'You're always the charmer, do you know that?' As they stood in each other's arms Charlie thought back over her comment. He had known how deeply Portia had been in love with her late fiancé and rather than be offended by her reminder that she had loved someone before him, it made him happy to know she felt relaxed enough to be open with him about her feelings.

'Where are you both?'

Charlie tensed on hearing Remi's voice. They moved apart hearing his footsteps.

'It's fine,' Charlie said giving her a reassuring smile.

'There you are,' Remi said, walking in carrying two loaves of bread. 'I baked you soda bread. I thought you might like to have it with some soup later.'

Charlie thanked him, feeling guilty about what he had to do. He would do his best not to upset their lodger but couldn't forget they still needed to get the driveway, front lawn and a small living room to use upstairs ready in time for the first event.

'They look and smell delicious, Remi.' Portia leant forward and smelt the freshly baked loaves.

Charlie knew he had to speak to Remi before he tried any more plastering. 'Remi,' he said. 'Would you mind if we have a brief chat?'

'Is this about the plastering I did in here?' Remi said sheepishly.

Charlie saw him look down at the loaves and realised that they were an apology for Remi's lousy job. 'Yes,' he said, smiling. 'I think we might need you to help us in other areas from now on.'

16

PORTIA

Portia's mobile vibrated against her leg in her trouser pocket. Relieved to have an excuse to take a break from removing old wallpaper from the living room wall, she took it from her pocket and read the text.

Supper tonight at ours. Come at around 6.30 p.m. for food, wine and some exciting news.
Lexi xx

Excited, she ran to the kitchen where Charlie was still plastering and held her phone in front of him so that he could read the invitation.

'I presume we'll be going?' He gave her a cheeky wink.

'Absolutely.' Portia quickly typed her response to Lexi. 'Unless you want to cook a tin of soup over that Primus stove we bought the other day?'

'Not if we have options. I always enjoy their cooking and it'll be great to be properly warm again for one evening.'

'I was thinking the same thing.' She turned to look at his hand-iwork. 'You're doing really well.'

'Thanks. It's coming along slowly.' He rested his hands on his hips and stared at the wall he had just finished working on. 'You know, I have to admit that when we decided to do this work I didn't take into account how big these rooms were, or how long it would take to do each one of them.'

She had been thinking the same thing as she struggled to remove the wallpaper in the other room. 'And the ceilings are so damn high, aren't they?'

Charlie grinned. 'Maybe next time we should stick to reno-vating a modern bungalow.'

She knew he was joking and sighed. 'That would be a sensible idea. Although I'm not sure you and I are all that sensible.'

'We can't be to have taken this on.' They stared at each other for a few seconds, each lost in their own thoughts until he spoke. 'Then again, how dull must it be not to take any risks.'

Portia tilted her head from side to side. 'Maybe we should aim for being more risk averse after we've finished these renovations. It's going to be a relief not to feel grubby for a while.'

'Agreed.' He blew a kiss at her. 'Right, enough chit chat. We're going to have to keep going if we're ever to finish any of these monstrous rooms.'

Portia returned to the large living room with its three floor-to-ceiling windows and set to work removing what was left of the old wallpaper. They had agreed to leave the room in its most basic state for the Christmas party, which was a relief. After all, their guests were coming to see the place and hopefully the worse it looked then the more dramatic the difference when they unveiled their handiwork at their opening.

* * *

Come in, come in,' Lexi said, hugging each of them as Portia, Charlie and Oliver entered the cottage.

'It was so kind of you to collect us,' Portia said for the second time. 'I hadn't been looking forward to walking here in the dark.'

'Even if I hadn't thought about coming to fetch you, Lexi would have insisted one of us did.' Oliver took Charlie's coat and waited for Portia to remove hers.

'Let's hurry up and get into the living room,' Lexi said. 'It's lovely and warm in there.'

Portia followed her in and went to stand in front of the roaring fire. 'This is utter bliss,' she said, rubbing her cold hands together and wishing they wouldn't have to return to the freezing chateau at the end of their evening. She caught Charlie's eye and wondered if he was having the same thought.

'I've cooked us a beef stew,' Lexi told them. 'With dumplings. I know you like them, Portia.'

Portia smiled, her mouth watering at the thought. 'I never imagined I'd enjoy something like that until you made them for me several months ago. Who knew something called 'dumplings' would actually be light and tasty.'

Oliver laughed. 'Sit yourselves down and get comfortable. You must both be shattered.'

'We are a bit,' Charlie agreed. 'I'm impressed with my girlfriend and how hard she continues to work though.'

'Us women are tougher than you might sometimes think,' Lexi said, giving Portia a wink as she walked over to the kitchen side of the room.

Portia watched as her friend raised the lid on a large pot on top of the oven and stirred the stew. Her stomach rumbled noisily. 'Gosh, sorry about that. I'm a bit hungry tonight. I've been looking forward to this meal ever since receiving your text inviting us here.'

'Me, too.' Charlie rested a hand on his stomach.

Oliver held up a bottle of red wine for them to approve. 'Will this do?'

'Perfect,' Charlie said.

'Is there anything I can do to help with the cooking, Lexi?' Portia asked, nodding her thanks to Oliver as he poured her a glass of wine.

'No.' Lexi shook her head. 'You two take it easy for once. We can eat whenever you're ready, but I'm happy to wait if you'd like to relax for a bit.'

'No chance,' Portia said, taking the glass of wine Oliver held out to her and carrying it to the dining table. 'Where do you want me to sit?'

Lexi picked up a ladle and began serving their supper. 'Wherever you wish.'

When they were all seated and Oliver had helped carry across bowls of steaming stew to the table, he and Lexi sat down to join them. She unfolded her napkin and placed it across her lap but Portia didn't miss the smile on her face and could tell Lexi was looking forward to giving them some news.

'You'd better tell them before you burst with excitement,' Oliver said quietly.

Lexi grinned at Portia and Charlie. 'Bella has spoken to Megan Knight about coming over to the island to open your chateau to the public.'

'And can I take it from the cheerful grin on your face that you have good news?' Portia forgot her hunger for a moment while she waited for her friend to share Megan's answer.

Lexi clapped her hands together. 'Apparently she was thrilled to have an excuse to return to the island.'

Portia gasped. 'She is?' She grabbed Charlie's wrist, almost making him spill his drink. 'Did you hear that?'

'I did,' he said, lowering his glass back onto the table. 'It's very kind of her to agree.'

'Apparently she was very excited about the whole thing,' Oliver added.

'She must love the island then.' Portia couldn't get over this incredible news.

'There's that, of course,' Lexi said. 'But it was also the idea that there's a chateau here.' Her face clouded for a moment.

'What is it?' Portia asked, noticing Oliver give Lexi a subtle nod.

'It's just that she has one stipulation.' Lexi took a mouthful of wine from her glass and swallowed.

Anxious to hear what that might be, Portia leant forward. 'Well?'

'She said she wants to stay in the chateau while she's on the island.'

Portia could tell Lexi wasn't sure how she and Charlie would react to Megan's request. She wasn't surprised. Both Lexi and Oliver knew how slow their progress was at the chateau since they were doing most things themselves to save money. Even with Remi's occasional help it was slow going.

'Stay. With us?' Charlie sounded horrified. 'But none of the rooms are anywhere near ready for guests, especially celebrity ones. I mean, she'll be used to smart hotel rooms, won't she?' He placed his fork down on the side of his bowl and caught Portia's eye.

Not wanting Charlie's concerns to ruin the opportunity, Portia knew she must push any concerns she might have aside and try to be the voice of reason. She reached out and took his hand in hers, trying to work out how best to persuade him to agree to Megan's request.

'It's fine. I'm sure we can do something to make one of the rooms acceptable for her,' she soothed. When he didn't seem convinced, she tried another tactic. 'Anyway, it makes good sense to me.'

'How?'

'Well, because having someone as well-known as her will surely bring our new venture to a much larger audience than anything we could ever hope to achieve.'

'I understand that, but I can't see how it's achievable.'

She gave his hand a gentle squeeze, aware she needed to try something else. 'We both expected to blow some of our budget paying her an appearance fee.' She looked across the table at Lexi. 'She didn't mention wanting one, did she?'

Lexi shook her head. 'No, I think she just wants to stay at the chateau.'

Charlie frowned thoughtfully. 'Are you suggesting we put the money we'll save towards contractors to help with the work then?'

'No. But if she only wants to stay in one of our rooms, then all we'll need to do is renovate one of the main bedrooms sooner than we anticipated, that's all.'

'And a bathroom,' he reminded her, staring into his wine glass as if it held some answers. 'I thought we were already busy enough.'

She wasn't sure if he was talking to himself. 'We can do this, Charlie, I'm certain of it.' She was glad her voice sounded more confident than she currently felt, but knew that they had little choice but to try and pull this off. 'If we find we're struggling, then we'll have to bring in someone to help us, but if we can save money by doing this ourselves, then I think it's worth a try.'

The three of them waited for him to respond. None of them moved until Portia, too hungry to wait any longer, began eating again.

'Charlie, you can do this,' Oliver said eventually. 'It's too good an opportunity to miss. Like Portia said, Megan will bring an enormous amount of attention to your venture and without any extra cost to you it seems. Don't forget, Lexi and I are happy to help where we can.'

Portia struggled to hide her amusement when Lexi shot him a stunned glance. 'Us? I'm not sure how good I'll be with painting and decorating.'

'Neither am I,' Oliver shrugged, taking a drink from his wine glass and smiling at each of them. 'But don't you think it'll be fun trying?'

Portia saw a doubtful expression pass across Lexi's face. It was close to Christmas and poor Lexi was already busy with her own guests staying in the cottages. Like most of the other locals, she would have a lot of preparation to do, buying presents, decorating the cottages, buying food and drink in for Christmas. The last thing she probably wanted at this time of year was work on a dusty building site.

'It's fine, Lexi,' Portia said, not wishing her friend to feel forced into anything. 'I'm sure we'll manage perfectly well and you've already got enough going on here.'

* * *

'Don't look so glum,' Lexi said to Portia as they did the washing up a little later. 'I'm happy to help wherever I can. But I wasn't kidding when I said I have no idea if I'll be good at anything.'

'Thanks, Lexi. I appreciate your and Oliver's support. I'm trying to figure out which room we should make ready for Megan. We have the largest two at the front of the house on either side of the first-floor landing. I suppose we should choose one of those and the small dressing room at the back could be turned into an en-suite.'

'Sounds good,' Charlie said, picking up a tea towel. 'I'll dry,

Lexi. You go and sit down with Oliver. I think he's looking up ideas for our website. He's offered to help me set one up for the business.'

'He'll be good at that,' she said, drying her hands and going to take a seat, leaving Portia and Charlie to chat quietly together.

'I'm glad he's doing this for us,' Charlie answered, lowering his voice. 'I wouldn't have a clue where to start setting one up.'

'Nor me.' Portia knew that Oliver understood website design and somehow succeeded in everything he put his mind to. She loved that he looked out for her since his brother had died and had become her closest friend. She always felt safe knowing he had her back, especially now he also lived on the island since falling in love with the place and Lexi the previous year.

Wanting to be certain that Charlie was happy about the news of their celebrity guest's visit for their official opening party, she turned to him and whispered, 'Are you sure you don't have any misgivings about the Megan thing?'

'Why do you ask?'

'Because you took time to reply earlier and I don't want you to feel you're being forced to agree to something you're not entirely happy with.'

He gave her a reassuring smile. 'You're lovely, do you know that?'

'Charlie, I'm trying to be serious.'

He scooped up a small amount of bubbles from the sink and placed them on the tip of her nose. 'I know you are. And I promise I'm fine with everything.'

She grimaced and snatched the tea towel from him to wipe the bubbles from her nose. 'If that's the case then why did you hesitate for so long?'

He took back the tea towel and finding a dry bit wiped a plate from the draining board. 'Because I don't make decisions nearly as quickly as you. I need a few minutes to think things through.'

Relieved he seemed happy to go ahead, Portia relaxed slightly. 'That's fine then.' She took the plug from the sink and let the water out before rinsing it to ensure it was clean. When she had dried her hands she noticed he was smiling at her. 'What?'

'Now we've determined that you make decisions quicker than I do I was wondering if you've already decided what room we should decorate for our honoured guest?'

'I have,' she admitted and explained which one she believed would be perfect and her thoughts on the en-suite.

Charlie laughed.

'What's so funny now?'

'Just that you can be so predictable sometimes, do you know that?'

Portia didn't like being thought of that way and nudged his side with her elbow.

'I don't mean it negatively,' he said, slipping his arm around her waist and pulling her to him.

'Is that an apology?'

'No,' he said, hanging up the damp tea towel. Then leaning closer to her he gave her a quick kiss on the lips. 'That's my apology.'

Portia peered over his shoulder and seeing that Oliver and Lexi were deep in conversation with their attention focused on the laptop, slipped her arms around Charlie's neck and kissed him properly. 'Apology accepted.'

17

PORTIA

After a restless night's sleep spent worrying about the extent of their renovations and how slowly they seemed to be working through them, Portia arranged to meet Lexi at the Summer Sundaes Café the following morning while Oliver went to help Charlie with some of the work. Lexi hadn't arrived yet, but as the café seemed busy as it usually was on a Sunday morning, Portia decided to put in her order. As she waited for Sacha to make their coffees and Jack to cook the bacon and eggs for their rolls, Portia went to stand at the window overlooking the sea.

Wave after wave rolled towards the beach and the beauty of the pale jade sea was mesmerising. She would never be able to see something like this if she still lived in London. 'I don't think I've ever seen so many white horses in the sea before.'

Sacha glanced over. 'It is rather spectacular, isn't it?'

'I'm hoping to go surfing in a bit.' Jack stepped out of the kitchen area and studied the busy café and lengthy queue. 'If this place ever dies down, that is.'

'It's probably a good thing we are busy.' Sacha raised her eyebrows at the woman who was next in the queue to Portia.

'Why?' Jack bellowed.

'Because that sea looks dangerous to me,' his sister replied. Portia could hear the tension between them but knew it was only because Sacha worried about her twin. 'Anyone else agree with me?'

There was a chorus of yes's and Portia added hers. Jack shook his head, clearly annoyed with their reaction and returned to the kitchen.

Portia didn't blame Sacha for worrying about her adrenaline-junkie brother and with Bella getting closer to having his baby she had supposed Jack would be a little more understanding.

Aware Jack needed to earn as much money as possible now he was about to be a father, it occurred to Portia that she might be able to please Sacha and Bella, while also giving Jack a reason not to go surfing. He was fit and strong and would be a great help if he were to agree to help them at the chateau. Excited at the thought but not wishing to go behind Charlie's back, she took her phone from her coat pocket and sent him a text asking what he thought of her idea.

Her phone pinged almost immediately:

Sounds great. Go for it. x

Delighted he agreed, she asked Sacha whether she might pop into the kitchen to speak to Jack about something.

'Go ahead,' Sacha said, putting the lids on the four reusable coffee cups that Portia had bought when they first moved into the chateau.

Portia stepped up behind the counter and went to stand at the kitchen entrance.

'You all right?' Jack asked, glancing at her before scooping their bacon and eggs from the frying plate onto the buns. 'Sorry, I don't mean to be snappy, but I'm going mad being stuck in here cooking for most of the day.'

'Then maybe you won't mind me making a suggestion.'

He stopped what he was doing and looked at her. 'I'm intrigued.'

'I was wondering if you might be interested in earning a little extra cash?'

He wrapped the individual buns in pieces of paper and then placed them into a paper bag. 'Sure. What would I be doing?'

She explained how Charlie was finding all the heavy work exhausting and why they needed to bring forward some of the internal jobs.

'We mostly need help in the garden pulling down the summer house and making everything look presentable. I thought that as the baby will be here soon and that your work is quieter now it's winter, and that Bella isn't planning on taking part in any antique fairs for a while that you might—'

'Need the money, you mean?'

'Yes.' She hoped she hadn't offended him by being so forthright.

Jack handed her the white bag containing her food order. 'I would love that,' he said with typical Jack enthusiasm. 'I still need to help Sacha here when Alessandro is off doing stuff for his gelateria, or archaeology work, but I'd still be able to put in quite a few hours each week, if that suits you? Obviously, I might have to dash off if Bella needs me or when she goes into labour.'

'That goes without saying,' Portia agreed, relieved he had accepted so readily. 'Bella and the baby come first.' She thought of her pretty friend and looked forward to being able to spend more time with her when they had completed more of their renovation work and she was free to take time away from the place. 'I'm so excited the pair of you are soon to be parents.'

'Thanks. I think we're both equally excited and terrified.'

'I'm sure that's only natural.' She lifted the bag, aware she needed to get a move on. 'I must catch up with Bella again soon, too. I haven't seen much of her since we've been back.'

'She'd love that.'

'Then I'll give her a call.' Portia turned to leave.

'You didn't mention when you need me to start,' Jack said.

'Whenever suits you.'

He followed her out of the kitchen and picked up several orders from the counter. 'I can start later today if you like?'

'That would be amazing.' The thought of Charlie having more help was an enormous relief. 'Charlie will be delighted to see you whenever you can make it.'

'Great. I'll make my way up to your place as soon as I'm finished here and after I've popped home to see Bella.'

Portia beamed at him. 'Thanks, Jack.' She breathed in the aroma of her breakfast. 'And these smell delicious.' She realised she was taking up his time when the café was busy and left to pay for the coffee, just as Lexi walked in and came to help her carry everything.

They waved goodbye to Sacha and, pulling their hats down over their ears and doing up their coats as high as each could go to keep out the strong bitter wind, left the café.

'You're looking very pleased with yourself,' Lexi said, walking next to Portia along the road towards the hill that would take them up to the chateau.

'That's because Jack has agreed to come and help us with the renovations. Well, help Charlie mostly, but I can't tell you how relieved I am to know we have a pair of strong hands like Jack's helping us.'

'I'm not surprised.' Lexi looked as if she was wondering whether to say something. 'I like Remi very much,' she said. 'But I noticed that he didn't seem all that on the ball about the building work the other day when Oliver and I came up to see you.'

'He's not.' Portia sighed. 'He's a great baker but not much good when it comes to helping out at the chateau, I'm afraid. We're trying to find what he's good at, bless him. Maybe with Jack helping Remi might not feel as obliged to do too much.'

By the afternoon, Lexi and Portia had completely removed all the wallpaper from the living room and Oliver had helped Charlie finish plastering the main kitchen.

They entered the living room, Charlie with an arm draped around Oliver's shoulders. He pointed at him, grinning. 'This bloke here is a dab hand at plastering.'

Lexi pushed a pile of discarded wallpaper into the wheelbarrow that was almost ready to be emptied into the skip outside. 'I didn't know you could do that?'

Oliver shrugged. 'Neither did I until I gave it a try. I'm happy to help out with other rooms in my spare time, if you like?'

'We would, very much,' Portia said quickly before he had a chance to reconsider. 'We need all the help we can get if we're to finish what needs doing.' Not wanting either of them to finish early, she added, 'As we're not bothering to repaper this room until after the party, I suppose you should both make a start on the bedroom we're preparing for Megan's arrival.'

Charlie lowered his arm to his side and looked at Oliver then back at her.

'I think that's us told,' Charlie said, looking amused. 'What will you two be getting on with next?'

'I thought we could start working on the dressing room to make it ready for the plumbing that'll need to go in there for the en-suite bathroom.'

Charlie nodded. 'Good idea. I'll relax a little bit when I know her accommodation is ready.'

'So will I,' Portia admitted. She noticed it was already dark outside and checked her watch. 'It's four thirty now. If you all don't mind working for another hour we could then get cleaned up and maybe pop out to the pub for something to eat?'

'Good idea,' Charlie said, smiling when Lexi and Oliver nodded their agreement.

'Or,' Oliver said thoughtfully, 'you could come to ours for something and I can show you the new website I've started setting up for you. I've got quite far along with it already.'

Lexi sighed. 'He's not kidding. He didn't come to bed until after two this morning.' She pointed at him. 'Oliver isn't good at leaving a project if he hasn't finished it.'

'That's true. I hope you like what I've done, but if you don't I can change it in any way you prefer.'

Portia was delighted. Everything seemed to take so long but on the other hand, she mused, they were seeming to be progressing quite well. At least if they had a website up and running then they could add photos of work as it progressed.

'I'm looking forward to adding before and after photos, so that prospective clients can see how well we're doing with the renovations.'

'Me, too,' Charlie agreed.

18

PORTIA

That evening, as she ate her Chinese takeaway in Oliver and Lexi's cosy living room, Portia was grateful Oliver had suggested that she and Charlie spend the evening at their cottage. They still had to get back to the chateau, but she knew Oliver well enough to know he would insist on driving them home.

She noticed Oliver had finished his food, picked up his laptop and was already logging on. She was excited to see his progress so far.

'This is very kind of you, Oliver,' she said. 'I know how busy you are with all your own projects, especially now, as your book did so well and you've been commissioned to write a series on – what was it again?'

'Succeeding in business.' He sighed. 'Not the most exciting topic.'

'It is for the people interested in that sort of thing, and you have so much experience it's wonderful that you'll be sharing it with others.'

'It does me good to step away from working on it though,' he said, without looking up. 'In fact, I really enjoyed myself working up at the chateau today. It did me good to do something physical again.'

Portia wondered if maybe Oliver was missing being in the Highlands where she knew he used to love going for long hikes with Alistair and their father before his brother died and his father became ill. 'I must admit, I expected to mind the hard work and lack of luxuries far more than I am doing.' As she said it, Portia realised it was true. Her childhood friends would be shocked to see her with broken nails and roughened hands, never mind that she hadn't been to a professional hairdresser since leaving London.

She realised Oliver was staring at her. 'What?'

'I was just thinking how different you are from a year ago.'

Portia wasn't sure what to make of his comment. 'In a good way?'

Oliver gave her an amused look. 'Well, let me put it this way. You know how fond of you I am, and we both know that you were always the most glamorous one of your London set. I've always known that underneath your perfect exterior there was a kind, beautiful heart, but I never realised how well you could adapt to a completely different lifestyle. And I have to admit I'm impressed. Massively so.'

Charlie held on to his plate of food as he leant sideways and rested his shoulder against hers. 'Oliver's right. I love the old you, but I think that this new side of you I've discovered recently is just as impressive, and I can't tell you how proud I am of you for coping with all that's been thrown at you.'

Her throat constricted with unshed tears. Portia was touched that Charlie and Oliver were impressed by her efforts, especially as she had been struggling more and more over the past few days. At least she had hidden her feelings from them. Not wishing to give in to tears and dampen the evening's atmosphere, she joked, 'If I'd known that all I had to do to impress the pair of you was to remove my manicure and make up and look like an old scruff in a pair of dungarees and work boots then I might have done this years ago.'

'You didn't know me years ago,' Oliver teased.

'Nor me,' Charlie laughed.

'And it's more than that anyway,' Oliver said. 'And you know it.'

'I do,' she agreed. She cleared her throat and took a deep breath. 'Right, are you going to show us what you've done for our website or are we going to have to wait longer to see it?'

'Finish your food first, then I'll set the laptop up on the dining room table and go through it with you.'

They did as he suggested and twenty minutes later all four of them were seated and staring at the screen. Portia felt Charlie take her hand in his. She could tell he was nervous; they were both grateful to Oliver for taking the time to create the site and neither of them wanted to admit it if they didn't like what he had come up with so far.

'Here you go.' Oliver clicked on a few things and pointed at the screen. 'This is the home page and there,' he added, 'is the logo I've designed.' He turned to them. 'No shyness about this, please. If there's anything you want tweaked, or even completely changed, it won't take me long to do it. I'd much rather you love what we put online than just accept something that's not perfect for you. Agreed?'

They nodded.

Portia stared at the intriguing announcement across the page saying, 'Top Secret – coming soon.' Underneath it announced that Megan Knight would be officially opening the chateau.

'What do you think so far?'

Oliver had created a brilliant site, but seeing it made what they were aiming for more real. Portia swallowed, trying to push away the panic rising in her. It was too late to change her mind about this now. Determined not to let them see how she felt, she grinned at Charlie. 'I love it. What do you think?'

'It's brilliant.' He sounded relieved. 'Really perfect. Thanks, Oliver.'

Oliver talked them through the next few pages, showing them the photos that he must have taken when he visited them. There was a photo of her and Charlie standing proudly on the front steps of the chateau. Their clothes were specked with paint and each were holding a paintbrush, their arms crossed. Remi was next to them, holding freshly baked loaves in his arms. Portia smiled, recalling that Remi had been loading his small van ready to start his deliveries.

'I suppose you've mentioned somewhere about him being a baker?' she asked, thinking how typical it was of Oliver not to miss a trick.

'Naturally. People love the thought of local food and especially artisan breads. I'm certain the thought of booking in to somewhere knowing you'll be treated to them during your stay can only be a positive.'

He was right.

She studied herself in the photo. She really had gone through some sort of transformation, she thought, as she peered at her image. No make-up, hair scraped back into a ponytail with strands falling loose around her face. Her dungarees were covered in dust and her sweater had a hole in it near the right shoulder where she had caught it on a nail while loading the skip.

'You look gorgeous,' Charlie whispered.

Portia laughed. 'Er, sure I do.'

'He's right, you do,' Lexi said, making Portia feel a little better about seeing herself the way others were about to. 'Only you could look that beautiful after spending hours working on a building site.'

'Thanks, both of you,' she said, feeling a little less insecure about everything.

'It's true. Unlike you, most of us,' Lexi said, grinning at Oliver, 'well, maybe not so much you, Oliver, but certainly Charlie and I are used to others not expecting us to appear perfect at all times.'

'Speak for yourself,' Charlie laughed. 'I'm only teasing. Lexi's right'

This new life of hers was somehow helping her worry less about others' opinions of her. Was it because she always felt less than perfect growing up? Always believing that if she looked better and achieved more, her parents might find her more interesting and make more effort to send for her during school holidays? It had never worked and she now wondered why she had tried for so long.

Charlie indicated some of the other photos. 'I like the ones of the rooms before we touched anything and those showing them *in progress*. This really is a great showcase for our renovations.'

'I'm glad you like it, but take time to think about it,' Oliver said. 'It's a work in progress. You might come up with other ideas along the way and I'll always be happy to change anything.' He smiled at them. 'Once everything is up and running and you have time to get to grips with it, I'll show you how to add photos and posts to the back end of the website.'

Portia wasn't sure she would be any good at that sort of thing but suspected Charlie might be more proficient given a chance to learn. He liked gadgets and would probably enjoy updating their website if he was taught how to do it.

She realised Charlie was waiting for her to say something. 'What?'

'I was saying the site looks perfect as it is and that we should let it go live. What do you think?'

She didn't see any reason to delay. 'Why not? Maybe people

might even start finding us on there among all the other places to stay.'

'I'm hoping fans of Megan Knight will find the site if they search for her name,' Oliver said, clicking on several things on the screen. 'It'll take a few hours to appear on the search engines, but if you're certain I can publish it now, then I'll do it.'

'Go for it,' Charlie said.

'Yes, do it.' Portia steeled herself against worrying that this was another step forward adding pressure for them to hurry up and finish their work.

Oliver clicked something, then sat back and rubbed his hands together. 'There. All done. Just keep taking photos as you progress with each room and send them to me. I'll add them as and when I can.'

'Well done,' Lexi said, getting to her feet. 'Now all we have to do is wait for the bookings to start flowing in.'

The thought of bookings terrified Portia. They were already limited for time and she was beginning to wish she hadn't agreed to hosting the Christmas party at the chateau.

'Don't look so concerned,' Oliver soothed when Charlie excused himself to go to the bathroom. 'It'll all be fine.'

'Do you really believe that?' She knew Oliver wouldn't lie to her and for some reason needed his reassurance right at that moment.

He patted her hand. 'I do. We're all here to help you and Charlie make this venture a success. I know you can do it and I want you to start believing it too.' He tilted his head to one side. 'You must be exhausted after working so hard, day in and day out. You'll probably feel better after a good night's sleep.'

He was right. 'I'm sure I will.'

'When Charlie gets back I'll give you both a lift home. It's

getting blustery out there and I saw on the news that snow is forecast over the next few days.'

'That's all we need,' Portia grumbled, her mood slipping. The
thought of being even colder in the chateau than they already were
was depressing.

'Did I hear you mention snow?' Lexi asked, carrying over cups
of coffee for them.

'Apparently it's due to hit the island in the early hours.' Oliver
gave Portia an apologetic look.

'Right, then I'll fetch you our spare duvet from the cupboard
and a couple of extra blankets to wrap around you when you're not
in bed.'

'Thanks, that'll be brilliant,' Portia said, relieved.

'Don't forget we do have the small fireplace in our bedroom,'
Charlie said, joining them. 'We can always wear beanies to bed to
keep our heads warm too.'

Portia laughed along with the rest of them, aware that however
messy she appeared in the photo on the website, wearing a beanie
to bed was going too far as far as she was concerned.

'Let's hope it doesn't come to that,' she said.

19

CHARLIE

Charlie heard the crash of something falling to the floor and, concerned for Portia, dropped the steamer he was using to remove wallpaper from the large bedroom wall and hurried into the dressing room to check she was all right.

'What happened?'

Portia waved her hand in the air and spun around to face him. 'I hit my damn knuckle on the doorframe.' She reached down an retrieved the paper scraper from the floor, then blew on her sore hand. 'It occurred to me that Megan Knight might change her mind about coming over now that the weather has turned. What will we do then?'

Relieved she seemed angry rather than hurt, he reached out and took her hand to check what damage she had done. Her hands were red and he could see the knuckle on her right hand already changing colour.

'You're going to have a nasty bruise there,' he said, taking care to rub it gently. He realised how cold her hands were. 'They're freezing. Where are your gloves?'

Portia mumbled something through gritted teeth.

'Sorry?'

'I said I got them wet working with the steamer, so took them off.'

He pulled off his own gloves and held them out for her.

'What are you doing?'

'You need these. Please put them on.'

Portia didn't take them and shook her head. 'No. You need them as much as I do. I'll find something else.'

Why she always had to argue with him about things, he didn't know. Charlie knew he mostly gave in to Portia when she was insistent about something but this time he had no intention of doing so. 'No. You wear them.'

'I'm fine.'

'Do you want to get chilblains?'

'What?'

He wasn't exactly sure what they were but knew his mother always used to threaten that he might get them if he didn't wear warm gloves and socks in colder weather. 'Chilblains. If you don't wear gloves in these temperatures you might end up with them. Now put these on.'

Relieved when she did as he asked, Charlie sighed. 'There, that's better. Now, maybe we should take a bit of a break and have a coffee or tea. Something hot to warm ourselves up a bit.'

'Good idea,' she said, smiling at him. 'I'll go and make it. Thanks for the gloves, Charlie. I do love how you look out for me, you know.'

'It's my favourite pastime.'

She smiled at him and blew him a kiss from the doorway. 'I'll bring biscuits up for us.'

He rubbed his hands together, aware that he needed to find other gloves to wear now that he had insisted Portia take his, and returned to the bedroom to continue working. Noticing the snow that had begun falling earlier that morning was now coming down faster, he watched out of the window for a few minutes as thick, white snowflakes swirled outside. If only they had managed to get as far as having the boiler repaired in time for this storm.

He turned from the window and seeing the fireplace decided to light a fire, hoping that the flue was clear and that the room wouldn't fill with smoke once he had lit it. He hoped her concerns about Megan not pitching up for the party were unwarranted. Surely she wouldn't agree to come and then cancel on them, would she? He thought back to how everyone seemed so impressed with her after getting to know her and decided that if Megan Knight could get to the island then she would honour her promise to do so.

By the time Portia returned to the room carrying a tray with two mugs filled with steaming coffee and a plate of digestive biscuits, he had a fire going in the grate.

'You clever thing,' she said, placing the tray down on an upturned tea chest that they had been using as a table. 'This should help warm the two rooms up nicely.'

'I've been thinking about Megan and believe she'll definitely be here.'

'I hope you're right.'

'I'm sure I am.' He decided to change the subject. 'It's getting bad out there now. I hope Remi will be all right getting home after making his deliveries.'

Portia handed him a mug of coffee and, taking a biscuit and her own cup, walked over to stand by the window with him. 'It's horrendous out there. The roads must be treacherous by now.'

'I can barely see much further than the first trees in the driveway.'

'Me neither. We'd better keep an eye out for him.'

'Maybe I should send him a text to check he doesn't need any help.' When Portia didn't answer he gave her a quizzical look. 'What?'

'I'm not sure how you're going to help him if he breaks down somewhere across the island. We don't have a car.'

'I hadn't thought of that.' It was another thing they would soon need to invest in, he thought miserably. They couldn't keep borrowing vehicles from their friends, or using Remi's van. Thinking of Remi, Charlie wondered if it might distract him to receive a text while he was driving. 'We'll check our phones in case he does contact us.'

'Yes.'

They finished their drinks and got back to work. Charlie knew that the sooner they were done preparing these rooms the sooner they would be able to stop for the night.

'Is it true you can't paint walls in very cold conditions?' Portia asked from the other room.

'Yes, unfortunately,' he answered, recalling looking it up over breakfast when he noticed how low the temperature was in the building. 'You're not supposed to paint outside when the temperature is below ten degrees Celsius and I gather that the weather shouldn't drop to freezing for the few days after that if you want the paint to stay on the walls.'

'But we're inside though.'

Charlie laughed. 'I know, but I don't think it's even as much as ten degrees in here right now.'

'Eugh, I hate this cold.'

He smiled to himself as he scraped off another piece of old wallpaper. 'You told me you love the snow.'

There was a few seconds silence, then Portia poked her head around the door. 'I meant I love going skiing.' She raised her hands and pointed to her woolly hat. 'When I'm wearing stylish skiwear, not dressed like a scarecrow from some old movie.'

Charlie saw the glint in her eyes and could tell she was amused despite her grumblings. 'You look gorgeous to me.' He cocked his head towards her. 'Now stop complaining and get on with stripping those walls otherwise we'll never get these rooms done in time.'

'I suppose keeping moving is one way to get a bit warmer,' she shouted from the next room.

Charlie lost all track of time as he slowly worked his way across the room. He was checking how much wallpaper stripping he still had to do when he heard a car hooting outside. Going to look out of the window, he spotted Remi's van. It was just visible but seemed to have stalled at the end of the drive just before the circular lawned area in front of the building.

Portia hurried over to join him. 'Is that Remi's van?'

'It is. It looks like it's stalled. I'd better go and help him push it closer to the house. If it's left out there it'll block the way for any other deliveries, should they make it here, and we don't want that.'

He ran out of the room, realising as he reached the bottom step that Portia was behind him. 'What are you doing?'

'I'm coming with you,' she replied, running past him and going into the dining room to grab her puffy coat.

Charlie didn't bother arguing with her but pulled on his parka over the jacket he was already wearing. Remi didn't need to wait for them to bicker before going to help him.

'This weather is horrible,' he heard Portia yell as she ran out towards the van.

They reached it and Remi got out. 'Sorry. It won't go further forward.'

'We'll push you down there,' Charlie said, pointing to a small area to the side of the chateau. 'It'll be out of the way and also slightly protected by the building from the worst of this weather.

'Thank you.'

'Portia, you get in and steer,' Charlie shouted, his voice almost lost against the strong wind and swirling snow. 'We'll push.'

She did as he asked and Charlie and Remi went to the back of the van and pushed. The snow was already almost a foot deep and it was harder than Charlie had expected to get the van all the way to the side of the house.

By the time it was parked, he saw Remi open the back of the van.

'You didn't manage to do your deliveries?' he asked, aware that this was Remi's only source of income.

Remi, his face red from exertion after pushing the van, shook his head. '*Non*. The roads, they were already impassable around here. I was stuck for a while, but Tony from the boardwalk, he helped me and told me I should return here as quickly as possible.'

'He was right.'

'Oh, no, your loaves.' She peered into the back of the van. 'Quick, let's get these inside before they get wet.'

They each carried trays of freshly baked loaves and rolls back into the chateau and took them into the dining room, setting them down on the table. The three of them stood back. Charlie wasn't sure what they were supposed to do with all the delicious smelling baked goods in front of them.

'It's not as if we have a freezer to put them in,' Portia said.

'We must eat what we can,' Remi said miserably. 'At least we won't starve if we get snowed in.'

Charlie rested a hand on Remi's shoulder. 'I'm sorry you weren't able to make your deliveries.' He tried to think what they might be able to do with the bread.

'If you couldn't do yours,' Portia said thoughtfully, 'then other deliveries won't have been made down at the boardwalk.'

'What are you thinking?' Remi asked, looking intrigued.

She glanced at Charlie and, seeing excitement in her eyes, he nodded. 'Go on, what is it?'

'Well, if you're happy for us to do it, Remi, I thought when this wind drops a bit we could each carry some down to Summer Sundaes Café. Maybe Sacha could sell them there. At least then you'll get some return for your ingredients and all your hard work.'

He looked impressed. 'I like this idea,' he said, glancing towards the window. 'But I don't think it will happen very soon.'

'As long as we have time to get them there and ourselves back up the hill and down this lengthy driveway before it's too dark that should be fine,' Charlie said, happy that Portia had come up with an idea that could help their friend and the people on the board-walk at the same time.

'Yes, we don't want to be out there too late,' Portia agreed, pulling off her hat and shaking the snow from it before taking off her puffy coat and hanging it on the back of one of the chairs. 'There aren't any street lamps from the boardwalk to here.'

Charlie knew they had little time to waste with the deadline they were working towards. He couldn't stand around chatting and neither could Portia if they were to complete the bedroom and bathroom in time for Megan Knight's arrival.

'Why don't you find containers to put the bread into to keep it dry, while Portia and I carry on with stripping the wallpaper. Shout for us if you notice the wind dropping or the snowfall easing and we'll drop what we're doing and go.'

It was less than an hour later when Charlie heard Remi calling for them. He switched off the steamer and set it down on the floor then turned to look out of the window. The snow was still falling, he thought miserably, but it didn't seem as thick and it looked as if the wind had dropped quite a bit.

'Should we leave now?' Portia asked, coming to join him in the bedroom.

'Yes, let's go.'

They wrapped up with extra layers and two pairs of gloves, each picking up two large bags of bread to carry down to Sacha's café. The snow was deeper than Charlie had expected but they would simply have to keep going. Remi relied on his sales and he hated to see all his hard work go to waste.

They walked in silence, each conserving their energy for trudging through the snow with their loads.

'I feel like a packhorse,' Portia moaned as they reached the edge of the boardwalk.

'Do you want me to take one of the bags from you?' Charlie asked, wishing she had said something earlier if she was finding herself overloaded.

'No, it's fine, thanks,' she said, brightening up as they neared the café, its lights reflecting out onto the snow. 'We're almost there now.'

Charlie reached the front door first and pushed it open, hearing the jangling bell announcing their arrival as the three of them entered the warm room.

Sacha's eyes widened when she saw them. 'What on earth are you three doing down here?'

'What's that?' Charlie heard Jack ask as he stepped out from the kitchen area before he had a chance to reply.

'We have bread,' Remi said when Jack hurried over to help relieve them of their packages. 'Many loaves that I was unable to deliver to my customers.'

'How lovely,' Sacha said, coming out from behind the counter to join them. She pointed to one of the larger tables. 'Put everything down on there and let's see what you've brought us.'

They did as she suggested.

'What's this?' Jools grinned at Charlie and gasped when she saw the containers of bread. 'They smell delicious.'

'Don't they?' Sacha agreed. She looked at Remi. 'Are you offering to sell them all to me?'

'Only the ones you are sure you will be able to sell on,' he said, looking sheepish.

Seeing how awkward Remi was feeling and wanting to help, Charlie stepped forward, about to fib and say that he had come up with the idea to bring the loaves to the café. Before he had a chance to do so, Portia admitted that the idea was hers.

'I hope you don't mind, Sacha,' she said, 'but I couldn't bear for all this delicious bread to go to waste and we supposed that if Remi couldn't carry out his deliveries, and that as you're down a fairly steep hill you might have the same issue getting supplies.'

'Please don't feel you should take it if you don't need it,' Remi added.

Sacha raised her hands. 'I think the three of you need to sit down and have a warm drink before we do anything else. You look perished with your pink cheeks and red noses. Get comfortable and I'll bring you all something, then we can chat about what we do with this bread.'

'I'll get the drinks,' Jack said. 'Coffees all round?'

They all nodded.

Sacha led them to a table and gave Remi a pointed look. 'I'm over the moon that you've brought these here.' She gave a sweeping wave in the direction of the loaves. 'My delivery was cancelled and I know that a lot of the residents on the boardwalk either rely on you or me for their bread. We should work out which residents have orders with you, so you and Charlie can deliver those. Then, I'll buy what's left to serve to my customers.'

'Please don't feel obliged to,' Remi said, looking sheepish.

'I don't. I'll definitely use them.' She looked from Portia to Charlie. 'I hope you kept a couple for yourselves?'

Charlie realised that they probably hadn't. 'Not that I'm aware of.'

Remi shook his head. 'I didn't think to do that.'

'Then you'll take two back with you for later. If this snow starts falling again as heavily as it did before and the wind picks up there's going to be snowdrifts and all these smaller lanes around here, and no doubt your endless driveway, will be impassable. Maybe for a couple of days. You don't want to go without.'

Charlie noticed Remi smile. 'I have ingredients at home and can always make many more loaves for us. We will never starve up at the chateau.' He laughed, and amused, the rest of them joined in.

He and Portia were luckier than they had realised having a baker under the same roof as them, Charlie thought, as Jack brought their coffees and bacon rolls. He decided that it had probably brought them closer together to help Remi too which was a bonus.

'Once you've eaten those I'll come and help you deliver your bread orders along the boardwalk,' Jack said. 'They'll be relieved not to have missed out. I know that I'm always happy as long as I can have toast or sandwiches every day. You can always make a meal when you have bread in the house.'

Charlie agreed. 'You're right, although living so close to the café and working here I doubt you'll ever have to worry about going without enough food, Jack.'

Jack gave him a playful punch on his shoulder. 'I was hoping for a little sympathy, for once.'

'Why?' Portia asked.

Charlie saw the questioning look in her eyes and realised that she had spotted something in Jack.

Jack's humour vanished. He waved goodbye to two customers and sat down at the table. 'I'm a bit worried, to tell you the truth.

The baby's due in a couple of weeks but the other day Bella was in pain from something called Braxton Hicks.'

'What on earth is that?' Portia asked.

Whatever they were, Charlie thought, they sounded uncomfortable.

'The doctor told us that they were the body's way of preparing to give birth,' Jack explained. 'Like sort of practice labour pains.'

'Sounds frightening.' Portia grimaced.

Charlie realised now what had been worrying his friend and hoped that Jack and Bella's baby wouldn't choose the next couple of days to make its appearance into the world. He caught Jack staring down at the tea towel in his hands and realised he was terrified that it might be exactly what would happen.

20

PORTIA

They were finishing their drinks after making the deliveries to the residents when Portia glanced out of the large café window overlooking the part of the promenade above the beach and groaned.

'What's the matter?' Charlie leant closer to her, his voice low.

'The snow,' she said, diverting her gaze back to look outside. 'It's thicker again. It looks like the wind has increased too.'

'You're right. We'd better get a move on if we're to get back to the chateau tonight.'

They stood.

'You're going already?' Sacha asked. She noticed three women walking towards the counter. 'I'd better see to these ladies.'

'The weather's got worse again,' Portia explained as she put on her coat and hat. 'We should be on our way.'

'We'll just settle up with you first.' Charlie zipped up his coat and retrieved his wallet from his trouser pocket.

Sacha put her hand out to stop him. 'No need. They were on the house.'

'No, you can't keep doing that.' Charlie argued. 'You're not going to make any profit if we keep eating and drinking here without paying.'

Sacha smiled at Remi. 'Thanks to you three trekking down here I now have bread for my customers.'

'All right then, but this is the last time. Thanks for the hot drinks and food though, it was all delicious.'

'It was,' Portia agreed, turning up her coat collar around her neck in anticipation of the freezing temperatures they were about to face outside. 'I certainly needed to be in a warm place for a while and being fed and watered was an added bonus.'

She leant forward and gave Sacha a hug, but was startled when the café door burst open and slammed against the wall, allowing a gust of freezing air to blow in. They turned to see who had made this dramatic entrance.

Portia saw Bella's mum, Claire, and was concerned to note she wasn't wearing a coat or hat and that her eyes were wide and her face ashen.

'What's happened?' Jack shouted, running towards her. 'Is it Bella?'

Claire had barely nodded when Jack tore out of the café without taking off his apron or a backward glance.

Sacha ran to close the door after him and, taking Claire's hands in hers, asked, 'Is she all right?'

'She's in labour,' Claire cried. 'I have no idea what to do. I was so young when I had her and it was all a bit of a blur.'

'I'll call an ambulance,' Charlie said, taking his phone from his pocket.

'I've tried that,' Claire said, close to tears. 'The roads down this way are impassable and they can't get here.' Tears began rolling down her face. 'I have to get back to her.'

'You can't go out there again without a coat,' Sacha said,

running through the café to the back room and coming out seconds later carrying a thick coat and a beanie. 'Put these on.'

'We'll come with you,' Charlie said.

'Yes,' Portia agreed immediately. She had no idea what use they might be but couldn't bear to leave Claire, Bella and Jack to deal with this alone.

'I'll lock up here and then come straight to the cottage.' Sacha hurried over to open the door for them all to leave.

Portia tried to think. 'One moment, Sacha. If the ambulance can't get here then we need to find someone medically trained in case there are complications.' She stepped away from her small group and addressed the few customers still in the café. 'Do any of you happen to be a nurse or doctor?'

She was disappointed to be greeted with shaking heads as an answer to her question.

'Do you know of anyone who might be?' Sacha asked, her voice shaky.

One of the women stood, getting ready to leave. 'Maybe you could ask Mrs Jones from Boardwalk Books. She knows everyone around here.'

'Or there's Betty,' another woman said before finishing her drink and standing to leave. 'If there is anyone with medical training around hereabouts she's bound to know.'

Happy to be useful, Portia offered to go and ask both of them. 'I'll come with you,' Charlie said. 'I doubt either of us will be any help cluttering up Bella's cottage with our fretting anyway.'

'I will close up the café for you, Sacha,' Remi offered. 'You must be with your friend and brother.'

'Really? You'll do that?'

'Of course. Now please go.'

Sacha gave him a grateful smile and rushed into the back room, returning soon wearing a coat and hat. 'Right, let's get going.' She took a set of keys from her pocket and handed them to Remi. 'Thanks for looking after the place.'

'It is no problem.'

'Let's go,' Portia said, not wishing to waste another minute. Her stomach was churning and the thought of Bella in pain and the advanced stages of labour was terrifying.

Sacha slipped as they walked along the snow-swept promenade, only managing to right herself when Charlie and Portia both grabbed her.

'We need to go more carefully,' Charlie said, as the three of them linked arms and slowed their pace. 'It's incredibly slippery out here and we won't help anyone if we hurt ourselves.'

Portia sensed Sacha's anxiety and hoped that she and Charlie could find someone to help them as soon as possible. 'We'll be there soon.'

They reached Bella's Bee Hive Cottage and knocked on the door to alert the occupants that someone was about to enter. Sacha opened it and anguished cries reached their ears. Portia exchanged horrified glances with her.

'Will you be all right in there?' Portia asked, her heart racing.

'I've no idea. I'm not very good with blood and that sort of thing.'

Portia saw the colour drain from her friend's face. 'I promise we'll be as quick as we can.'

'Yes, please hurry. She sounds as if she's in a lot of pain.'

'We'll do our best,' Charlie assured her. 'Try to remain calm. I think what Bella needs most is reassurance.'

Portia had no idea what the poor girl needed, but doubted having another person in a terrible state like Claire had been and Jack probably was, couldn't possibly be much help to Bella at that moment.

Charlie closed the door behind Sacha. 'Where should we start?' he asked, his voice loud against the wind.

'The bookshop is closest,' Portia said. She didn't know Jools well and had only visited the second-hand book shop a couple of times so hardly knew Mrs Jones, the proprietor and Jools's grandmother. She just hoped that the shop might still be open. As they crossed the boardwalk Portia presumed they would be at home. Surely most people would choose to be at home rather than out in this snowstorm and she was sure Lexi had mentioned once that the two of them lived in a flat above the shop. She hoped they did because it looked like the shop was closed.

'The lights are off,' Charlie said, obviously having similar thoughts.

Portia supposed they must have closed early. It wasn't even four o'clock yet, although she noticed it was already dark. 'I'm going to knock and hope they hear me,' she said, determined to find help for Bella. The thought of being in pain and giving birth at home where there was no one to give her pain relief terrified Portia. She shivered at the prospect as she reached out and pressed the doorbell.

She stepped from foot to foot trying her best to keep her feet warm. Charlie had his hands cupped together and was blowing into them.

'Roll on summer,' he said with his teeth chattering.

'There's a light.' Portia pointed as a warm glow appeared through the window. 'Thank heavens for that.'

The door opened and Jools peered at them. 'Come in,' she said, waving for them to do so. 'Quickly. Gran will be cross if we let in the cold, this place is a pain to keep warm with all the big windows overlooking the beach.'

They hurried inside quickly, closing the door behind them.

'Is something wrong?' Jools asked, looking them up and down. 'You're not hurt or anything, are you?'

'No,' Portia said, breathless from her barely suppressed panic. 'But Bella's in labour and neither her doctor nor an ambulance can get down to the boardwalk in the snow.'

Jools frowned, looking confused. 'Poor Bella, how frightening.' She frowned. 'She's not by herself, I hope?'

Charlie shook his head. 'No. Her mother, Sacha and Jack are with her.'

'That's a relief.' She looked from one to the other of them. 'I'm not sure what I can do to help.'

Portia heard footsteps coming down the wooden stairs from the flat. 'Is anything wrong?'

A handsome fair-haired man appeared and stood next to Jools. 'Hi,' he said, holding out his hand. 'I'm Marius.'

'Hi, Marius,' Charlie said. 'We were just telling Jools that her friend, Bella, is in labour.'

'She is?' He glanced at Jools. 'What can we do to help?'

Portia didn't want to waste any more time at the bookshop if they weren't going to be able to suggest someone. 'We were wondering if maybe your grandmother knew of someone who lived near here who might have medical training, so that we could call on them and ask for help.'

'We need to hurry, I think she's in a lot of pain.' Charlie took hold of Portia's hand and he could feel it trembling in his.

'I'll run upstairs and ask her,' Jools said, leaving them immediately.

Portia saw Marius take his mobile phone from his back pocket. 'I'll give my grandad a call. He hasn't been back on the island all that long but he's met a lot of new friends and he might know someone.'

'Thank you.' Portia was relieved she wasn't here alone.

'Thanks, Gran.'

Portia gave Charlie a hopeful look as she heard Jools's voice before her footsteps running back down to join them. 'Does your gran know anyone?' she asked before Jools had managed to reach the bottom of the stairs.

'Yes. Apparently Moira used to be a midwife. She's been retired for a few years now, but at least she should know what is supposed to happen and might be able to help.'

Portia sighed with relief. 'Thank heavens. Where does she live? We'll go to her place immediately.'

Jools pointed to the right. 'It's two houses before Betty's, which if you didn't know is the white one at the very end. So two up from that one.'

'That's brilliant.' Portia gave Jools a grateful hug. The look of fear on Claire, Jack and Sacha's faces haunted her and she hated to think how the time must be stretching for them and Bella while they waited for someone to come and help them.

'We'll go straightaway.'

'At least she should be at home,' Charlie said, the hope clear in his voice.

'I would think so,' Jools said. She went to open the front door for them. 'Do you need me to come with you to show you the right cottage?'

'No need for you to come out in the cold too,' Charlie said, leading Portia back out into the freezing wind.

'Thanks, Jools,' Portia shouted again. 'Please thank your gran for us.'

They walked hand in hand at a fast pace, slowing slightly when Charlie nearly slipped over. 'This is so frustrating,' he shouted over the howling wind.

'We'll be there soon.' Portia pulled her hood over her hat, holding it low to cover as much of her face as possible. She hoped

Moira was at home and wouldn't mind going with them to Bella's cottage.

'I think it's this one,' Charlie peered through the thick snow towards Betty's cottage, counting backwards until he pointed at Moira's home. 'Yes, it should be.'

He banged on the front door.

No one opened it and Portia wondered if there was anyone at home, when she noticed the curtain twitch from the corner of her eye. Someone was trying to see who was at the door, so she stepped back and pushed her hood back slightly so they would see it was a woman and hopefully would feel more inclined to answer. She raised her hand in a wave, giving what she hoped was a friendly enough smile before pointing towards the front door.

Seconds later it opened and a woman of around sixty-five glared at her. 'Yes? What is it?'

'Moira?'

'Who wants to know?'

This wasn't going very well, Portia realised. Then again, she and Charlie were complete strangers to this person and were banging on her door when it was dark. She wasn't sure she would be all that welcoming either if someone did the same thing to her.

'We're very sorry to bother you. I'm Portia and this is my boyfriend, Charlie. Mrs Jones from Boardwalk Books suggested you might be able to help us.'

'She did, did she?'

'Um, yes. You see, our friend Bella is in labour and urgently needs your help.'

'Bella? From the blue cottage?'

'That's right,' Charlie said. 'Her mother called for an ambulance a while ago, but they can't get down to the boardwalk in this weather.'

'They won't be able to get past the parish hall up the top of the hill in this,' Moira said confidently, sounding a lot friendlier. 'You'd better come inside while I grab my coat and a couple of things. Oh, that poor, dear girl. What a time for the baby to decide to be born.'

'Thank you so much,' Portia said, emotional with relief.

She felt Charlie's hand giving hers a gentle squeeze. 'There, you see? Everything's going to be all right.'

'Thank heavens,' Portia said, hoping he was right. 'I'm not sure what might have happened if we hadn't found Moira.'

'Let's not think about that right now.'

She realised Charlie was as terrified as she had been. 'No, let's focus on the positive.'

'I'm ready.' Moira appeared wearing a hat and coat and carrying a large bag. 'Let's get a move on, shall we?'

'I'll be back as soon as I can, Ted,' she shouted upstairs.

Charlie led the way to Bella's cottage and gave one knock before opening the door and holding it open for Moira and Portia to go inside.

'Shut that door,' Claire shrieked. 'We're trying to keep this place warm.'

Portia heard Claire's fear before she had a chance to take off her coat and hat. 'We've bought Moira to help,' she said, hoping to calm her.

'Moira?'

'Yes, dear, it's me.'

Claire stared at the woman who only lived a few houses down from her own. 'What are you doing here?'

'I'm a retired midwife,' Moira explained. 'If you hadn't been living away all these years, you'd know as much. Anyway, these two thought I might be able to help your lovely daughter.'

There was an anguished cry from upstairs.

'I think by the sounds of things you'd better take me straight up to her.'

Portia watched Claire and Moira go up the narrow staircase. 'What should we do?'

Charlie seemed as uncertain as she felt. 'I'd like to get going home, but I don't want to leave them in case they need us.'

'Let's warm up while we're waiting to find out what they want us to do,' Portia said, going to stand in front of the fire. 'Ahh, this is bliss.'

They were so intent on warming their hands and feet that neither of them heard Sacha entering the room.

'You guys are amazing,' she said, surprising them and making Portia gasp.

'How's Bella?' Portia asked.

'Much better now she has someone competent looking after her.' She shrugged. 'I didn't realise you knew Moira.'

'We don't.' Charlie explained about Mrs Jones making the suggestion that they ask her.

'I can't tell you how relieved the three of us are to know Bella's in safe hands.'

'I can imagine,' Portia said. 'She seems like a nice lady too. Very calm.'

'She was telling us that she's delivered hundreds of babies in her time and that the rest of us need to leave Bella with her for a while. Claire's on her way down but Jack refused to leave Bella's side.'

'I don't blame him,' Charlie said, his cheeks reddening when Portia gave him a surprised look.

She liked the thought of him not leaving her if she was ever in Bella's position. It was a sweet thing for him to say and she liked to think that Charlie was protective in this way. 'Dear Jack,' Portia said, picturing the muscular, fun-loving man whose love of surfing had always been his priority until he and Bella had become a couple. 'He must be in a terrible state seeing Bella in pain and not able to help her in any way.'

'Moira has Jack keeping her focused on breathing techniques,' Claire said, joining them. 'It's helping Bella keep on top of her pain somehow, and Jack finally seems a little calmer too, thankfully.'

Portia wondered if maybe now might be a good time to leave. It was a small cottage and they didn't need to be cluttering up the place. 'Will you want us for anything else, or would you rather we left?'

'You two can go,' Claire said, walking over to get the door for them. 'But thank you very much for all you've done for my daughter. We all appreciate your help so much.'

Sacha hugged Portia and then Charlie. 'I'll give you a call when we know something, but I think you'd better go and fetch Remi now. You should make your way back home as soon as you can. By the look of that weather you're going to have rather a difficult trek on your hands.'

'Don't worry about us,' Charlie said. 'I'm sure we'll be fine.'

Portia thought of the café keys. 'We can drop the keys off to you on our way.'

'No need,' Sacha said. 'I have a spare set. Just ask Remi to keep them up at the chateau for now and I'll fetch them from you in a day or so.'

'Will do.' Portia zipped her coat as high as it would go once again.

'Do you have a torch?' Claire asked.

Charlie frowned thoughtfully. 'Good question. We have the ones on our phones, but they tend to run the battery down quickly. I'm not sure if they'll all last long enough for us to reach the chateau now I think of it.'

'Wait there.'

They watched as Claire disappeared into the kitchen and

emerged with two hand torches. 'These both work, so hopefully they'll be all right until you get home.'

They took one each and thanked her before stepping outside. When the door closed behind them, Portia looked at Charlie and puffed out her cheeks. 'I don't know about you, but I'm glad to be going home now after all that excitement.'

'We've got a way to go before we'll get there unfortunately. I'm looking forward to taking these outer clothes off and changing into something a bit more comfortable.' Charlie grinned. 'I suppose we'd better go and fetch Remi and get up that hill.'

21

PORTIA

Portia was incredibly grateful to finally step into the hallway of her new home. For once she didn't mind that it was cold with an icy draught brushing past them through the hallway. She unzipped her coat, barely stopped to drag off her hat and practically threw it and her coat at a dining room chair before kicking off her boots and running upstairs to hers and Charlie's bedroom.

It had taken them far longer to walk home than it had to walk down to the boardwalk earlier. The snow had been much deeper on their way home and walking in the dark had not been fun. She had fallen over twice and Remi once, and by the time they reached the start of the driveway their moods had been so low none of them had anything much to say.

She hoped that they didn't have many more of these lengthy, arduous days. She was exhausted after these weeks working at the chateau and today had almost finished her off. She stripped off her damp jeans and discarded the rest of her clothes. Wanting to warm their bedroom, she set about lighting the fire in the small fireplace. She needed to sleep. The emotional and physical activity had been almost overwhelming and nothing other than sleep was going to help her feel better. This must be what exhaustion felt like, Portia thought as she struggled to light the fire.

As soon as it was lit, she grabbed her towel and night clothes and ran down the cold corridor to the bathroom. She turned on the taps and was already so cold that she barely noticed the freezing water as it splashed over her naked body. Maybe she was too tired to mind, she wondered, as she quickly soaped then rinsed her aching body.

She dried herself and dressed hurriedly, slipping her feet into her slippers and running back to her bedroom, hoping it had warmed slightly. She dragged one of the two chairs Charlie had brought up to the bedroom from the dining room so that it was closer to the fire and brushed her hair, willing it to dry so that she could put it in a ponytail. Now that she was beginning to thaw out she slowly began to relax.

The door opened and Charlie walked in. 'Hello, sweetheart. You look cosy in here.' He bent to kiss her cheek. Then, walking over to the window, pulled the wooden shutters closed on either side blocking out the snowy night. 'I'm not sure this will make the room much warmer, but it's worth a try.'

'Any difference to this cold will be worth it,' Portia said gratefully.

He put the other chair next to Portia's and sat before untying the laces on his boots. He took them off and held the soles of his feet near to the fire, wriggling his toes. 'You look a lot better than I feel.'

She knew he was trying to be cheerful and tried to smile but it seemed to take too much energy. She closed her eyes and leant her head against his shoulder. 'I'm so glad to be back home again, aren't you?'

'I am now that I'm in here with you. The rest of the place is freezing though.'

'Where's Remi?' she asked, hoping he was also somewhere getting warm.

'He went to his room, so he's probably lit a fire in there by now. I hope so, because it's the only way any of us are going to start to feel a bit more human.'

Portia felt Charlie's hand on hers and opened her eyes to see him watching her, a look of concern on his handsome face.

'Are you all right?' he asked. 'You look very pensive.'

'I can't stop thinking about Bella,' she shivered. 'She sounded so frightened.'

'I know, but she did seem better once Moira went up to help her.'

Portia nodded. She had. 'I'm relieved we found someone to help her. I couldn't bear it if we hadn't.'

'I agree.' He smiled at her. 'But we did and we've also left her in very good care. Claire and Jack will be with her all the time, and knowing Sacha she'll make sure everyone is well catered for. I doubt any of them will want for anything.'

He was right. 'I hope she has the baby soon,' Portia said, wondering if she would ever have the courage to have one herself after today's dramas. She admitted her concerns to Charlie.

'As long as you don't have to give birth in the depths of winter you should be fine,' he said matter-of-factly. 'Just plan to fall pregnant so that your baby is due in the summer.'

She wasn't sure what it was that tickled her, whether it was being over-tired, or the rollercoaster of emotions she had experienced throughout the day, but Portia felt a wave of laughter flicker through her and within seconds was laughing hysterically.

Charlie looked aghast. 'What's so funny?'

'I'm not sure. I think it's the serious look on your face when you were advising me about planning for a baby.'

He let go of her hand and sat back in his chair and Portia

realised she had hurt him. 'Oh, Charlie, I wasn't being mean,' she said, still unable to stop her laughter. She covered her mouth and took a deep breath trying to control her emotions. 'Sorry. It's not what you said exactly.'

She realised he was smiling. 'It's fine,' he said, not looking bothered. 'I think after today almost anything could make me laugh.'

'Or cry?' she asked, now feeling the urge to sob. What the hell was wrong with her?

Charlie leant forward again. 'Hey, don't be upset on my account. I was just a little taken aback for a moment there.'

'It's not that,' Portia said, as tears filled her eyes and began falling down her cheeks. She wiped her eyes with the backs of her hands. 'For pity's sake. I'm a mess and I don't know why.'

Charlie stood. 'You're exhausted and I'm not surprised.'

'But you're not crying, nor is Remi.' She hoped he wasn't, anyway. She would hate to think of him being upset without anyone to comfort him.

'There's a lot of pressure on us all at the moment and we all deal with it in different ways,' Charlie said. 'I take out my energies by hitting hammers against walls as I'm working.'

'I'll be fine soon,' she assured him, determined to gather herself as quickly as possible. 'Do you think Remi is all right though?'

'Tell you what, I'll go and make us a cup of tea and will ask him if he needs anything before I do so I can see if he's OK. All right?'

'Thank you. That's kind of you.'

'It's fine. Would you like anything to eat? Don't forget we have Remi's bread to eat and I can make us some toast or something?' He raised his eyebrows as if he had had a brilliant idea. 'There's some delicious honey in the cupboard. Shall I put that on the toast when I make it?'

The thought of warm toast and butter with honey over it cheered her enormously. 'Yes please.'

Charlie was as tired as she was and Portia didn't like to think he was doing all the work looking after her and Remi. 'What can I do to help?' she asked, getting to her feet.

'You can stay here where it's warm and keep putting logs on the fire. I need the room cosy for when I get back. Then we can eat and drink in front of the fire before going to bed.'

'That sounds perfect.' A thought occurred to her. 'Although if Remi isn't feeling very cheerful maybe you should invite him here so we can eat together. He might need company for a bit.'

'Will do.'

She watched Charlie leave the room and sighed. He really was the most caring man and although they had a lot of hard graft in front of them, Portia decided that she couldn't do something as testing as these renovations with anyone other than Charlie. She was grateful he didn't treat her like a princess but also that he seemed to know when she had reached her limit and was always understanding. She wondered how she could have been so lucky as to find two men in her life who loved her the way Alistair had done and now Charlie was doing.

'I must be the luckiest woman in the world.' She sighed deeply.

Dear Alistair. She had loved him with all her being and had believed her life over when he was killed. It was only Oliver's insistence that she would find a reason to carry on that had kept her going. Now, she was even more grateful to him for giving her the strength to keep on living because now she had Charlie and she was happy again, as Oliver had assured her many times that she would be. It was something she had never expected to feel and certainly not this completely.

She thought of Jack and the way he had dropped everything to run from the café to be with Bella when he heard she was in labour. How was Bella? Portia wondered, hoping they might hear news of her and the baby very soon. How frightened she must have been to discover she wasn't able to get to the maternity ward where she had imagined she would be to give birth to her baby? She gave a shuddering sigh.

The door opened a while later and Portia got up to help Charlie carry in the two mugs he was holding in one hand and two plates held awkwardly in the other.

They put them onto the tea chest and he rubbed the side of one finger. 'Phew, that was a bit hot though.'

She looked at the mug of steaming liquid and the plates of toast with honey. 'Either one?'

'Help yourself.'

She carried her food and drink and sat on her chair in front of the fire. 'Thanks for this,' she said gratefully to him. 'It's exactly what I need right now.' She took a bite of the delicious, sweet honey on top of the crispy, perfectly toasted bread. 'Heaven.'

'The perks of having a baker living in our home.'

At the reminder of Remi, Portia asked how he was.

Charlie finished his mouthful of toast. 'He's fine. Said he wasn't hungry and just wanted to get some sleep because he'll be up early again to bake if the snow has melted at all.' He thought for a moment. 'I suspect he's struggling a bit.'

Portia wasn't surprised. 'It can't be fun doing this by himself. At least we have each other to bounce things off when things get tough.'

'Mmm. I think we're going to have to make an effort to include him in more things. He's a quiet chap at the best of times, so it's up to us to draw him out of himself and help him when he needs it.'

She agreed. 'Definitely. I feel a bit mean this didn't occur to me before now.'

'Me, too.' Charlie ate a bit more of his toast. 'I suppose we've been so wrapped up in hard work we haven't noticed him finding life a bit difficult.'

'Yes. Poor thing, losing his bakery and flat above. Such a shame the owner wanted to redevelop it.'

'It is, but he has us and our kitchen and now he knows he has the support of our friends too. He'll be fine. And in future we'll take care to look out for him more. Agreed?'

She raised her mug before taking a tentative sip of her hot tea. 'Yes.' Portia realised they had been living and working in the same place for a couple of weeks, yet she knew very little about Remi. 'I think the first thing I'm going to do over breakfast is ask him more about his family and how he came to live here. Get to know him a bit better.'

'Good idea. Hopefully he'll be happy to tell us and it might get him opening up about other aspects of his life.'

'Perfect. Then that's what we'll do.'

Charlie's phone buzzed. He put his plate and cup on the floor and took it from his pocket. 'It's Jack,' he said, looking at the screen and answering the call.

Portia tensed, willing Bella and the baby to be fine.

'Hi mate,' Charlie said, staring at Portia unsmiling as he took Jack's call. 'How's everything going?'

Portia leant forward to try and hear what was being said. All she could pick up was some sort of excitement in Jack's voice, but knew that could be concern as much as happiness. She frowned at Charlie, hoping he would give her a clue about what was being said. Then Charlie's face relaxed and his mouth drew back in a wide smile. He beamed at her and nodded.

'That's amazing news, Jack. Congratulations from all of us here. Please give Bella and the little one all our love. And don't forget to let us know if there's anything we can do for you all.'

He finished the call and grinned at Portia. 'They're both fine.'

'I presume you mean Bella and the baby.'

'Yes.' He laughed and picked up his food and drink.

'Well?' she asked impatiently.

Charlie looked confused. 'What? They're fine.'

She closed her eyes briefly in frustration. 'Is the baby a boy or girl?'

'Oh, a girl. Apparently she's a bit wrinkled but Claire is sure she's going to look just like her mother.'

Portia sighed and relaxed for the first time that day. 'I'm so relieved they're both fine.'

'Me, too.'

'Maybe we can go and visit them tomorrow or the next day,' Portia suggested, surprised at herself for being interested. She hadn't been interested in babies before. Then again, she reasoned, she hadn't been around many. 'I feel like we've stepped into the next phase of our lives now this has happened.'

Charlie looked at her thoughtfully. 'Really?'

She nodded. 'It's all rather exciting, even though this baby isn't really anything to do with us.'

'Maybe it's because we're close to Jack and Bella.' He shrugged. 'Who knows? I'm just happy that we can go to sleep tonight and not have to worry about how things are going down at Bella's Bee Hive Cottage.'

So was she.

22

CHARLIE

Charlie woke to the sound of buzzing and it took him a few seconds before he worked out that a call was coming through on his mobile. He reached out to take it from the floor by his side of the bed. Squinting, he peered at the screen.

'Oliver?' He noticed the time and seeing it was a little after seven groaned inwardly. He could have done with an extra hour asleep after the efforts of the previous day and knew that even if this call only took a few minutes he would be unable to drift off to sleep again.

'Did I wake you?' Oliver sounded apologetic and Charlie suspected by the sound of his friend's alert voice that he had probably been up working for a while already.

'No, not at all.'

Oliver laughed. 'Sorry, I can tell by your croaky voice that I did. I can call back later.'

'It's fine. I need to get up and get going anyway,' he fibbed. Pushing back his side of the duvet he swung his legs out of the bed and sat up, shocked by the temperature in the cold room. 'Is something wrong?'

'No. The opposite in fact, which is why I couldn't wait to call you.'

'Go on.' Charlie was intrigued to hear Oliver's news.

'I checked the website this morning and you have a booking.'

'Really?'

Portia moaned softly next to him and he felt her hand on his back. 'What is it?' she murmured, still half asleep.

'It's Oliver. He says a booking has come through on the website.'

'What!'

He heard her move to sit up. 'Go on, Oliver. When is it for?'

'That's the thing,' Oliver said. 'It's for Liberation Day.'

'Liberation Day?'

He looked over his shoulder at Portia who seemed to be scowling. When she didn't comment on the date he realised she was struggling to remember when the annual holiday was held on the island.

'May ninth,' he whispered.

Portia's eyes widened. 'But that's only five, no four and a bit months away! We'll never get the place finished in time.'

'You may as well put me on loud speaker,' Oliver said.

Charlie did so. 'OK, we can all hear each other now. Go ahead.'

'Morning, Portia.'

'Hi Oliver.' Portia rubbed her eyes and Charlie knew she was trying to wake herself up as much as possible. 'This is exciting.' She pulled a face at Charlie. 'But I don't see how we can possibly get this place remotely ready in such a short time. You must know that better than we even do.'

'I do,' Oliver replied. 'However, you're not in a position to turn bookings down.'

Portia cringed. 'I know. What do you suggest we do?'

'Wasn't it you who mentioned a while ago that you could renovate certain areas for events and keep areas that aren't ready closed off?'

'Sort of. Yes.'

Charlie gave her an encouraging nod. 'That could work, couldn't it?'

'I think so,' Oliver said. 'Thanks to the work you're already doing on the rooms for Megan Knight's visit, you'll already have a bedroom for the host and hostess to stay in after their party ends.'

'Party?' Charlie asked, confused. He had presumed the booking would be for a wedding.

'Yes. Didn't I say? It's for a sixtieth birthday party. Apparently the place they initially booked has had to close for unexpected extensive building works.'

The irony of the situation wasn't lost on Charlie. 'A bit like what we're doing here,' he joked.

Oliver laughed. 'Yes, and they probably have far less work to contend with.'

Charlie couldn't hide his amusement, until he noticed Portia's expression. Clearly she wasn't feeling as positive as he and Oliver.

'Can we focus on practicalities?' Portia asked, her voice quaking with emotion. 'I'm not sure we can take anything on this early in our schedule, Oliver. It's too much pressure.'

Charlie understood her concerns and slipped his arm around her shoulders when she climbed over to sit on the edge of the bed next to him. 'I don't see that we have any choice, sweetheart,' he said. 'Not if we're to make this business work.'

'But what if we accept the booking then end up having to let the people down? I couldn't bear to do that.'

Neither could he. 'Then we'll have to make sure that doesn't happen.'

'Charlie's right,' Oliver said. 'I know you're both new at this kind of thing, Portia, and it's bound to be frightening at times. Unfortunately though, you've started this now, you've invested heavily into the project and you're going to have to start saying yes to whatever bookings you think are feasible. I know you'll find a way to make it work.'

Charlie winced, wishing he was as brave as Oliver when it came to insisting Portia do things. Then again, he reasoned, Oliver was Portia's friend, whereas he was her partner and it isn't always as easy to be firm with someone you love as much as he loved her, regardless of how necessary it might be.

'Oliver's right,' Charlie said softly. 'We'll find a way to do this. Don't forget we now have Jack on board to help us and I'm sure he's going to make a huge difference to the amount of work we manage to get through in the next few months.'

Portia sighed. 'He's only just become a father though, and his priorities will have changed, at least for the foreseeable future.'

'Bella's had the baby?' Charlie heard Lexi's excited voice in the background. 'When did this happen?'

Charlie presumed Lexi must have taken Oliver's phone from him. Happy for the distraction, he handed his phone to Portia and, realising he was shivering with cold, got up, hung Portia's discarded dressing gown around her trembling shoulders and quickly dressed before sitting back down again and waiting for her and Lexi to finish their conversation.

Portia said goodbye to Lexi after arranging to meet up with her in the next few days and handed the phone back to Charlie.

'So, what do you want to do?' Charlie asked her, not wishing to keep Oliver from his own work. 'Oliver is going to have to get back to them about the booking before they try elsewhere.'

She looked anxious for a moment. 'I don't suppose we have much choice.' She leant closer to the phone. 'Please message back to say we'll be in contact with them about their details in the next few days. That should give Charlie and I time to work out some ideas for their party.'

'Great idea.' Oliver sounded satisfied. 'I'll do that now and then let you have their contact details so you can speak to them directly. Unless you want to log on and get back to them yourselves now?'

'We don't have Wi-Fi here yet,' Charlie said, glad not to have to keep an eye on the website just yet. He had more than enough to contend with. 'I don't fancy trying to log on to the website from my mobile. Is that OK with you?'

'It is. I'll speak to you soon. Good luck with the work.'

The call ended and Charlie moved to face Portia. 'I know this frightens you a bit,' he said, wanting to comfort her. 'But this is how it's going to be until we get this place up and running.'

She took his hand and rested it on her lap. 'I know. And I'm grateful that you have more confidence in our abilities than I do.' She took a deep breath and he could see she was trying to calm down. 'I'm sure I'll be fine once we've done the first few events here. I think I just got the wobbles a bit now that it's all becoming very real.'

Charlie hugged her, unable to help smiling. The Portia he knew in London was always perfectly presented, contained and in control yet here she seemed to have far less confidence. It was strange seeing her this way and he was determined that by the time they had a proper event space he would make sure that she felt ready to face their new business, just like she always seemed to be when she had run their lives in London.

'Let's go and tell Remi our exciting news,' Charlie said, as Portia quickly dressed. He hoped that if he acted positive that some of it might rub off on Portia's mood.

They found Remi downstairs in the dining room eating some of his toasted bread. Charlie was relieved that his reaction to the booking was one of enthusiasm. 'You must be very excited.'

'Um, yes, I suppose we are.' Portia nodded. 'I have to admit, I had a bit of a fright when I heard how short a time we have to get things ready.'

Charlie was glad she seemed to be coming to terms with the idea. 'It's daunting for me too, but the difference is that I have more experience thanks to working in hotels.'

'Would you like me to fetch a notepad and pen?' Remi asked, getting up from his seat when Charlie nodded. 'It might help if you talk through your ideas and thoughts on which rooms you wish to work on next.'

'Yes,' Charlie agreed, feeling more enthusiastic. 'And what we hope to offer these first clients of ours. And how much we'll need to charge them so we don't scare them off, or end up leaving ourselves out of pocket.' Never mind him trying to reassure Portia, he thought, the money part was the aspect that troubled him most of all.

'Yes, I'd forgotten we still need to do that,' Portia said, pulling out a chair and sitting on it. 'And it's not just the rooms we'll be using for the party that have to look right, don't forget. The rest of the areas that they'll pass through in the grounds and the chateau will need to look presentable too.'

Remi returned to sit down with them. 'I will help you when and where I can. I think it is a good idea you now have Jack helping with all this work. Everything will need to be as perfect as you can make it. I hope that nothing goes wrong for you.'

'Don't say that,' Charlie said, feeling his anxiety rising. 'On an island this small we can't afford to let anyone down, least of all our first proper clients, otherwise word of mouth will get it around in no time and our business will be a failure before it has even had a chance to get going.'

He realised he had said too much when he saw the horror on

Portia's ashen face. He took a deep breath and forced a smile. 'We will make this work though, so don't worry.'

Charlie saw Remi and Portia exchange uncertain glances and wished he had thought before speaking his mind. He was going to have to be a lot more careful voicing his concerns in front of her in future.

23

PORTIA

'I can't believe our party will soon be here,' Portia said as she held the ladder for Charlie as he carefully hung the wallpaper they had bought earlier that day in St Helier. It wasn't exactly what Portia had envisaged being in this room, nor was it the perfect colour she had hoped for, but the pale blue subtle pattern fit the period and anyway, she mused, they had little choice so it would have to do.

'You shouldn't worry so much,' he said, positioning the piece so it matched exactly the other already glued to the wall. 'When Megan sees the rest of the chateau I'm sure she'll be happy this is where she'll get to go and relax at the end of the day.'

He had a point, Portia mused, recalling how they had spent almost an hour that morning at the breakfast table watching a tutorial on tiling while eating their toast.

'I wonder how Remi and Lexi are getting along with the tiling in the bathroom?' she whispered, glancing over her shoulder, aware they couldn't hear any chat coming from the room. Portia had been surprised when Remi insisted he had experience of tiling a bathroom and that he could do a reasonable job of it. Charlie hadn't been convinced and neither had she, but eventually they had given in to Remi's protestations, anxious that they had little time to make good any errors he made or to waste arguing.

'The most important thing is,' Charlie said, brushing over the sheet of paper before stepping down from the ladder, 'that the bedroom and bathroom are finished today. Then everything can be cleaned and the furniture brought in and set up.'

Portia was looking forward to that bit most of all. She had pictured how this room would look so many times since their arrival at the chateau that the need to see it looking its best was almost overwhelming.

'I'm glad I have my smartest bedlinen and bedspread to dress this room. The last thing we need is Megan telling people the bed was uncomfortable or sharing photos of the room looking unappealing.'

'True. And we must have a fire going for when she arrives and enough wood next to it so that she can add to it whenever she wants.'

Portia felt a surge of excitement. It was the first time she had felt anything other than concern or fear for some time and it was a welcome feeling. *Maybe this was how it would feel going forward when they began to reach some of their goals for the venture?* The sensation gave her the incentive to keep working even though after days with little rest she was beginning to wonder if she could remember how it felt not to have aches and pains in every muscle.

They hung the final piece of wallpaper and then stepped back to survey their efforts.

'What do you think?' Charlie asked, scanning the room.

Portia was happier than she had expected. 'You were right, this does look amazing in here.' She kissed his cheek. 'You've done a fantastic job. It looks perfect. Very plush.' She recalled him saying he had never hung wallpaper before.

'How did you know what to do?'

He seemed happy with her praise. 'I remember helping my granny wallpaper her back bedroom when I was about ten and that helped a little, but I basically looked it up on YouTube, as I've done with every other job I didn't have much idea about.'

She picked up a couple of scraps of paper from the dust sheet covering the floor. 'Well, it did the trick. I suggest we leave it to dry for a little while then bring in the bed and rest of the furniture to dress the room.'

They didn't have as much furniture as she would have liked but Portia reasoned that Megan was expecting the place to be far from ready and hoped she would understand if there were some shortcomings. As it was, their guest would be sleeping in the most expensive bedlinen Portia owned and that alone should help make her night's sleep a restful one.

'Shall we check on Lexi and Remi? Then we can start fetching the pictures we cleaned up from your great aunt's room.'

'Sounds good to me.'

They stood at the doorway of what had been the old dressing room and Portia couldn't believe how well Remi and Lexi had got on.

'This looks amazing,' she said, staring at the large ceramic cream tiles that now almost completely covered the walls and floor. 'You're almost finished, too.'

'We are,' Lexi said, standing and pointing to Remi. 'I can't take much of the credit though, Remi has been the one to line everything up and cut the tiles to size. It does look pretty impressive though, doesn't it?'

'It looks wonderful.' Charlie nodded. 'I can't tell you how relieved I am that we'll have these two rooms ready for Megan's arrival tomorrow.'

'It was a good thing the plumber had a cancellation and could install the new sanitaryware in time for us to finish this bathroom,'

Remi said, finishing his final tile and wiping it before standing to survey his hard work.

'It was kind of Oliver to find him for us,' Portia said grateful to her friend for always being there when she needed him.

'It looks great,' Lexi said, folding her arms. 'Oliver was a bit anxious that he might not find someone who was free to do the work for you at such short notice.'

Portia relaxed slightly. She knew Oliver well enough to feel sure that if this plumber hadn't been available someone would have been found to replace him very quickly. Oliver Whimsy wasn't used to letting people down and if necessary he would help Charlie do the work himself. Somehow.

'Right,' Lexi said. 'I don't know about you three but I'm parched. Why don't I drive Portia down to the boardwalk to fetch us all some of Sacha's delicious coffees and maybe a couple of pastries to keep us going?'

'I love that suggestion,' Portia said, looking forward to getting away from the chateau for the first time in days. 'At least the snow has stopped falling now and the roads have cleared a bit.'

She and Lexi would still have to walk down the long driveway to where Lexi had left her car just to be safe. It would be worth it though, simply to have a break from the chateau. 'We should pop in to see Bella and the baby while we're down there.'

Lexi's mouth drew back in a smile and Portia realised that was what her friend had been hoping to do all along.

Portia looked up at Charlie. 'You can spare me for a while, can't you?' she asked guiltily. He also hadn't had a break from the place. Only Remi had been out during the day to deliver his bread to customers.

Charlie grinned at her. 'You enjoy yourself. Remi and I have enough to keep us busy here while you're gone. In fact,' he said, turning his attention to Remi. 'Maybe we could fetch the furniture and set it up in the bedroom while Portia is out and unable to boss us around?'

She knew he was teasing her. 'Ha, ha,' she said sarcastically. 'I'll leave you to it then. Come along, Lexi, let's go before they change their minds and decide to join us.'

* * *

Sitting in Bella's warm living room with a mug of tea in her hands and a plate of delicious homemade biscuits one of the neighbours had dropped off for Bella and Claire, Portia felt more comfortable than she had in days. She and Lexi watched as Bella fed her tiny daughter and Portia couldn't get over how instinctively her friend had taken to motherhood.

'You both look so content,' she said wistfully, wondering if she and Charlie might ever be parents.

'You do,' Lexi agreed. 'And she has to be the prettiest baby I've ever seen.'

Bella looked up. 'Do you really think so?'

'Yes, we do,' Portia said.

'Jack and I feel the same way, but then we're biased.'

There was a knock at the door and Claire went to open it. 'Sacha, come in. What have you got there?'

Sacha walked into the room carrying two bags, placing her free hand over her heart as she peered down at the baby girl dozing in her mother's arms. 'This is so amazing.'

Portia could hear by her friend's voice how besotted she already was with her niece. 'You're the first of us to have a baby, Bella, and she's perfect.'

'That's what we were saying,' Lexi said. 'What have you got there?'

'Oh, these are pastries. I thought you might need them.'

Portia was surprised. 'You knew we were here?'

Sacha shook her head. 'No, I brought them for Bella and Claire, in case they were peckish, but there's enough for all of us.'

'Lexi and I were coming to the café to buy coffees and pastries once we'd seen the baby. We've left Charlie with Remi. They're working hard up at the chateau and we promised to return with treats.'

'I'll go to the café with you when you leave.' Sacha perched on the side of Portia's chair. 'Have you and Jack decided on a name for my baby niece yet?'

Bella looked at them. 'We have, but you must promise not to tell anyone outside of this room until I've had a chance to tell Jools and Betty.'

They promised to do as she asked.

'So what name have you chosen?' Portia asked, fascinated to know.

'We're calling her Maia.' She looked from one to the other of them.

'What a beautiful name,' Portia said. 'What does it mean?'

Bella smiled. 'It means great, or mother. Jack insists it means water.'

Claire joined them having taken the bags of pastries to the kitchen and placed them neatly onto a large plate. 'He also said that Maia was the mother of Hermes in Greek mythology, or some such thing.'

'I love it whatever it means,' Sacha said, clasping her hands together and gazing down at the baby. 'Hello, Maia.'

'I'm so thrilled you all like it,' Bella said, lowering her head to kiss the top of her baby's head. 'We think it suits her.' She looked up and smiled at them all. 'And it's easy to spell, so that will be an added bonus for her when she starts having to write her name.'

Bella looked content and unflustered and Portia imagined how perfect her little family must look when Jack was with them. She felt mean for being the cause of Jack having to spend time away from his new family and her guilt made her address the issue with Bella.

'Would you rather Jack spent more time at home with you?' she asked, without stopping to consider how best to put across her question.

'Pardon?'

Bella, Claire, Sacha and Lexi's heads all snapped around to look at her and Portia realised her question had come out of the blue.

'What I mean is, seeing you here with baby Maia made me feel selfish.'

'Why?' Bella shook her head in confusion.

'Surely Jack wants to be here, instead of helping us up at the chateau.'

Bella stared at her for a moment longer before smiling. 'Ahh, I see. No, don't be silly.' She shrugged. 'Of course I'd like him to be here as much as possible, but we need the money. Please don't feel guilty, we're grateful to you and Charlie for giving him the extra work when he needs it most.'

Relief washed through her. 'Really?'

'She's right,' Sacha said. 'I never need Jack for as many hours at this time of year and I know things are quiet for Tony with the fishing thanks to the bad weather we've been having on and off since October. Jack was only telling me this morning how happy he is that you've asked him to help at the chateau. And,' she grinned, 'he loves physical work and I know he'll be looking forward to when you start working on the garden. He's happiest working outdoors.'

'That's all right then,' Portia said, deciding she must relay Bella and Sacha's assurances to Charlie.

Bella covered her mouth and Portia realised she was trying to hide a yawn.

Lexi stood. 'Talking of Charlie, I suppose we should go and get those coffees and pastries we promised to take back with us.'

'Yes, We should get a move on.'

'I'll come with you,' Sacha said, standing.

'You don't all have to go, do you?' Bella asked.

'We do,' Sacha insisted. 'You need your rest while Maia is sleeping and I really must get back to the café. I'll pop back a bit later.'

The girls blew kisses to Bella and her baby and Claire showed them to the door.

'Thanks for coming, girls,' she said quietly as they fastened their coats and pulled on hats. 'Bella was thrilled to see you all but you're right, she is exhausted. I'm going to try to persuade her to go and take a nap.'

'We'll be back to see you again soon,' Portia promised before leaving with the others.

24

CHARLIE

Charlie woke when his hand rested on the cool sheet where Portia usually slept. He opened his eyes, wondering where she could be. Listening for a few seconds, he didn't think she was in the bathroom, so got out of bed, pushed his feet into his trainers and grabbed the blanket they had left lying on the chair nearest to the fireplace. Wrapping the blanket around his shoulders he went to look for her.

Not wishing to wake Remi, Charlie crept to the bathroom first, in case she was in there. Assuming she might have gone downstairs for some reason, he made his way down the staircase, stopping for a second when one of the steps creaked loudly underfoot before continuing on.

When he didn't find her in the living or dining rooms, he battled not to panic. She must be here somewhere, he thought, hurrying through the hall to the kitchen. The door was open and he saw a dim light on the tiles just inside the room. Stopping at the doorway, Charlie watched her silently. She was sitting at the table, a cup of tea in her hands, staring straight ahead. He didn't want to startle her, but noticed she was shivering, so had little choice but to let her know he was there.

'Portia?' he whispered, walking up to her and pulling the blanket from around him.

She looked up at him, not seeming to register it was him for a moment, before looking away again. 'Sorry Charlie, I hadn't meant to wake you.'

He draped the blanket over her shoulders, wondering how long she had been sitting in the cold room. 'You look frozen.'

She looked up at him. 'I suppose I am.'

Taking the cup from her he realised the tea was cold. 'I'll make you another one of these, then I want you to come back to bed where it's warm and tell me what's wrong.'

'Wrong?'

'Why you're sitting here in the cold in the middle of the night.' He checked his watch and saw that it was after three in the morning.

Charlie pressed the kettle on and went back to her, putting his arm around her shoulders to try and warm her. He covered her bare legs with one end of the blanket before sitting down on the chair next to her.

'What is it, sweetheart? What's the matter?'

She looked down at her hands for a while.

'Portia, please tell me. I can't help if I don't know what's upset you.'

She looked him in the eye and held his gaze and Charlie could tell she was trying to decide what to say to him. Wanting her to open up to him, he waited for the kettle to finish boiling so he could make them both a hot drink, hoping she might be ready to open up to him when he sat at the table again.

'Here, this should help warm you.'

Charlie noticed she was crying. 'What is it?' He took one of her hands in his and rested his other palm lightly on her shoulder. 'Please tell me.'

Portia wiped her nose on the back of her hand and took a steadying breath. 'I'm frightened I'll let you down.'

It wasn't what he had expected to hear. 'You could never do that, sweetheart.'

She sighed. 'I didn't think this would be so hard,' she said quietly. 'I don't know if I can do this after all, Charlie.'

His heart dipped. It hadn't been easy, he knew that. 'Working in these conditions isn't ideal and it doesn't help that we have such a tight deadline,' he said. 'If it helps, I also struggle to keep going at times.'

'I don't want to disappoint you.'

He hated to see her distraught. 'You could never do that. Look, if this is too much for you, I can carry on by myself,' he soothed, aware that wasn't the answer she wanted when she gasped. 'I have Jack helping now, and of course, there's Remi doing some of the work.'

She shook her head. 'But that's not the point.'

'Then what is?' he asked as gently as he could manage.

She withdrew her hand from his and went to fetch some kitchen towel. Portia wiped her eyes and blew her nose before returning to sit next to him. 'Ignore me. I'm fine.'

'No, you're not. We need to be open with each other about how we feel.'

'It's fine.' She took a tentative sip from her cup. 'Really. I think something woke me and I panicked.'

'It's more than that,' Charlie argued, wanting her to be honest with him.

Portia rested her head on his shoulder for a moment. 'Honestly, Charlie. I had a moment's panic, that's all. Talking to you has reminded me that I'm not alone here. I'll be fine. Really I will.'

'But Portia—'

She stood. 'No, Charlie. Please forget this ever happened. Now, let's take our drinks up to the bedroom and get some sleep.' She pulled the blanket towards him, so that he could wrap it around his shoulders too. 'Look at you with barely anything on. I'd never forgive myself if you froze because I was having a wobble.'

Charlie knew when it was time to give in. 'Fine. Let's go back to bed and try to get some sleep before the alarm goes off.

* * *

That morning, Portia initially seemed much happier. Later as they worked in the hall, he noticed her trying to mask her anxiety but he hadn't missed how she kept twisting the ring on her index finger as she frowned thoughtfully.

'The hall doesn't have to be perfect,' he reminded her, hoping to reassure her. Then, studying the tiled floor he had just finished cleaning and the washed paintwork that was drying, he had to admit that the room really could have done with a fresh coat of paint. 'We don't have time to do anything more with it, not before Megan arrives.'

Remi picked up the mop and bucket to take it outside. 'There's no point in doing any more to the hallway anyway,' he insisted. 'We have lots of people arriving tomorrow night for the party and they're only going to spill things and make a mess. They all know that nothing is totally finished and as it will look when it's done anyway.'

'But I was hoping for it to look more welcoming than this.' Portia stood by the closed front door, her hands resting on her hips and Charlie could tell she was picturing something that would no doubt mean extra work for him. 'Surely there's something we can do to help it look a little less unloved.'

'Like what?' he asked, dreading her suggestion.

'We need people to have a good first impression as they arrive.' She tilted her head to one side in contemplation.

Charlie was relieved they had no spare time to add anything else to their list. 'Yes, well, next year we can put up a Christmas tree in here,' he said, picking up dusters he had been using earlier and going to walk to the back of the building to put them away.

Portia gave a strange shriek. 'What did you just say?'

Shocked, Charlie stopped and turned to her. 'Who? Me?'

'Yes.'

He thought for a second sensing he might regret his flippant comment. 'Something about next Christmas?'

She pointed at him, excited and her mind raced with possibilities. 'That's it! We need a Christmas tree.'

Charlie puffed out his cheeks and groaned. 'You mean now, don't you?'

'I do. Don't you see? A Christmas tree will make the place smell of pine instead of plaster dust and it will be a focus point to detract guests' view from the state of the place.'

'I suppose you're right.' He wished she wasn't.

'I know I am. Surely you can find a tree somewhere in the garden. It doesn't have to be too enormous and we do need to thin trees out in places, you said so yourself.'

'I did?' Why had he said that to her?

'I can see you're not happy about this. Look, we don't have much time. Will you ask Remi if he can go with you to find a tree for us? Now?'

Charlie knew when it was quicker to give in and nodded. 'I don't see why not. But do we have any decorations here?'

'No, but I'm sure I can find some from somewhere, or borrow them.'

Charlie shook his head. 'Portia, it's almost Christmas. I assume that whatever decorations people might have they will have already used them in their own places.'

'Fine, then I'll ask Lexi to drive me to the shops. We can try and buy something that will pass for decorations.'

'Are you sure this is necessary?' he said in one last attempt to deter her. 'We still have to clean Megan's bathroom now the tiling is finished in there and also tidy up the kitchen. And we need to bring in the pots with small trees for the living room and dining room, too. Never mind getting all the food and drink ready.'

She raised her hands in the air. 'I'm aware of the lengthy list we still need to work through before Megan arrives at six thirty. But I also know I am right about having a Christmas tree in the hall.'

Charlie withheld a groan. 'Fine. You go and sort out decorations and I'll ask Remi to come and help me.'

'Thank you. I promise you'll be glad you did it once you see the effect it'll have in this hallway.'

Half an hour later Charlie and Remi carried a slightly wonky tree in through the entrance. Charlie was tired and sweaty from working almost non-stop all day and regretted agreeing to the party at all.

'It's not perfect,' he said before Portia could suggest they go and find a better one. 'But it'll have to do.'

He and Remi stopped in the hallway.

'That looks impressive,' Remi said, turning to Charlie, a smile on his face.

'Thank you,' Portia said, looking very pleased with herself, a pair of gardening pruners in her hand. Charlie studied the ivy she had woven back and forth between the banister rods and had to admit it had given the hallway an ambience it desperately needed.

'It does look good.' Charlie gave her an appreciative smile, glad he had been wrong to doubt her idea.

'I also found these strings of white lights in the small boot room at the back of the house where we had stored outdoor decorations I'd already bought for the place. I'd forgotten that I had them.'

Charlie looked down at the bundle near the stairs.

'I thought you two could hang a string of them on either side of the entrance way to light up the route to the front door.' Charlie puffed out his cheeks at the thought of yet more jobs being added to his already teetering pile. 'That leaves one string for the tree and two others to be strung up in the living room and dining room.' She grinned at him. 'Don't worry, I'll do those.'

'Let's set this thing down,' Charlie said. 'It weighs a ton.'

'That's clever.' Portia pointed to the base he and Remi had made from two blocks of wood and nailed into the bottom of the trunk.

'It should be enough,' Charlie said, hoping he was right. 'Okay, if you stand over there, Portia, you can tell us which way to turn the tree to make sure it looks as good as possible.'

'I think it's perfect as it is,' she said, surprising him. 'Thanks, guys. This is just what we needed.' She rested one hand on her hips. 'I feel much better about this place now and think everything is coming together pretty well.'

Charlie smiled. His face felt hot from the exertion. 'Let's get those lights set up outside while there's still some daylight,' he said, motioning for Remi to join him. Then, recalling decorations, he turned to Portia. 'What about the decorations for that?'

She followed his finger as it pointed to the tree. 'We don't need many, not with a load of white lights wrapped around the branches.'

By the time Charlie and Remi had set up everything outside and each carried in two small trees and shrubs they had found in pots in a greenhouse at the back of the property there were bright lights twinkling on the tree. They both stopped as they entered the hallway and noticed them.

Charlie was impressed. 'You're right, Portia, that was a great idea.' He raised his eyebrows. 'It does look impressive. Very much so.'

'*Merveilleux*,' Remi said, looking equally as surprised as Charlie had done.

'Well, if our guests are as impressed as you two, then I'll be very happy.'

'Right,' Charlie said, looking from one tree in his hand to the other. 'Where do you want these placed?'

Portia climbed down from her chair and returned it to the dining room. 'Two of them can go there—' she pointed '—and there, Remi,' she said, pointing to areas in the room.

'Charlie, if you bring those two into the living room.'

He followed her, putting them down where she indicated.

'What do you think?' she asked, narrowing her eyes.

'I have to admit you really do have an eye for these things.' He studied the lights hanging across the wooden shutters and the carefully placed pots.

'I'm glad you think so. I do have a certain amount of experience making things look good, don't forget.'

He knew she did. He walked up behind her and, slipping his hands around her waist, kissed the back of her neck, causing her to shiver. 'I know you do. I promise not to be such a misery next time and to listen to your suggestions without moaning.'

She turned to face him, still in his arms. 'I'll believe that when it happens. You're as strong minded as me when it comes to believing you're right.'

'True.'

'I think that as time goes on we'll both work out each of our strengths and maybe stop wasting so much time arguing before letting the other one do their thing.'

'Are you two ready to carry on with everything?' Remi asked, surprising them and causing Charlie to turn to him. He noticed the weary smile on Remi's face as he stood waiting for them at the living room doorway.

'Sorry, Remi,' Portia said, moving back from Charlie. 'Charlie's just coming to help you.'

'Help with what?' Charlie frowned.

'We need another couple of trees brought in. Just little ones. Shrubs even. I just want lots of greenery to hide the scrappy look of the undecorated rooms. Then we can get on with the food and drink, clean Megan's bathroom, then each take a shower.'

'So not much left to do then?' Charlie laughed, longing for everything to be done so he could relax a little.

'Not much.'

25

PORTIA

Portia checked her watch for the fifth time in as many minutes. 'How long do you think Oliver will be collecting Megan from the airport?'

Charlie put an arm around her shoulders as they stood in front of the huge living room window. 'She's coming over by private jet, so I don't think we can check its arrival on the usual website.' He kissed her cheek. 'Everything is ready for her though, so try not to worry too much.'

Charlie was right, as he had been when she had voiced her fears about letting him down, and about Megan cancelling her trip over to the island. She needed to try and remain calm. Anyone who knew her from London would be surprised to see her acting any other way and if she was honest with herself, there wasn't too much that fazed her; but this was important to them both and more than anything she wanted to do her best to ensure everything went well for Charlie's sake. He had worked so hard up until now – they all had, even kindly Remi – and she had no intention of letting herself down by panicking, especially in front of Megan Knight.

Portia had to admit it was an enormous relief to at least know that Megan had arrived on the island. Oliver explained before leaving to fetch her that Megan had sent a text letting him know when her jet was about to take off from London City Airport. The fear that the weather would close in once again and stop her getting to Jersey had caused Portia's anxiety to shoot up but now she was here, and the rooms they had prepared were ready for her, all Portia had to worry about was ensuring Megan's stay at the chateau was an enjoyable one. It was vital if she were to share photos and positive thoughts on her social media accounts, to her friends, and hopefully maybe mention the chateau in the occasional interview after she returned to London.

They both needed her experience with them to be perfect – well, that and their party going to plan. Portia longed for the next couple of days to pass so she and Charlie could go back to work on the chateau. She was amused to think she was looking forward to the messy work instead of being excited about a party. How times had changed.

'Is that Oliver's car?' Remi asked, coming to join them.

Portia peered out of the window and spotted dappled lights flickering through the trees as a car drew down the driveway. 'She's here, Charlie!' Portia took a deep breath and patted her chest, immediately forgetting her intention to remain calm.

Charlie gave her hand a squeeze as he leant closer to the window to check. 'Yes, that must be them.'

Excitement vied with nerves in Portia's stomach as she prepared to meet this woman who could potentially make an enormous amount of difference to the success of their business venture. Portia grabbed her coat and slipped it on, going immediately to stand on the front steps after Charlie, so they could greet their VIP guest.

Oliver parked the car and walked around to the passenger's

side to open the door. It took a moment for Megan to appear at the front of the vehicle and as soon as Portia saw the bright, friendly smile coming her way, she felt much better. Of course Megan was going to be nice, she thought, returning the friendly gesture and stepping forward with her hand outstretched to introduce herself. After what sounded like a bit of a shaky start, everyone on the boardwalk seemed to have taken to Megan, and hadn't she offered to come and stay for free to help them?

'Megan, how lovely to welcome you to Chateau de Caesarea. We've been looking forward to meeting you.'

Charlie stepped forward and shook Megan's hand. 'Thank you for coming and being not only our very first guest, but also for helping us launch our new venture. We really are very grateful to you for doing this.'

'It's my pleasure,' she said, her free gloved hand holding the faux fur collar of her camel coat close to her throat.

'It's too cold to be standing here chatting,' Portia said, motioning for Megan to accompany her inside. 'Not that it's much warmer in the chateau, I'm afraid. The fires have been lit in an attempt to warm the rooms we'll be using but our heating doesn't yet work. I hope you're going to be warm enough.'

Megan batted the comment away with her hand. 'Don't worry about me,' she said. 'I'm tougher than I look. A bit of cold isn't going to bother me.' She looked up at the front façade of the building. 'This is an impressive place, though. I'm excited to be here. I'm looking forward to being shown more of it in daylight tomorrow.'

'We can't wait to show it to you,' Charlie said, giving Portia a smile when Megan wasn't looking.

'Come along,' Portia said, opening the door and indicating for Megan to go in. 'We've prepared chicken pie with all the trimmings for you.' She gave Megan a conspiratorial grin. 'I say *we* but by that I mean Charlie made it. He's an excellent chef.'

'Really?' Megan smiled at him appreciatively. 'I'm so hungry and that's one of my favourite dishes.'

'I know,' Charlie said. 'I contacted your manager and asked for food suggestions. We want to make your stay here as comfortable as we possibly can.'

Portia could see that Megan was charmed by Charlie's thoughtfulness and why wouldn't she be, she mused. He knew how to look after guests better than anyone else she had ever met and never seemed to be fazed by people, no matter how influential or affluent they might be.

Remi pushed the door wider with his foot as he entered the chateau carrying a piece of hand luggage and a case. Oliver followed carrying matching cases. How many items of clothing did one person need for a two-day trip? Portia wondered before reminding herself that even six months ago she would probably have felt the need to pack almost as much as Megan for the same amount of time.

Portia closed the door behind them, not wishing the freezing temperatures to come sweeping into her home.

'I'll show Oliver where to take these,' Remi said as he passed her. 'Then we'll come down to join you.'

'Thank you both so much.'

Megan was staring at the Christmas tree. 'How beautiful.'

'I'm glad you like it,' Portia said, walking up to stand next to the complimentary woman. 'We thought this room needed something to bring it to life for your visit and the party seeing as we haven't been able to decorate the area yet.'

'Well, you've done the right thing. It is perfectly Christmassy. I love it.'

'May I take those from you?' Charlie asked as she undid her opulent coat and unwound the cashmere scarf from her neck. She handed them to him before removing her hat and passing that too.

Portia watched as Megan ran her fingers through her shiny hair to give it a bit more bounce after removing her hat.

'Let's go into the dining room,' Charlie suggested, leading the way and draping Megan's hat, coat and scarf neatly over the back of one of the chairs.

'It's lovely and warm in here,' Megan said politely.

It wasn't what Portia would describe as warm but it was more pleasant than the hallway had been. She also noticed with delight that either he or Remi had added more logs to the fire and someone had laid the table while she had been putting final touches to Megan's bedroom and bathroom. She made a mental note to excuse herself before they finished their meal to add extra coal and logs to the fire that she had lit earlier in Megan's room.

'I adore your wooden shutters,' Megan said, walking over to stand closer to the fire. 'I've always fancied a place that has those. And you can't ask for more with this gorgeous fireplace. So perfect for a frosty evening like this one.' She rubbed her hands together in front of the dancing flames. 'And that cornicing, it's stunning. In fact, I'd go so far as to say you're very lucky to find a chateau with so much character still in it.'

Portia looked at the shutters, now closed across the window and blocking out the black night sky. It made a nice change to see the place from fresh eyes. The room did seem much cosier with everything as it now was. It was the first time she had seen it with this much atmosphere and it made her proud to welcome their guest into this special space of hers and Charlie's.

'This is lovely,' Megan sighed, still looking around the room. 'I was looking at chateaux in France this summer but nothing appealed to me as much as this one does.'

Charlie pulled out a chair and waited for Megan to take a seat. 'You haven't seen the rest of it yet,' he laughed. 'I wouldn't make your mind up too soon.'

'He's right,' Portia agreed, taking the seat opposite her. 'We've only decorated a couple of rooms so far and one of those is your bedroom.'

Megan chuckled. 'That's so funny.' She became thoughtful. 'Then again, if the atmosphere is this magical when the place has had little work done to it imagine how enchanting it's going to be when you've finished it all.'

She had a point, Portia mused, delighted that Megan seemed to have taken to the place as much as she had done. 'I'm so pleased you like it,' she admitted. 'We knew we were taking a chance asking you to come here, and to be honest, I'd already started thinking of smart hotels I could phone and beg for a room for you if you did take one look at the place and decided you couldn't stay here after all.'

She caught Charlie giving her a concerned look as he lifted two logs ready to place in the fire but wasn't sure what he was trying to tell her.

Megan seemed thrown by her admission. 'Really?'

Portia sensed she had said something wrong and hoped she hadn't offended her. 'I didn't mean to imply that you wouldn't stay here, only that you might prefer a little more luxury.'

Megan stared at her silently for a few seconds then shook her head slowly. 'No. I'd never do that. I might wear expensive clothes and spend a ridiculous amount on facials and haircuts, manicures, that sort of thing, but I would never cancel like that.' She glanced at Portia's hands.

Aware that her once perfect nails were ruined, Portia bent her fingers to hide them from view.

Megan looked embarrassed to have caused her reaction. 'I haven't always been used to this way of life though,' she said with a slight shrug. 'This is very exciting for me. An adventure. Since becoming a celebrity I've seen and done many things I never expected to do. I fully intend making the most of them all.' She smiled. 'And if one of those things is helping friends while staying in a beautiful chateau, then I'm happy to do it.'

Feeling a little as if she had been put in her place, Portia decided to be more careful about her presumptions in future. She couldn't afford to offend Megan. They needed her far too much, and, Portia reasoned, she did seem very pleasant. She sighed inwardly. She had an awful lot to learn from Charlie about this hospitality life.

She heard Oliver and Remi's voices and was relieved when the two of them entered the dining room. 'Come and sit with us,' she said, looking up at Oliver. 'Feeding you is the least we can do to thank you for collecting our lovely guest.'

Oliver walked over to stand behind Portia, resting his hands on each of her shoulders before bending to kiss the top of her head. 'I'd love to stay longer but I promised Lexi I'd be home for supper. I'll be back tomorrow with her to help you prepare the place for the party, though. I'll be off now and leave the four of you to get to know each other better.'

Portia smiled up at him. 'Thanks, Oliver. Please give my love to Lexi.'

He said his goodbyes and Charlie saw him out.

'Would you both like something to drink?' Remi asked, walking over to a fifties drinks trolley that Portia hadn't noticed being in the room before. She had no idea where it had come from and presumed Charlie must have found it somewhere.

'I'd love a glass of red wine, if you have one,' Megan said.

Charlie entered the room carrying a crystal decanter quarter-filled with a rich-looking red wine. 'Was someone wanting a glass of this?' he asked, clearly knowing what Megan liked to drink as well as her favourite meals. He gave Portia a wink as he passed behind Megan and poured each of them a glass before placing the decanter on the table.

Megan took a sip. 'Mmm, now that is delicious. In fact,' she added, looking surprised, 'that's...'

'Your favourite wine?' Portia asked, smiling gratefully at Charlie. 'Someone has been a very busy man.'

'You are a dream host,' Megan said before taking another sip.

'I aim to please.'

Portia shook her head, amused. He really was even better at this hosting business than she had imagined.

Having drunk a small amount from his own glass, Charlie stood. 'I'll go and fetch supper now. I'm sure we could all do with eating straightaway.'

Later, as each of them sat back in their chairs sipping wine after finishing their meal, they continued chatting amiably.

'I've really enjoyed this evening,' Megan said, sounding a little tipsy, but looking, Portia was relieved to note, content.

'I'm so happy to hear you say that,' Portia said. 'I think we're probably all nearly ready to go to our rooms and was thinking that we could meet down here for breakfast at whatever time suits you. Then we'll show you around the grounds and the rest of the chateau after we've eaten, if that works?'

'Jack and Alessandro are coming over shortly after breakfast,' Charlie explained. 'You know them, of course, and you'll see Sacha and Bella later at the party. They won't be here until then because both of them have a lot on tomorrow. And you'll meet Jools tomorrow evening for the first time, I gather, but the guys wanted to come up and say hello and see if you needed anything fetched from anywhere.'

'I can't wait to see them again. Everyone is so lovely over here. I can't believe they're coming here just to see me?' She looked amazed and Portia couldn't help thinking how unassuming she was not to expect special treatment from anyone. 'They were both so kind to me when I was here last year and I've been looking forward to catching up with everyone again and meeting Jools.'

'It should be a lot of fun tomorrow night,' Portia said, feeling much more relaxed about the party than she had done up until then. She took a last sip of her drink.

'I'm sure it will be,' Megan agreed, finishing her wine and placing her glass down with purpose onto the table. 'Well, that's me.' She got to her feet. 'If you don't mind, I think I should turn in for the night. This sea air has wiped me out just like it always seems to do.' She covered her mouth as she yawned.

'I'll show you up to your room.' Portia stood as Remi went to pull back Megan's chair.

I hope you're going to be comfortable enough in here,' Portia said when they entered the freshly decorated bedroom as she scanned the room yet again to ensure nothing had been forgotten or was out of place.

Megan yawned again. 'I'm sure I'll sleep like a baby. This room is beautiful and so cosy with the fire lit.' She turned to Portia. 'Thank you for inviting me here. You really have a stunning home. I must admit I'm quite envious of you.'

Portia was surprised to hear Megan saying as much but the warm sensation wafting through her on hearing the positive words gave her a boost she realised she needed. 'Thank you. I don't think you probably realise quite how much your visit means to Charlie and me. You coming here and giving our place the seal of approval is the very best encouragement others can need to persuade them that Chateau de Caesarea is the perfect place for their important celebration, and the two of us can't thank you enough.'

Portia thought of the cost of Megan's flights. 'I know Oliver said you didn't want any payment for coming here,' she said, embarrassed to have to broach the subject of money. 'But we insist that you let us cover the cost of your flights to and from the island. It's the least we can do.'

Megan shook her head. 'No need.'

'But you can't pay to come here as well as being our special guest to welcome people to the chateau at the party. That's far too much.'

Megan opened her suitcase and pulled out a pair of silk pyjamas. 'Rubbish. Anyway, I wasn't the one who paid for them, Oliver did that. He arranged everything.'

Portia couldn't think what to say. 'He did?' Why hadn't he mentioned anything to her? How typical of him to be so generous.

Megan gasped and covered her mouth. 'Hell, I wasn't supposed to say anything.'

What else had he paid for that she didn't know about? Portia wondered, hoping the flights were everything. They were already far too much.

Megan took Portia's hand in hers. 'Please, don't be angry with him. I know you mean the world to him and he would be furious with me if he knew I'd told you what he'd done.'

Portia took a deep breath, determined to look unfazed. She was over-tired and exhausted from all the hard work over the past few weeks and knew her emotions were only just being contained. It wouldn't do to let herself down in front of Megan. She gave a tight smile. 'If you don't want me to say anything, then of course I won't.'

'Thank you. I'd hate to cause close friends to fall out on my account. Anyway,' she said, giving Portia's hand a gentle pat before returning to her unpacking. 'Do you know what I'd be doing if I hadn't come here today?'

Portia shook her head, intrigued. 'No.' She hoped Megan wasn't about to make her feel guilty by telling her that she had turned down an important engagement, or maybe a family Christmas get-together.

'Nothing.' Megan lifted two brightly coloured dresses from her suitcase.

'Sorry?'

Megan draped the dresses over her left arm and raised her eyebrows, looking sad. 'I would be sitting in my posh flat with a bottle of something expensive and one glass.'

Portia pictured the glamorous photos of Megan at one impressive party after another, always on the arm of a gorgeous man. 'I don't understand,' she said, going over to the wardrobe, opening it and taking out a couple of padded hangers. Portia took the two dresses from her guest and hung them in the wardrobe. She passed another two to Megan waiting for her to continue speaking.

'All I mean is that there must be photos of you smiling and appearing to be having a wonderful time?' Megan didn't speak for a couple of seconds. 'Always with a friend as perfectly turned out as you, and probably a couple of handsome guys looking dashing as you all smile at the camera.'

Portia thought about what Megan was saying. She had a point. 'I suppose so.'

'Were those nights always that awesome? That perfect?'

Portia thought back to how she had felt most of those times. Since Alastair's death she had always felt like she might be letting someone down if she did as she would have rather done and stayed at home alone but she had always done what was expected of her. She had dressed up, gone out and socialised and shone as well as she knew how regardless that she would have much rather been wearing Alastair's favourite grey cashmere sweater and crying as she poured over photos of the two of them together, grieving for the future that had been snatched from them.

She felt a hand on her arm and took a deep breath to bring herself back to the present. 'Sorry, I was miles away.' She realised Megan looked stricken.

'I've made you cry.'

Portia hadn't realised she was crying.

'Oh Portia,' Megan said. 'I feel terrible. I always assumed your life was perfect.' She groaned. 'Which is ironic when I'm trying to make a point about people not believing everything they think they see when I look happy in photos.'

Furious with herself for letting her emotions get the better of her, Portia wiped away tears she hadn't realised had been running down her cheeks. 'It's not your fault,' she insisted. She cleared her throat. 'I don't know what came over me. Probably too much wine after a tiring few weeks. I'll be fine. Anyway, I was thinking how right you were. That I was only playing a part and looking happy because that was what had been expected of me, too.'

'Just like I do when I'm out at parties, I attend because it's expected of me,' Megan said. 'Anyway, are you sure you're all right?'

Portia exhaled sharply, embarrassed to have made a scene. 'Perfectly. It wasn't anything you said, it just took me back to a sad time in my life that's all.'

'It was stupid of me.'

'Not at all. It's the time of year. Christmas is the anniversary my late fiancé's death. He was Oliver's older brother.'

Megan's mouth opened in shock. 'I had no idea.'

Portia needed to get their chat back onto a guest and hostess keel. 'Anyway, that's all over really. I have Charlie now and I'm very happy with him.'

'He is lovely,' Megan agreed. 'But you've had a difficult time and you're bound to be emotional occasionally. I am certain this place is going to be perfect when you do open it to the public though. You're a lovely couple and deserve to do well.'

'That's very kind of you and I hope you're right,' Portia said proudly. She realised Megan had been trying to make a point when she mentioned smart parties a short while before. 'And to answer your question, I do understand what you were saying about the parties. But I had imagined you might have a significant other to spend Christmas with.'

'Not any more. And to be honest, I'm not sorry, not now I'm here. Do you know, I think we're going to be good friends.' Megan smiled.

'And I think you could be right, although...' Megan laughed doubtfully.

'What?'

'You wouldn't say that if you'd met me a year ago.' Megan shook her head. 'I was a right brat then.'

'I can't imagine that.' Portia couldn't. Megan seemed so thoughtful and kind.

'It's true. Ask Bella. I met her when she was hired to be my hands.'

'Hands?' Portia watched as Megan held out her hands, turning them back and forth.

'Bella had to stand close behind me for a photo shoot, so it looked like her hands were mine and I was a complete pain. I've grown up a lot since then, though.'

Portia decided Megan must have endured a lot in suddenly having to get used to the constant attention after her stint on the reality TV show that shot her to fame. Portia wanted her to feel like she could confide in her. The woman might have a manager and presumably family somewhere and friends, but hearing her compare their two lives as far as appearances were concerned, she wondered if maybe she needed a confidante. 'I had thought you were in a relationship with a singer.'

'Actor,' Megan unzipped her make-up bag and rummaged around looking for something. 'I thought he was about to propose when he took me out for a special meal two weeks ago.' Her voice lowered so much that Portia struggled to hear what she was saying.

'And he didn't, I imagine,' she said.

Megan sighed deeply. 'No. He said he was taking me out for our last meal together. Apparently he wanted it to be special because he had been offered the role of a lifetime in Hollywood. He said he knew I couldn't leave my work here in the UK and thought it better if we ended things between us.'

'You couldn't?' Portia asked, certain that if Charlie had to leave to work in the States for whatever reason that she would find a way to be with him, at least part of the time.

'We could have found a way,' Megan said sadly. 'But I quickly realised that he had no intention of even trying to work something out. I think he was looking forward to having fun out there and the last thing he needed was a girlfriend getting in the way.'

Portia's heart ached for her new friend. 'I'm so sorry. That's a horrible thing for him to do.'

'Thank you. I thought so too, but then this evening, as we sat in your undecorated but gorgeous dining room, it occurred to me that I would rather be with genuine people like the three of you, than yearning for a man who didn't care enough for me to at least try and fight for our relationship.'

'You're very wise,' Portia said, surprised when her comment seemed to shock Megan.

'You really think so?'

'I definitely do.'

26

PORTIA

'This toast is delicious.' Megan bit into another mouthful while Portia, Charlie and Remi watched in amusement. 'And the butter is heavenly. I forgot how scrumptious Jersey butter tastes. I must take some home with me when I leave.'

Portia pictured the Jersey butter she had seen in shops on the mainland. 'I'm certain you can buy it in UK supermarkets.' Portia thought back and wondered why she hadn't thought to buy any for Charlie as a taste of home when they were living in London.

'Can you?' Her eyes were wide with delight. 'Then I must order a load.'

Portia watched her and saw how much younger than her Megan actually was. The evening before, with her immaculate make-up on her face, she had appeared to be in her late twenties, but this morning she was fresh faced and Portia thought she looked younger than her twenty-three years.

'So,' Megan said, taking a sip of her tea. 'What's the plan for today? I want to help.' She pulled a cheeky face. 'Nothing too mucky though, but if there's something I can help with I hope you will let me know.'

'We will.' Portia had no idea what preparations needed to be done that wouldn't involve getting a bit messy, but decided to worry about that after breakfast.

Charlie walked over to the window and folded back the shutters, immediately letting more light flood into the already sunlit room. 'I think that's Sacha arriving.' He turned back to them looking very happy. 'She's brought Jack and Alessandro with her, too. I'll go and let them in.'

Portia was surprised that instead of wanting to go and greet the new arrivals, Megan stayed at the table and took another piece of toast from the toast rack Remi had just carried into the dining room. 'I'll catch up with you all later, this stuff is too good to resist.'

Portia noticed Megan indicate for Remi to sit and join her and liked that she was paying him attention. By the pink shade his cheeks had gone he didn't mind one bit.

'There's no way I'm going to forgo this delicious bread, toasted or otherwise. You, Remi, are a magician when it comes to baking.'

Remi blushed. 'I am not.' He shook his head and looked down at the last remaining piece of toast but Portia could tell he was delighted.

It gave her an idea. 'Would you mind if Remi quotes you on our website, Megan? I'm sure that the review will make a lot of difference to sales and we will be buying our bread from him when we open properly.'

'If you think it'll help.' She seemed doubtful.

'Absolutely. You have the ear of a younger audience.'

Remi nodded. 'It is those who have not yet discovered my produce.'

Megan spread a thick layer of the rich, yellow butter onto her toast before taking a large bite and closing her eyes ecstatically. 'Then they don't know what they're missing.' She finished eating. 'Yes, go for it. Use my quote with pleasure.'

Portia grabbed Remi's arm in excitement. 'You see? Your baking is a marvel. I wish you'd understand how much we all enjoy it.'

His cheeks reddened even further and he smiled. 'That is kind of you to say.' He stared at Megan, still eating the toast in her hand. 'You are very kind. Thank you.'

She waved her free hand in the air. 'Rubbish. You deserve all the praise. My only worry is that your bread might get too popular and there won't be enough for me when I next come to the island.'

'I will make certain there is always some available for you alone.'

Portia enjoyed seeing Remi looking so happy. For some reason she hadn't yet been able to fathom, he seemed to have a sadness about him that concerned her. Was it a broken romance that none of them knew about, or something else? She wasn't sure but she decided she needed to make an effort to find out, when the time was right. She might even be able to help bring some happiness back into the sweet Frenchman's life. For now, though, his day had clearly been made by Megan's praise and for that she was extremely happy.

Hearing footsteps and happy voices, Portia began tidying the table. 'Sorry, Megan. I know you're still eating but I should take this dirty crockery to the kitchen out of the way, in case the others need the table for anything.'

Megan swallowed her mouthful and held up the last remaining bite. 'Don't mind me, I'm almost done anyway. You go, I can bring my cup and plate when I'm finished.'

Portia was enjoying having such an affable guest staying with them. She hoped most of their future guests would be as charming and helpful, but doubted they would be. Then again, if they were expecting guests to pay for the privilege of staying at the chateau they could hardly expect them to help out too.

'Megan,' Jack cheered as he entered the dining room with his arms wide. 'It's great to see you again.'

She finished her mouthful and took a sip of her coffee before standing and going to greet him. 'Still the same old Jack; noisy as ever.' She stepped into his arms and hugged him back. Then spotting Alessandro behind him, let go and went to hug him.

'Is very good to see you again.' Alessandro held out a white paper bag.

'It's lovely being here.' She pointed at the bag. 'For me?'

'Yes.' Sacha entered the room and gave Megan a kiss on the cheek. 'I thought you might like a Jersey Wonder.' Portia saw her friend glance at the table still with remnants of their breakfast on it. 'Maybe you could have them later with a cup of tea?'

'That sounds perfect.' Megan took the bag and had a quick look inside. 'Looks tasty, and still warm. What a shame. I'm full after making such a pig of myself over breakfast. I'll bring these through with me to the kitchen.' She picked up her plate and cup. 'I won't be long, Sacha. Take a seat if you like and I'll come to join you in a minute.'

'Don't worry about that,' Charlie said, taking the bag and crockery from her. 'You four catch up with each other and I'll follow Portia through. We won't be long.'

Portia left the room and heard Charlie following behind. 'I'm a bit worried about the amount we need to get through to be party ready.' She resisted glancing into the bare living room as they started to make their way through the hall.

'Stop panicking,' Charlie soothed. 'There are enough of us to work through the preparations, especially now we have extra hands helping us.'

'I'm so grateful to them.' Portia entered the kitchen and took the used crockery over to the sink, turning on the tap and pouring in some washing up liquid.

Charlie placed what he was carrying on the draining board next to her before taking the bag of freshly baked Jersey Wonders and placing them into one of the newly cleaned cupboards to keep them for later. 'I doubt Sacha will be able to stay and maybe not Alessandro if he's going to be helping her at the café, but I know Jack is here for the day because he sent me a text earlier telling me that's what he'd be doing.'

'That's a relief.' It was. Jack was strong and used to helping Sacha with her place. She knew he needed the money that they would pay him for however many hours he worked with them. She tested the water and began washing the dishes.

Charlie picked up a tea towel and dried and a few minutes later they had put everything away. 'Why don't you go and see the others and I'll fetch the list I drew up for all we need to do today?'

'Fine.' As Portia walked back through the house to join the others she felt a lurch of excitement in her stomach. Tonight would be the first party she and Charlie would host. She decided that instead of being anxious about it that she was going to do her best to enjoy every moment. Then, if there were any mishaps, she would put them down to experience and learn from them.

After working through the list and designating jobs to everyone, Portia watched Charlie, Alessandro and Megan go out of the front door, each wrapped up against the cold and Megan wearing Portia's wellington boots. Portia knew Charlie would give their friends an entertaining guided tour of the grounds and closed the front door.

She went back to the living room where Remi and Jack were waiting for her. Studying the room with its bare, patchily filled, paperless walls and freshly painted woodwork, she took a calming breath. 'I think the first thing we need to do is bring in wood and set up a fire in the grate. Even with our guests here tonight it'll probably be cold in here, and if nothing else the fire will give the room a welcoming vibe.'

'It will,' Remi agreed. 'I'll start bringing in the wood and make a pile next to the fire.'

'Thanks, Remi.'

'I'll bring in a couple more small trees that Charlie and I planted into pots the other day.' Jack pushed his jacket sleeves up his forearms. His jacket wasn't nearly as thick as everyone else's coats, Portia noticed, reminding herself that as someone who surfed all year round he must be hardened against the cold.

'Great. I'll bring in a mop and bucket and wash the floors. Then you and Remi can help me hang the rows of lights across the room when you're both finished.'

'It's going to look great in here, Portia,' Jack said, looking about him as if picturing the scene. 'You just wait. Everyone's going to love it.'

She hoped he was right.

27

CHARLIE

Charlie took Megan's hand to steady her as she carefully stepped over an old fallen tree trunk. Letting go, he indicated the heavy canopy of trees making up the wood at the side of the driveway leading down to the back of the property. 'We need to thin this lot out,' he explained, not looking forward to the strenuous task in front of him and Jack.

'You're cutting down these trees?' Megan looked horrified.

'Only because we have no choice if we want the healthier ones to survive.' He understood her shock and even though he knew what he intended doing was for the best, it still wasn't something he relished. 'Trees need light and some of these, like this one—' he rested a palm on a skinny tree that was struggling to compete with larger ones around it '—will die anyway. So we need to make sure they don't kill nearby trees before we have a chance to rectify the issue.'

'I didn't realise it took so much planning to look after places like these.' She gazed around her. 'It's fascinating. I'll have to come back to see what it all looks like when you've finished.'

Charlie looked forward to when the work had been done, too.

'Let's find our way back to the driveway and I'll take you down the side of the building to the back garden, then I can explain what I'm hoping to do there.'

He caught sight of the window to the room he had discovered on the other side of the dining room the previous evening when Portia had been showering. It was through a door he had assumed belonged to another large cupboard but until then hadn't dared look inside, not wishing to find yet another place filled with odds and ends that he would need to sort out.

The sight of the walls covered with built-in mahogany shelves, each laden with neatly arranged books, most of which had been leather-bound and all with a thick layer of dust covering them, had surprised him. There was an old leather-topped desk, its inlaid leather tooled in gold, a worn green leather captain's chair facing a large double floor-to-ceiling window. Whoever had enjoyed the room must have had a perfect view of the once ornate garden. To the side of the room was a fireplace with an Italian marble surround.

Charlie wondered whether the room might make a perfect office for either him or Portia. Maybe they could each have a desk in here, he mused.

He had gone back downstairs before Portia had woken that morning and spent two happy hours going through several books on garden management. As he flicked through the yellowing pages looking for anything that might help him correctly carry out the necessary work in the grounds, it occurred to him that Portia might want to help with some of the outside work.

Unsure if he was right, he continued his search for useful information. It had been an unexpected thrill to discover the room and old books in what could probably have been his great uncle's library, or maybe the vast array of dust-covered books belonged to his great aunt? How many other surprises was this place going to reveal, he wondered, excited at the prospect of coming across the next one.

'Another wilderness,' Megan teased, bringing him back to the present. She stopped, resting her hands on her hips. 'I don't envy you guys sorting this lot out. I thought the chateau was going to keep you busy but where on earth will you be starting out here?'

Charlie scanned the overgrown mess that had once, he presumed, been a back garden. He looked to the left of them at the ivy-covered bricks. 'I imagine this was the kitchen garden.'

'You don't know for certain?' Alessandro asked, joining them.

Charlie shrugged. 'I haven't found the entrance to it yet.' Charlie was amused at their stunned expressions. 'I fear there's a lot we have yet to discover about this place.'

'I'm not sure whether that would excite or terrify me,' Megan laughed. She narrowed her eyes. 'I can tell it excites you though.' She walked over to the brick wall and pulled away a little bit of ivy. 'I love old red bricks.'

'So do I,' Charlie admitted.

'I'd be interested in looking for remnants of what it once looked like,' Alessandro remarked.

Megan frowned. 'Like what?'

Charlie nodded, liking the idea. He gave her question and Alessandro's comment some thought. 'It wouldn't be in this area, but some of these old larger gardens had follies built.'

Megan burst out laughing. 'What on earth is a folly?'

'It could be a small tower, or a ruin, maybe a small castle built for amusement.'

'But why would you do that?'

'They were built for amusement mostly, weren't they, Charlie?' Alessandro asked.

'I believe so.'

'Now I really am intrigued.' Megan began walking again. 'Come along, you two, I want to see everything.'

'You enjoy yourself,' Charlie said. 'I'd better try and find a way into the walled garden.'

* * *

'Charlie! Quick!'

Hearing Megan calling his name, Charlie ran in the direction of her voice. He had been so lost in his thoughts that he hadn't noticed her disappearing into the overgrown ivy deeper into the garden. 'Which way are you?' he called when he couldn't see her immediately.

'We are this way,' Alessandro replied, groaning as if he was trying to lift something.

Charlie pushed his way through thick strands of ivy and eventually reached them. 'A door?'

'I found it,' Megan cried, clapping her hands together. 'We can't open it though. I think the hinges are rusted up.'

'We didn't like to chance breaking the old wood forcing it.' Alessandro gave him a frustrated look.

Charlie was grateful to them for considering his door. 'Good thinking. Stand back and I'll see if I can budge it. If there's no other way to open it I'll have little choice but to kick the door in.' He hoped he could repair the door if he didn't completely obliterate it. If the wood was that rotten, it would need to be replaced anyway. He inspected the door handle and metal hinges. His friends were right, they were completely rusted.

His impatience to see inside the garden increased as he tried to picture how it might look once it was cleared and new beds planted with crops they could harvest for guests' meals. 'Step back, I'm going in.'

'Careful you don't damage yourself,' Megan shouted. 'You won't be popular with Portia if you hurt yourself before the party tonight.'

She was right. 'Maybe I should use my foot instead of my shoulder,' he said, almost to himself.

'I think that's wise.' Alessandro moved out of his way.

Charlie stepped back, then braced himself before kicking the door as near to the hinges as possible. He couldn't believe it when it didn't shift at all. 'This is going to be harder than I thought.'

'Do you want me to kick with you?' Alessandro suggested. 'With both our strength we have a better chance.'

'Hopefully that will work.' His impatience was getting the better of him. He also knew there was a lot more work to do in preparation for their party and had little time to waste here. Wanting to return to the house with exciting news for Portia he knew he needed to discover what exactly they had found.

'After three.' They linked arms. 'One. Two. Three.'

Both men kicked as hard as they could at the same time and the door opened a little way but didn't fall over.

Charlie stepped forward and peered around it. 'More ivy. It's holding it up.'

'Shall I try and get inside?' Jack asked, walking up to them.

'We could have done with your help getting this thing open,' Charlie said, wondering where Jack had been.

'I was inspecting the pond at the front of the house in case there was a quick way to improve how it looks before tonight.'

'And was there?'

'Nope.' He rested a hand on Charlie's right shoulder and peered past him to see what was through the open doorway.

Charlie moved out of his way to let him have a better look. 'You can try and get inside if you want, but you're a bigger build than me and I doubt you'll be able to squeeze inside if I can't.'

'How about me?'

Charlie turned to look at Megan. 'Not a chance.'

She scowled, clearly indignant to have been refused. Charlie realised he had inadvertently offended her.

'Sorry, I didn't mean that to come out as it did. Of course you can, if you want to, but I can see vicious brambles in there and I'd hate for you to hurt yourself.'

She folded her arms grumpily across her chest. 'I suppose you're right. I can't exactly turn up to your party bleeding and covered in scratches.'

Jack groaned as he squeezed his top half back from the slight opening. 'Charlie's right. We can't have the guest of honour being damaged, especially not when there's bound to be loads of photos taken of you.'

'Why don't you go to find Portia and tell her what we've found. I'm sure she'll want to come and see it for herself. Jack and I can try to cut down some of the thicker ivy and clear a few brambles. Then hopefully we can all have a good look inside.'

She seemed to like that idea. 'Will do. I won't be long though, and we don't have too much time if we're to help make the rooms ready for the party tonight, don't forget.'

Charlie wished he still had another day until the party was to take place. Discoveries like this were far more fun than greeting and making small talk with lots of people. He would much rather spend the next few hours working in the walled garden than doing anything else.

'We'll get going straight away,' he heard Jack say with assurance.

When Megan had gone, Jack nudged him. 'I know what you're thinking,' he laughed. 'We can come back here tomorrow when everyone's gone and work on here for as long as we like and make good headway without anything else to think about.'

Charlie nodded, aware that Jack's baby was probably going to need his attention before a garden did but didn't like to say anything. 'I'll leave you here to see what you can do while I go and fetch a couple of saws and something to cut through the vegetation.'

'Better bring some thick gardening gloves while you're at it,' Jack shouted after him. 'We also don't need to damage ourselves before the party.'

'OK.'

By the time Megan returned to the garden with Remi and Portia who, Charlie noticed with pleasure, were carrying two bottles of beers for him and Jack, he was ready for a break. Cutting their way into the garden was far harder than either of them had anticipated. Charlie estimated that they had probably only been working for twenty minutes but both of them were tired and sweaty despite the freezing temperatures.

He took the bottles from Portia and thanked her, handing one to Jack.

'Well? What do you think?' He realised the place was so over-grown that it was difficult to see very much, but it was obvious from the little the two of them had cleared so far that the garden was bigger than he had initially imagined.

Portia stood, gloved hands on her slim hips as she stared around her. 'It's huge. It's going to take us months to clear this place though, let alone taking it back to how it must have looked in its heyday.'

'True, but it's a brilliant find, don't you agree?'

'It is very impressive,' Megan said. 'I can't wait to come back and see it in all its glory when you've worked your magic.'

Charlie took a mouthful from the bottle in his hand. 'I remember when I was a boy, I came in here once,' he said, thinking back. 'It was overgrown then, but not like this.' He smiled at the memory. 'I came here to hide from my father.' He tried to recall why, then remembered only too clearly.

'What is it?' Portia asked quietly.

Charlie took another mouthful of beer to gather himself. 'Dad was impatient for us to leave the island. It was when we were emigrating to New Zealand. My mother was heartbroken at the thought of leaving her aunt, the island and what had always been her home, but he had made up his mind and so the rest of us had little choice but to go with him. I remember running away and hiding in here for ages. I could hear them all calling for me, but hoped they would have to leave without me.'

He thought of his father dying several years later from a second heart attack and his mother shocking him and his older brother by remarrying someone she barely knew instead of doing what she had always insisted she wanted to do and returning to Jersey. She had never seemed happy since then and Charlie always felt guilty for not being able to help her financially and pay to bring her back to the island. Not that she probably would ever have admitted she had made a wrong decision in marrying that second time, he thought miserably.

Portia rubbed his arm. 'Poor little boy. What happened?'

He gave a long slow sigh. 'My great aunt's companion at the time found me and promised me some toffees if I went with her to my parents' car. I didn't want to accept at first, but she was a kind lady and promised me that I would be back one day.'

'And that was the last time you were here?' Megan asked. 'When you were small?'

'I came back when I was sixteen for a summer when my father had his first heart attack, but never to this walled garden.'

'Why not?' Her voice was low and there was an emotion in it that surprised Charlie.

'Maybe because it was in a worse state when I got here than it had been when we first left, I don't really remember.'

Portia slipped her arm around his waist. 'Well, soon you'll be able to come here whenever you wish. You never know, if you and Jack sort this place out soon enough, you'll be able to plant vegetables and maybe harvest some of them in time to feed our first guests.'

Megan pulled her hat down over her ears. 'Yes, and hopefully I'll be one of those guests.' She laughed. 'If I don't freeze to death before then.'

'That's a good point. We should be getting back inside,' Portia reminded them all. 'We still have last minute bits to get ready before the party and we'll all want showers before we dress up.'

'Come along then,' Charlie said, regretting having to leave the garden. 'Hand those to me,' he said to Jack, indicating the loppers his friend had been using. 'I'll return them to the store room and we can get on with sorting this party out.'

28

THE PARTY

Portia

Portia stood to one side of their honoured guest with Charlie next to her and Remi on Megan's other side as they listened to her short speech. Even though Charlie was smiling she suspected his earlier reminiscing in the old walled garden was still playing on his mind. He was pushing himself so hard trying to make their venture work. She understood his determination to make it a success but doubted he realised that by pushing himself so hard, she also felt obliged to do the same and she wasn't sure how much longer she could keep going.

Megan raised her glass of champagne. 'All that's left for me to do now, is toast our delightful host and hostess and wish them all the luck in the world for this amazing new venture at Chateau de Caesarea and hope it is a massive success for many years to come. To the chateau,' she cheered as everyone joined in and raised their own glasses.

'To the chateau,' their guests chorused.

Portia fixed a smile on her face and raised her glass with everyone else.

'Thank you,' Charlie said, smiling at Megan and then at Portia and their guests. She felt him take her hand in his. 'We are very grateful to you for your good wishes, and for coming here tonight to open the chateau and welcome our guest of honour. Portia and I are aware that we have a huge amount of work still to undertake but wanted you all to join us and celebrate our first Christmas here.'

Portia watched him give one of his most appealing smiles. She loved him, but maybe they had taken on too much. She couldn't help feeling that Charlie's obsession to take the chateau back to its former glory was somehow driving a wedge between them. It might have been her idea initially, but she now knew she had been naive to think they could do this without damaging their relationship. Her heart ached at the thought that their dreams might end up pulling them apart.

'And show you our plans for our new business.' He indicated Oliver, standing with his arm around Lexi's shoulders. 'Thank you, too, to our dear friend Oliver Whimsy for setting up the website, which you are all very welcome to look through, and,' he said grinning cheekily, 'through which you may book any events you might be contemplating holding here.'

There was laughter and Portia noticed a few of their guests whispering to each other with enthusiasm. They were probably considering making a booking with them. She knew she should be pleased, but the thought of being committed to this venture when all she wanted to do right now was run away, terrified her.

She turned back to watch Charlie enjoying speaking to their sixty or so guests. She was trapped. Look at him, she thought, always so charming and relaxed in front of people. She was proud of him and wanted the best for her darling Charlie. Portia knew she couldn't let him down, she loved him too much. She would have to find the strength to see this through. It might be daunting, she reasoned, and she couldn't imagine immersing herself in anything this daunting with anyone other than Charlie. But she was doing this with him and she would have to find a way to keep going.

'You look gorgeous,' Charlie whispered to her, his arm around her waist and she realised their guests were giving him a round of applause.

'Thank you. So do you.' She kissed his cheek, spilling tonic water onto her other hand. She noticed Betty and her friends. 'We should offer to refresh their drinks.'

'We should. Let me take those for you, then you can pour some of the mulled wine for Betty and the two women who've come with her.' Portia glanced at the corner close to the fire where the three elderly women were sitting chatting on the chairs she had carried in from the dining room earlier.

She did as he asked, hoping people would stop arriving soon so that she and Charlie might be able to slow down and take a moment alone with each other. They both needed to eat something. Neither of them had time to have a snack before the start of their party and her stomach grumbled loudly.

Her feet, neck and back ached from all the work and although she knew she had scrubbed up pretty well, Portia knew the pair of them deserved to have a bit of fun. She would begin by taking her mind off her troubles and stopping to chat to a few of her friends from the boardwalk.

She placed the warm drinks on a small tray and carried them over to the three ladies and placed them on the small table in the middle of them.

'Enjoying yourselves, I hope?'

'Very much,' Betty said, picking up a glass and taking a sip. 'This is an enchanting place you have here. I remember coming here, ooh, about fifty years ago, it must be now.'

'You do?' Portia was intrigued.

Betty nodded thoughtfully. 'I was helping out at a party, but it was smaller than this one. I think it might have been a wake, now I come to think of it.'

Portia wondered if it could have been for Charlie's great uncle and shared her thoughts.

'Yes, I think you're right. It was a sad occasion. I seem to recall his widow having to go to lie down in her bedroom before the guests began leaving.'

'Poor lady.' Portia hated to think of anyone being distraught but to lose a husband suddenly, as she seemed to recall Charlie mentioning that his great aunt had done, was sad.

'That wasn't my first time here, now I think of it,' Betty said, clearly to the other two ladies' surprise.

'It wasn't?'

'No. I was here just after the occupation.'

'Occupation?' Something rang a bell in Portia's memory. 'Wasn't that during the Second World War?'

'That's right,' Betty confirmed. 'Did you know that the Channel Islands were the only places in Britain that were invaded by Nazi forces?'

Portia seemed to recall something, but wasn't sure what exactly. 'Did they come to the chateau?' She should try to discover some of the history of this place.

Betty cocked her head to one side. 'It was the headquarters of one of the senior officers. I seem to recall coming here with the previous owners when they returned after the liberation to help tidy up and try to find some of their furniture and paintings they had hurriedly stored in the attic before being evacuated with their two children.'

Portia was fascinated. 'Charlie's great aunt wasn't the owner then, was she?'

'No, I seem to recall her husband bought it from those other owners. They found it hard to settle back here after the war with the thought of who had lived in their home for those war years. I think it was the wife that wanted to move to somewhere smaller.' Betty thought for a moment. 'Places like these were easier to run when there was a bigger staff, but after the war, finding people still wanting to live a servant's life wasn't easy, so probably added to their reasons behind selling up and downsizing. They probably sold it for far less than it was worth prior to the war. There would have been quite a lot of work to do to bring it back to its original smart state, I should think.'

So that was how Charlie's relations had managed to acquire this place. She was about to ask what else Betty remembered when the music was turned up and Charlie called for everyone's attention.

'I think the time has come for us all to take to our unpolished floors and have a bit of a dance, don't you?'

Their guests clapped and some immediately stepped forward. Others took their partner's hands and soon most of them were having fun dancing.

'Enjoying yourself?' Charlie asked, slipping his arms around Portia's waist.

'Yes, thanks.' She looked around at the smiling, rosy faces of everyone in the large living room. 'I think tonight has gone very well, don't you?'

'Couldn't have gone any better.'

She spotted Remi dancing with Megan. 'Ooh, look.' She

nodded her head in their direction. 'I think those two might rather like each other.'

'I suspected there might be a bit of a spark between them,' Charlie said triumphantly.

'Really? When did you think that?' Why hadn't she seen anything pass between them? She realised Charlie was grinning at her. 'What?'

'You're cross you missed it, aren't you?' he teased.

'No, I'm not.' It was a lie and she knew that Charlie was aware of it. 'Fine,' she whispered. 'Maybe a little.'

Charlie threw his head back and laughed. 'You are so competitive sometimes.'

'No, I'm not.'

'No?'

Portia sighed and twirled in front of him. 'I'll admit to being a little competitive,' she said as she came back to face him again. 'Sometimes.'

29

PORTIA

The following morning, Portia carried the last tray of glasses through from the living room to the kitchen and placed it on the worktop near to where Charlie was washing up.

'I'll go and give the floor a sweep,' she said, bleary-eyed from their night ending just after two that morning. She grabbed the broom and dust pan and walked to the doorway.

'Have you seen Remi and Megan anywhere?' Charlie asked, a tea towel over his shoulder ready to dry anything that wasn't glass. 'I haven't seen them since breakfast and I wasn't sure when she had to leave for the airport.'

Portia realised she hadn't seen them either and told Charlie, 'I'll have a look for them when I've finished in the living room. Maybe they're still chatting over their breakfast. I haven't cleared up in there yet.'

She walked back through the hallway and peeked into the dining room to see if she could spot them but there wasn't any sign of them. They must have been in there though, because the pastries she had left in a tub had gone and the breakfast crockery was stacked neatly on a tray and the table wiped. Where could they be?

Portia was almost finished sweeping the floor when she heard a squeal coming from outside. Intrigued, she hurried to peer out of the window. The snow was still thick on the ground and the front garden looked like a winter wonderland. 'So pretty,' she whispered.

Seeing movement near the far end of the lawn, she leant forward as close to the windowpane as possible to get a better look. Squinting, she peered at something in pink. It was on the ground and she gasped as she realised that the pink was Megan's coat.

Frightened to think that their guest had fallen, Portia dropped the broom and raced into the hallway, grabbing her coat but not daring to waste time changing out of her trainers to put on her boots. 'Please don't be hurt,' she prayed, bellowing for Charlie just before running out of the front door.

She ran as quickly as she could manage in the two feet of snow, her feet instantly wet as the icy cold seeped in through the mesh on the top of her trainers, soaking her socks. 'Megan!'

As she neared the line of trees separating the lawn from the driveway, she spotted Remi with a cheerful smile on his face. He was gazing at Megan, then seemed to spot Portia running towards them and his expression immediately changed. 'Portia, something is wrong?'

She stared from him to where Megan had been lying and saw she was slowly sitting up. As she reached her, Portia saw concern register on Megan's face.

'Is everything all right, Portia?'

Confused, Portia looked from them and noticed impressions in the snow on either side of Megan's body and realised what had been going on. 'You've been making snow angels?'

'Yes, isn't it fun?'

'Yes,' she laughed, relieved. 'I imagine it is.'

She heard the front door close and footsteps cross the gravel driveway towards them. 'What's happened?' Charlie bellowed. 'Is anyone hurt?'

Aware that she had unintentionally caused a bit of a scene, Portia raised her hands. 'Sorry, I saw Megan's coat on the ground from the window and panicked, thinking she had fallen and hurt herself.'

'We were making snow angels,' Remi explained. Portia saw the spark in his dark eyes. 'I did not know what they were until Megan showed me.' He reached out and, taking Megan's outstretched hands, pulled her to her feet, brushing snow from her expensive coat.

Megan grimaced. 'Sorry. It didn't occur to me how it might look from inside.'

'It's not your fault,' Portia assured her, clocking Charlie shaking his head in amusement. 'I shouldn't have assumed the worst.'

Charlie frowned at Remi. 'What on earth have you got there?'

The three of them stared at the strangely shaped piece of wood in Remi's hand.

'For the snowman's nose,' Remi said, holding it up.

'Snowman?' Portia looked around to see where it might be.

Megan laughed. 'We haven't made it yet. Now the two of you are out here, you can take a break from your hard work and help us build one.' When Portia and Charlie didn't instantly respond, she pursed her lips. 'And I won't take no for an answer. I'm leaving in a couple of hours and it'll do you both good to have a little fun for a change.'

'We had fun at the party last night,' Charlie argued, clearly not having much enthusiasm for Megan's suggestion.

'That was work,' Remi said. 'Even if it was enjoyable.'

Portia thought about what Megan had said and decided she was right. They did need time doing something silly and fun. 'I can't remember the last time I made a snowman. Come along, Charlie. If we make a good effort, we can take photos once it's finished for the website. Show people that staying here in the winter will be just as much fun as in the summer months.'

'Not that we usually get snow in the winter,' Charlie reminded her.

'Stop being a misery.' Portia argued, noticing the dark circles under his blue eyes. Like her, he was tired and stressed. She realised her feet were soaking wet and getting colder by the second. 'I'd better go and dry my feet and change into some boots, but I'll be back with something for the snowman's eyes and for around his neck. He has to look impressive if he's going to make an appearance on our site.'

Charlie sighed but she could see he was amused. 'I'll come and put on a coat before I get hypothermia. You two can start building him while you're waiting for us.'

Happy, Portia took Charlie's hand and ran with him back inside.

'Wait there and I'll fetch you a towel and some dry socks,' he said. 'Take those wet things off straightaway.'

Not wanting to delay getting outside again, she shook her head. 'You go and fetch something for the snowman's eyes and mouth and I'll sort myself out.' She kicked off her soaking trainers, pulled off her wet socks and ran upstairs to dry her feet. Having put on her warmest socks, she went to find one of her older bright scarves to wrap around the snowman's neck. This was exciting, she decided, and the perfect way to spend Megan's last few hours with them, as well as quality time with Charlie.

'Wow, you're doing well,' Charlie shouted when they joined Remi and Megan again.

They were, Portia agreed. The snowman was growing fast and soon the four of them had finished making his rotund body. They added a head, the triangular piece of wood for a nose and two large bolts that Charlie had brought for his eyes and a piece of curved copper tubing left over from the heating pipes that he had replaced the previous week for the mouth.

Portia loosely tied the red scarf around his neck. 'One minute,' she said, studying their masterpiece. 'He needs better arms.' She pointed at Remi. 'You fetch a couple of small branches that have been cut from the thinned trees and I'll run inside for something else.'

She returned shortly after carrying a Santa hat someone had left behind the previous evening that she had found when tidying up the living room. Placing it carefully on the snowman's head she stepped back. 'It works well with his scarf, don't you think?'

'Perfect,' Megan said, linking arms with her. 'Well done. He's amazing. I don't remember having this much fun in years.'

'Me neither.' Portia could only recall one instance when she helped build a snowman and that had been with Alastair and Oliver in Scotland one Christmas several years before. She pushed the memory away, wanting this to be all about her, Charlie and their friends.

'Right, now for some photos,' Charlie insisted, waving for them to take places round their creation.

Two hours later, as they waved Megan off in Oliver's Range Rover, Portia sighed happily. 'I think she really enjoyed herself here.'

'She told me it was one of the best times she's ever had,' Remi said quietly.

Portia turned to look at him. He seemed sad to see her go but there was an inner happiness about him that she had never seen before. Charlie was right, Remi really did like Megan. It cheered her even more to know that their friend had found someone he was attracted to. The haunted look that seemed always present in

Remi's dark eyes had lifted slightly and Portia thought this was the best present she could have received this Christmas.

She linked arms with him and Charlie. 'Our first guest has just left us. Her visit and the party were a success. I'm so relieved.' She grinned at Remi. 'And I suspect she'll be back again very soon.'

'I think you could be right,' Charlie agreed.

They stared after the car as it disappeared into the trees down the long drive.

'Right,' Charlie said. 'Time to go and tidy up. It's Christmas Day tomorrow and we should make the most of having a day off. Then the hard work begins again straight afterwards.'

'Eugh,' Portia grumbled, not looking forward to getting her hands dirty again after the festivities were over.

30

CHARLIE

Charlie woke early, wanting to take Portia breakfast in bed for their first Christmas together. She had been a little distant over the past few days and he wondered if she was just tired or if their project was getting to her. Hopefully his plans for the day would go some way to cheer her up. He knew he was pushing himself hard and that she was trying to keep up with him, but if they were to succeed then he didn't think they had any other option but to keep going as they were.

He thought of the turkey with trimmings he had sneaked out to buy the day before, and how he had secretly asked Oliver, Lexi, Sacha, Alessandro, Bella, Jack, Claire and Betty to join them. Betty thought it would be too much for her and Claire offered to take care of the baby to give Bella and Jack a few hours' break and have Betty over to join her and Tony for a quiet Christmas lunch with his two children. He was sad that Jools and Marius weren't able to leave her grandmother and his grandfather, but understood that Mrs Jones traditionally spent the day in her flat above the second-hand bookshop with her dog, Teddy.

Still, he thought, it should be a fun day.

Portia woke as he entered their bedroom carrying the tray with two plates of eggs Benedict for them, a glass of Buck's Fizz each and a cup of coffee for her.

She stretched and smiled up at him. 'You spoil me, do you know that?'

He placed the tray down onto the trunk and bent to kiss her. 'You deserve it.' He plumped up her pillows and waited for her to settle back against them. 'Ready?'

'Yes. That looks and smells delicious.'

He opened the shutters to let the sunlight into the room and they sat and ate their breakfast, leaning against the headboard. 'I think we should make a plan to do this every year,' he suggested. He wasn't certain if he had imagined it but it seemed as if sadness clouded her face for a split second.

'I like that idea, but it will have to be much earlier than this if we have guests staying.'

'Always so practical,' Charlie teased, taking a sip of his Buck's Fizz. 'But you're right, of course.'

'I feel a bit bad that Remi is in his room alone with nothing to eat,' Portia said after swallowing a mouthful.

'He isn't. Who do you think baked this bread?'

'He's already in the kitchen?'

Charlie nodded. 'He is and he's eating the same as us. I didn't leave him out when I made our treat.'

She leant her head against his arm for a moment. 'You're always so kind.'

'I do my best.' He kissed the top of her head. 'Now eat up before it gets cold. As soon as we're done with this lot we need to shower, dress and start preparing for our lunch guests.'

'Typical of you to make an occasion out of today.'

He hoped she was amused rather than put out. If he was completely honest he would have also rather spent the day relaxing with Portia in their room, or making the most of sitting in front of the fire in their bright living room, but he had invited everyone now and they would have to wait until later to do that.

He was looking forward to getting downstairs and giving Portia the gift he had placed under the tree for her. It wasn't very romantic but he had something planned to cover that in few days' time.

'What's that?' Portia asked as soon as her feet touched the hall floor from the stairs. She glanced at him, narrowing her eyes suspiciously. 'Wait here.' She ran back upstairs, returning moments later, a small package in her hands. 'You see, Charlie? You're not the only one full of surprises today.'

'How do you know the present under the tree is from me?' He laughed. 'Or for you, for that matter? Maybe it's something for Remi?'

She shook her head. 'Because I know you rather better than you think I do.' She went and placed her present next to his. 'We can open these at the same time, later when everyone has gone.'

'What if I don't want to wait that long?'

She slipped her arms around his waist and hugged him tightly. 'You have little choice. We still have an enormous amount to do before our friends arrive for lunch.'

* * *

That evening, when everyone had left and Remi had retired to his room telling them he had calls to make, Charlie took Portia's hand. 'Shall we open our gifts to each other now?'

'Let's bring them in here and make the most of this glorious fire.'

'I'll fetch them.' He wished he could have bought her something expensive, but he hoped she liked what he had found for her.

He joined her back in the living room and sat next to her on the cushions that they had placed on a rug on the floor in front of the fire. 'Here you go,' he said, handing her his gift and keeping the beautifully wrapped one she had placed under the tree for him.

'This is exciting,' Portia said, watching him. 'I'm trying to guess what's inside.'

He wasn't surprised. Realising she was waiting for him to start unwrapping her gift, he pulled at the gold ribbon and then tore at the paper. He opened the small box and saw a silver hip flask. 'I love it,' he admitted. 'And I'm going to use it when I'm working outside in the cold. I could do with the odd snifter when it's really freezing like it is now.'

She rested a hand on his. 'But only when you're not using tools and might end up hurting yourself.'

Charlie laughed. 'I agree. I promise I'll use it sensibly.' He indicated her box. 'Hurry up, I want to see what you think of your present.'

She finished tearing off the paper and opened the box, lifting out the pair of leather work boots he'd bought her. She held one up and beamed at him. 'Oh, you clever thing, I love them.'

'They should fit, Lexi helped me with the sizing.' He watched her remove her slippers and slide her feet into each one, then helped her tie them. 'How do they feel?'

Portia got to her feet and walked back and forth a couple of times. 'Wonderful. Thank you, Charlie.'

'My pleasure. They also have steel toecaps, so should protect your toes from most things.'

She bent down, took his face in her hands and kissed him. 'I love you, do you know that?'

He pulled her down onto his lap and kissed her back. 'I do, and I love you too.'

* * *

It was the briefest Christmas break and Charlie couldn't help feeling a little guilty for insisting Portia get straight back to work on Boxing Day. Remi didn't seem to mind helping them and Charlie presumed that was because he was used to supplying his baked goods most days throughout the year. Portia, on the other hand, was looking decidedly glum, he noticed. She hadn't spoken much that morning. He had left her painting the hall woodwork a couple of hours before while he had been tiling in the kitchen and thought she could do with some sort of refreshment.

He made three cups of coffee and, placing the cafetière onto a tray with them for anyone who might want a second cup, he added a plate of biscuits left over from the party and a small jug of milk. Charlie carried it through, stopping as he reached Portia sitting silently on a cushion as she concentrated on her painting.

'I've brought us something to snack on and a drink.' She didn't react and for a moment he thought she might not have heard him, then realised she simply wasn't in a mood for chit chat. 'I'll take them through to the dining room.' He paused. 'What's wrong?'

Portia lowered her paintbrush and shrugged.

'Is it something I've done, or said?' Charlie willed her to open up to him.

She rested the brush on top of the tin lid and turned to him. 'It's just that when I first pictured us renovating this place I had imagined we would be spending more time working together, but we seem to spend most days in different rooms, or you're outside while I'm in here and I miss you.'

So that was it. Charlie gave her comment some thought. 'Maybe we could work outside together today, then? You could try out your boots in the snow, see how well they hold up.'

'Doing what?'

'Digging up an unnecessary area of concrete that I spotted near the side of the house.'

Portia laughed. 'I don't think I have the strength to dig up concrete and I'm pretty certain I'll be dangerous working any sort of digger.'

'You could hold a pneumatic drill straight though, couldn't you?'

'A what?' She stared at him for a moment. 'Do you mean one of those things I've seen workmen using to dig up roads?' she asked, aghast.

Charlie nodded. 'I do. Would you like to give it a go?'

'I'm not sure. Do we have one I could try using?'

'Not yet,' Charlie said, kissing her on the forehead. 'Leave it with me to track one down. I might have an old friend who could lend one to us for a few days while his company is off work over the holidays.'

He placed her cup of coffee down on the table. 'Right now though, we need to get on with the inside of this place,' he said, leaving her to continue painting, excited to think of them working together on something a little different. Pneumatic drills were heavy but Portia was strong enough to hold one. At least he hoped she was. He would soon find out.

31

PORTIA

'What is it?' Portia asked, standing at the side of the house, pulling on her gloves as she stared at the rather large metal contraption set on the concrete next to a skip that hadn't been there the day before. Then it dawned on her. 'This isn't one of those road digging machines you mentioned borrowing, is it? For that concrete bit you want removed?'

'That's right,' Charlie said, not taking his eyes off the thing that had been delivered at some point without her noticing. 'A mate of mine said we can borrow this for today, but that's all.'

That's enough, Portia thought. 'So, how does it work?' she asked, wanting to appear interested but wishing she could get back to the house and out of the icy wind.

'He's gone through it with me.' He looked up at her, clearly excited about something. 'Isn't this fun?'

'What?'

'This. You wanted us to work together on something.'

'You really think I can work this thing?'

'Why not?' Charlie walked up to her and took hold of her

upper arms. 'I thought it would be fun trying out something new together.'

Portia's idea of fun hadn't included something this difficult, but Charlie was trying to find work for them to do together and she didn't like to put a damper on things.

Why hadn't she kept her thoughts to herself? 'I didn't think you were serious about this thing.'

Charlie laughed and pulled her into a hug. 'Don't worry,' he said. 'I've listened to my mate and looked it up on the internet, so I know what to do.' He let go of her and rubbed his hands together gleefully. 'Shall we make a start then?'

Aware she might as well get this over and done with, Portia forced a smile. 'Go on then, what do we do?'

She watched as Charlie took the pneumatic drill to the area he wanted them to remove. Holding it upright he pressed the lever in one of his hands and made Portia jump when it noisily began hammering into the concrete at his feet.

After a few moments Charlie cocked his head for her to go over to him. 'Here, you take this and carry on, while I shovel the broken bits into the skip.'

Resigned to doing what he wanted, she stepped forward, her hands replacing his and shrieking when the weight of the machine took her by surprise.

'Don't panic, I've still got hold of it,' Charlie soothed. 'Right, I'm letting go now.'

She braced herself. 'I think I've got it.'

'If you're sure, I'll switch it on.'

'Yes,' she said nervously.

Charlie turned it on and Portia clung tightly to the handles as the enormous pneumatic drill sprang into life. In seconds it had broken up the concrete at her feet. 'It's actually rather satisfying,' she yelled, surprised at how much she was enjoying what she was doing.

She glanced up to see Charlie standing back, a proud expression on his face as he watched her work.

'Don't just stand there,' she laughed. 'Get shovelling. I'm not sure how long I can keep this up.'

They worked together for a while and Portia was certain she had control of the machine until the hammer got stuck and surprised her. The drill began tilting to one side and although she tried to hold it upright Portia instantly realised that she couldn't take the heavy weight, so lowered it as slowly as she could to the ground.

'You okay?' Charlie said, reaching her side.

She explained what had happened. 'But if you stand it upright again I'm happy to carry on.'

'You're doing a brilliant job, you know,' he said, his voice filled with emotion.

'We all are.' She looked pointedly down at her feet. 'Now, if we're to finish this work before your friend collects this thing later, I think you should lift it up so I can get going again.'

Portia wasn't minding the work nearly as much as she had expected to do and knew that this was Charlie's way of trying to bring them together again. Why hadn't she given more thought to how it was going to be working on this vast building in winter? It had been an ambitious project from the start without taking into account how they would both feel living in such a rustic way while working manually, something neither of them were used to doing.

'You all right there?'

She gave Charlie what she hoped was a reassuring smile. 'Fine, thanks.'

He didn't seem convinced and she wasn't surprised. She was

getting tired and her muscles ached. It was also a little draining being cold. All the time!

Three hours later, it was a relief when Charlie took over from her. 'You look frozen. Why don't you go inside and warm up with a hot shower and change of clothes.'

'What about you?' she asked, guilty that she was about to leave him to finish the work they had started together.

'I'm happy to carry on. Now, off you go. I won't be much longer.'

'Thanks,' she said, moving away from the drill when his hands took over from hers. 'I'll see you in a bit.'

She didn't look back but could sense him watching her as she returned to the house. If only she could muster the energy to put on a brave face, Portia mused as she closed the front door behind her and leant against it. She barely had energy for much these days and she wasn't sure if she was tired from all the hard physical work or simply worn down by the disappointment of having misjudged her expectations when they had started this project.

32

CHARLIE

Charlie was painfully aware that his attempts at making work fun with Portia hadn't turned out as successfully as he had hoped. She had been quiet all morning and he wondered if maybe having Megan staying, then a day relaxing, might have spotlighted how different her life was now to how it had been before they had moved to the island.

He was unsure what to do to rectify the situation, but knew he needed to stay focused if he were to keep up momentum with the renovations. The skip had been removed the previous evening and his friend collected the pneumatic drill first thing that morning. He thought he had heard Remi arriving home a bit earlier from his rounds and was hoping to ask him to help Jack with more of the heavy outside work so that he and Portia could sit and discuss plans for the rest of the day.

Charlie ran up the stairs, expecting to find Remi decorating the next bedroom on their to-do list. He wasn't there, but Charlie was relieved to find half of the old wallpaper stripped off. He went back downstairs to look for him but he wasn't in the old utility room that had now been set up as his small bakery either.

'If you're looking for Remi,' Portia said, pouring water from the kettle into her porcelain mug, 'he came through here earlier. Said he was going outside to help Jack clear the walled garden.'

'Great, thanks.' He noticed she seemed a little more cheerful than she had done earlier. Deciding to make himself and the other two a coffee, Charlie took three mugs from the cupboard and spooned coffee granules into each one. The coffees made, he decided to go and fetch them and give them a break inside the building, out of the extreme cold.

'Don't let your coffee go cold,' he shouted as he ran outside without bothering to put on a coat. 'Bloody hell,' Charlie grumbled when the cold wind hit his face. He hesitated, wondering if maybe he should return to the house to fetch something to put on over his paint-spattered sweater, but decided against it, preferring instead to find Remi and Jack and invite them inside for something to eat and drink.

'Hey, guys where are you?' Charlie bellowed as he neared the red brick wall with the open door.

He hated to think that the shine of their plans for the chateau was fading for Portia. It worried him that she didn't seem like her old self. Working over the holidays was something he was used to after years in hospitality, so it hadn't bothered him. In fact, he liked making the days special for guests whenever he was at the hotel. Most people though, and especially Portia, hadn't had to work over the festivities and not having a proper break or enjoying the usual traditions might be, he thought, what was getting her down. He hoped it was just that and nothing more. Unfortunately, this year they little choice but to keep going. They had far too much still to do and too little time before their first event for them to spend any time taking things easy.

'We're in here,' Jack bellowed. 'Come here a sec, will you?'

Gritting his teeth to stop them chattering, Charlie did as his friend asked and hurried through the doorway. At least the wind wasn't so fierce within the four walls and he was glad of some respite. 'What's the matter?'

'Look at what we've found.' Remi waved him over from what looked like some sort of brick bunker, a look of excitement on his face.

Intrigued, Charlie joined them. 'Is it a coal hole?'

'More of a storage space, I think,' Jack said.

'In there.' Remi pointed down at an opening near to the ground. 'Look closer.'

Charlie crouched down and for a moment wasn't sure what he was supposed to be looking at. It was dark inside the square brick storage space. He bent lower and waited for his eyes to acclimatise to the darkness inside, then noticed what looked like a small oak chest among the detritus and weeds. 'I see it now. What do you think it is?'

'We aren't sure,' Remi said. 'But I know it's not something I'd expect to find out here.'

'Do you think it could have been hidden here by someone and then forgotten when the garden fell into disuse?'

Remi shrugged. 'Maybe. Let's pull it out.'

'Careful,' Jack said, standing. 'It's been there a long time by the look of things and could be fragile.' He handed Remi a spade. 'Hook the top of this through the metal handle on the side closest to us.'

He stood and stepped back slightly to give Remi enough room to hook the spade handle around the metal hook at one end of the trunk. Jack nudged him and raised an eyebrow, looking as excited as a schoolboy. Charlie understood how he felt; he was rather intrigued himself.

'Take it slowly, Remi,' Jack said quietly.

They waited while Remi did what he had to and shortly after the oak casket appeared through the hole.

'It only just fitted through that,' Charlie said, excited. 'Look, guys, it's freezing out here and I came to tell you I've made coffee and biscuits for us. Why don't we put this in a wheelbarrow and take it inside and Portia can see what you've found?' he suggested, thinking that she might be waiting for them to join her for their elevenses.

'Good idea,' Jack said. 'It looks pretty dodgy and we don't want it falling to pieces as we carry it to the chateau, and whatever's inside spilling out.'

Remi didn't look so convinced. 'I'm not sure taking it inside is the right thing to do.'

'Why not?' Charlie shivered, irritated with himself for not putting on a coat after all. 'If you're worried it'll make a mess, I really don't mind,' he said, too impatient to discover what might be in the trunk to be fazed. 'Anyway, we can open it in the rear hall by the back door. At least it'll be warmer in there.'

'Agreed.' Jack went to fetch the wheelbarrow, waiting for Charlie and Remi to carefully lift the oak trunk and lower it slowly into it.

'What have you got there?' Portia asked as Charlie entered through the backdoor.

She and Charlie watched as Remi walked in backwards pulling the wheelbarrow as Jack lifted it up over the steps.

Charlie hoped the excitement of their find might take her mind off whatever was bothering her. 'The guys found something in the walled garden.'

Her eyes lit up, just as he had hoped, and she went to have a look.

'I've made us coffees,' Charlie said. 'They're on the worktop.'

Jack and Remi didn't move to get their drinks.

Portia gasped. 'What's in it?'

'We don't know yet.' Remi gave her an excited smile.

Charlie fetched the tray of drinks and biscuits, aware that the others had little intention of leaving the chest until they had opened it.

'I'll get some newspaper to put on the floor,' Remi said. 'For any mess when we lift the box from the wheelbarrow.'

Portia grumbled something under her breath as she waved away the offer of biscuits. 'I think it's too late for that.' She indicated the muddy trail from the wheelbarrow. 'Let's just open the thing, then we can all carry on with what we were doing.'

Charlie looked sideways at her. The chateau renovations had been her idea and he had suspected for a while that she had grasped at the opportunity to make him happy, but nothing made him more miserable than seeing her this troubled.

She and Jack were watching Remi trying to prise open the lid. 'The hinges are rusted shut,' Remi grumbled, leaving the room for a short while and returning with a chisel and hammer to try again.

Jack stood, a biscuit in one hand and his coffee cup in the other. 'This is fun, don't you think?' he asked, looking from Charlie who returned his smile to Portia who gave a half-hearted shrug. Jack frowned. 'You OK, Portia?'

'Fine,' she said, sounding anything but.

Jack caught Charlie's eye and raised his eyebrows.

'I think we're all probably a bit tired from the build-up to the party,' Charlie suggested, attempting to make light of things.

'Got it.' Remi placed the hammer and chisel onto the tiled floor and, gritting his teeth, pulled up the lid with an effort that reddened his face.

Portia peered over his shoulder. 'Another box? It looks like a jewellery box.'

Charlie bent down to have a look. 'You could be right.'

'This is exciting.' Jack rubbed his hands together theatrically. 'I wonder what we'll find in there.'

'You should open it, Charlie,' Remi said, moving back to let Charlie get closer to the box. They watched as he carefully lifted the smaller box from the other one, placed it on the floor, undid the catch with a little difficulty and opened it. '*Mon dieu.*'

Inside the jewellery box were smaller boxes that even Charlie's untrained eye recognised as ring boxes, together with several slightly bigger leather boxes he presumed contained larger pieces of jewellery.

'Let's take this through to the dining room,' Portia suggested, seeming far more interested in the contents.

She led the way through and when everything had been taken from the jewellery box and set down on the table, the four of them took a seat and waited for Charlie to do the honours.

He picked up the first box and looked from one to the other of them.

'Go on,' Portia encouraged. 'I assume they belonged to your great aunt and as she left you as her sole beneficiary they must be yours now.'

He was unsure but supposed what she said made sense. He lifted the lid, holding the box forward for each of them to study the contents.

Portia gasped. 'That has to be the most exquisite diamond solitaire I've seen in a very long time. May I?' She held out her hand and Charlie placed the box onto her palm.

He watched her inspect it. Charlie had no idea about jewellery but even he could see that this diamond glinted impressively in the daylight. It was rectangular in shape and looked bigger than any other diamond he recalled seeing before. 'Let's see what else is in here.'

A few minutes later they sat in stunned silence staring at an array of gold and platinum, or so Portia insisted. It looked the same as silver as far as Charlie was concerned, but he didn't argue.

'There must be twenty pieces here.' Portia inspected an art deco necklace for a third time and looked up at him. 'I think you're going to have to find a way to confirm these pieces did in fact belong to your great aunt. Just to be certain.'

'Who else would they belong to?' Jack asked, without taking his eyes from the shiny haul. 'No one would surely come here and leave stuff behind, not in a walled garden people who weren't from here wouldn't even know existed.'

He had a point, Charlie decided. 'It could have been someone who worked here in the past maybe?'

'I doubt anyone working here would own such a splendid selection of jewellery though.' Portia pushed the necklace away from her. 'It could simply belong to your great aunt like we all suppose it must.'

'How will you find out though?' Remi stared at the jewels on the table.

Charlie wasn't sure. 'There's a lot of stuff stored up in the attic from when she lived here, I seem to recall. Maybe there's a portrait of her wearing some of it.'

'That's a brilliant idea,' Portia added, with more excitement in her voice than Charlie had heard in days. 'There could be a couple of photo albums with photos of her wearing it, too. Or receipts that your great uncle kept when he bought some of the pieces.'

'What if I can't find anything to substantiate that they did belong to her?' Charlie asked, hating to think he might claim something not rightfully his.

Jack took another biscuit and ate it thoughtfully. 'If you can't then I suppose you'll have to contact the police and ask them to check their records to see if there was a burglary reported during the time she lived here. They should be able to trace who they belonged to if it wasn't her stuff.'

Remi nodded. 'Yes. First, maybe look in the attic.'

Charlie thought that the wisest thing to do. "I'll do that. You guys carry on in the walled garden, if you will. Portia, may I have a quick word with you?'

Jack and Remi finished their drinks and left through the back-door, taking the wheelbarrow with them.

Charlie noticed Portia give him a withering look. He had never seen her so down and it was disturbing him. Her initial excitement seeing the jewellery had vanished.

Portia led the way back to the kitchen and turned once inside. 'What is it, Charlie? Not happy with my work?'

He took her by the hands. 'Don't say that, Portia. I'm concerned.'

'Why?'

He felt the tenseness in her hands soften slightly. 'You're unhappy and I think it's because you're exhausted.'

'We all are.'

'But you're unhappy and that worries me. Don't you want to do this any more?'

She looked him in the eyes for the first time and sighed deeply. 'I'm not sure.'

His stomach lurched at her reply. He heard the emotion in her voice and also something else. Was it disappointment? Was it because their dream to do this work wasn't as satisfying in reality as she had maybe imagined it to be? He pulled her gently into his arms. 'Sweetheart, you are allowed to change your mind about doing this, you know.'

She pushed him away from her.

'What? I didn't mean—'

She raised her hand to stop him continuing. 'Are you insinuating I don't possess the tenacity to see this venture through to the end?'

He was about to argue the point, then realised that was exactly what he had been thinking. 'I just hate to see you so obviously unhappy, that's all.'

'I'm fine,' she snapped, turning on her heels and marching out of the room.

'You're obviously not though,' he murmured at her retreating back. He was at a loss as to what to do. How could he address this situation properly if Portia was refusing to admit how she really felt?

33

PORTIA

They decided to keep the news of their discovery between themselves until Portia had helped him bring down box after box of photos and paperwork from the attic to their bedroom. They decided it would be safer to keep the jewellery there than in the library just in case they had any unwelcome visitors. So far, though, they hadn't come across anything that helped prove the jewellery had belonged to his great aunt.

Portia was sitting cross-legged on the bed looking through yet another folder of receipts and letters when she heard Charlie call up to her from downstairs. 'You've got post, Portia. It looks like an invitation.'

Was that excitement in his voice? Since Charlie had shared his concerns about her wish to continue with their venture the previous week, Portia had made a concerted effort to appear more cheerful. It wasn't Charlie's fault she was struggling to keep her enthusiasm for the renovations. She hadn't meant to upset him either and hated to think he believed himself at fault in any way.

She was the one who had imagined she could do this with no experience of working on a property before. The only time she had been near any renovation work she had employed others to do it for her. It had always seemed far simpler watching contractors rather than physically doing it herself. Every muscle in her body ached, she was covered in bruises and had blisters on most fingers and her palms.

She decided to go and see who had sent her something. Few people knew her address here, so she was more than a little intrigued. She reached the hallway and lifted the cream envelope from the hall table where Charlie had left it, turning it over in her hands, enjoying the feel of the quality paper.

She studied the beautiful handwriting but didn't recognise it, so opened the envelope and withdrew another envelope from inside it. This time her London address was written on it. Next to the address was a note.

Apologies. My darling husband opened this by mistake and forgot to tell me that the invitation wasn't for us. I hope you receive it in good time. V x

Portia opened the second envelope and took out the single card inside.

'Is it an invitation?' Charlie joined her from the dining room, paintbrush in one hand. He gave her an expectant smile and she realised he was hoping it was something to cheer her up. So, he had seen through her forced happiness. Her heart swelled and she turned and kissed his cheek, hating to be the cause of his concern.

'What was that for?' he asked, smiling, his free hand rising to touch where her lips had brushed his skin.

'Because you are the sweetest man and far too good for a misery like me.'

'What rubbish.' He cocked his head towards the invitation. 'Anything exciting?'

She held it up for him to see. 'Yes, actually. It's an invitation for me and a "plus one" to attend my friend Cressida's thirtieth birthday party. She sent it to my old address.' Portia supposed it served her right for not bothering to send out change of address notes to all her friends. Then again, her address book was bulging with names and the thought of having to contact each of them wasn't something she had time to do. Not when she and Charlie had so many other things they had needed to plan before leaving London.

'You should go,' Charlie insisted.

'But not you?' She wasn't sure why she was asking; she could see by the look on his face that he had no intention of leaving the chateau yet. She understood why. Charlie was determined to do as much of the work himself, hoping to keep some of her money intact. Maybe if they could pay some contractors, life wouldn't be quite so exhausting for them both right now. Jack was a great support but he was only one man and as much as Remi did his best to help he had his own business to run.

He shook his head. 'Not this time. Do you mind?'

'No,' she said honestly. Maybe some time apart might do them both good. 'Although I don't really want to go without you,' she added for his benefit.

He studied her for a moment. 'I think you should.'

A flicker of fear shot through her. 'Why?'

Charlie stroked her right arm. 'Because you need a break from all this plaster dust and mud, Portia. I think a few days in London reconnecting with your friends, dressing in beautiful clothes instead of paint-smeared dungarees and attending glamorous parties is exactly what you need. Don't you?'

He had a point. She noticed her nails again. She could have a much-needed manicure and pedicure, get her hair trimmed while she was there. Now that she thought about it she was yearning to spend some time back in her favourite city, catching up with friends and wearing heels again.

'You wouldn't mind me taking the time off?'

He shook his head. 'Of course not. You deserve it.' He smiled affectionately. 'How you've gone this long without seeing the city lights, or visiting a theatre, I've no idea.'

'You make me sound very shallow.'

'I don't mean to. It's what you're used to though, and that's nothing to be ashamed of.'

'What about you?'

He shrugged. 'I admit the constant mess can be a bit tiresome and I wouldn't mind decent central heating for a few days, but apart from that, I'm fine.'

Should she go? She studied Charlie's face and decided that he meant what he said. He seemed happy enough for her to leave him behind here and travel to London and have some fun.

'All right then,' she said, feeling more excited about going to London by the second. 'I'll let Cressida know I'm coming over.' Her mind raced with all she needed to plan. The party was that weekend. 'It's awfully soon though.'

'So what? It's only a thirty-five-minute flight from here to London most of the time. Why don't you book a ticket and make plans.'

'You really don't mind?'

Charlie shook his head. 'You know I don't. I want you to be happy, Portia. You need this. It's come at the perfect time as far as I'm concerned. Now, stop worrying and start planning what you need to do. You have very little time to get organised.'

'I feel a bit like a rat jumping ship leaving you here to carry on working while I gallivant in London.'

'I told you, I'm fine. Anyway, I'm not here by myself – I've got Remi for company and Jack comes in every day at the moment.' He grinned at her. 'Hopefully we'll be able to surprise you with all the work we get finished while you're away.'

She liked the thought of that. 'All right. Then I will go.' She flung her arms around his neck causing him to drop the paintbrush. 'You are the best boyfriend, do you know that?'

'I do now,' he laughed, pulling her tightly to him and kissing her.

Portia lost herself in the moment, aware she felt happier than she had done in at least a week.

'Maybe Venetia will offer for me to stay in my old spare room. I'd like to see what they've done to the place.'

Charlie laughed. 'I'd like to see her find an excuse not to invite you.'

Portia heard tyres on the gravel outside the front of the chateau. 'Who can that be?' She went to the window and looked out to see Lexi getting out of her car. 'It's Lexi. She looks excited about something, too.'

'Let's go and find out what it is then, shall we?'

She followed Charlie to the front door. 'Lexi,' she said, waving her friend inside. 'What's brought you here?'

Lexi ran up the front steps and into the chateau. Portia closed the door behind her.

'Come into the dining room,' she said. 'The fire will still be going a little in there from breakfast so it'll be warmer than anywhere else.'

Lexi took her laptop from the bag she was carrying over her shoulder and set it down on the table. 'I have stuff to show you.'

'I'm intrigued,' Portia laughed, wondering if what they were about to see were photos that Megan had shared on her social media accounts.

'I'll fetch Remi, he might want to see this.' Charlie left the room without waiting for either of them to respond.

Lexi looked at Portia. 'I hope I haven't interrupted anything.'

Portia shook her head. 'No. We were chatting about a party invitation I received today.'

'Party? Here?'

'In London. Charlie insists I should go and make the most of catching up with friends there.'

'You should,' Lexi replied, giving her a strange look.

Confused, Portia suspected something was on Lexi's mind. 'What is it?' When Lexi didn't immediately reply, she added. 'You think I'm wrong to leave Charlie here doing all the work while I go away and have fun, don't you?'

Lexi looked shocked. 'I wasn't thinking anything like that.'

'Then what?' she asked guiltily. 'I know there's something you're not saying.'

Lexi shrugged. 'I think you should go.' She smiled, then hesitated. 'Now I don't want you to take this the wrong way...'

'Go on.' Portia tried not to feel defensive as she waited for Lexi to confide in her.

'Well, it's just that what you've been doing here, all of you, is mucky work. Hard, physical work.'

'You don't think I'm up to it.'

'Stop being defensive, Portia. That's not what I'm saying at all. I don't know how you've done it, to be honest. I wouldn't want to spend day in and day out up to my arms in dust and rubble. I think you're doing an incredible job. The pair of you are. But I believe Charlie's right to encourage you to take time out and go and have a bit of fun.' She narrowed her eyes and took a deep breath. 'You're looking tired, and as much as you're more than a match for the guys, you do need to give yourself a break occasionally. There's nothing wrong in going and enjoying yourself for a few days.'

Portia was grateful to her friend for being so direct. 'Thanks. I know you're right.'

'You seem hesitant though. Why?'

Portia hadn't realised she was being so but could see that Lexi had a point. 'I'm not sure. I think I'm worried that if I take a break from here and remind myself how much I love London life that I might be reluctant to return.' She glanced at the door, hoping Charlie hadn't heard her comment. Lowering her voice, she added, 'I feel like I've lost who I am being here. Like I don't know who I'm supposed to be any more. Does that sound really dreadful?'

Lexi rested a hand on Portia's wrist. 'No. It sounds very honest.'

The door squeaked as it opened and Charlie entered the room. 'Remi is on his way. He won't be a second.'

Portia saw him glance at her and suspected he had noticed they had been confiding in each other about something. Instead of saying anything, he pulled his seat closer to Lexi's other side and sat looking at her laptop screen.

'*Pardon*,' Remi said breathlessly as he burst into the room. He closed the door behind him and sat in the spare chair next to Portia. 'What is this that you are to show us, Lexi?'

She typed something into her search box and tens of photos popped up onto the screen, all of which, Portia noticed, included Megan. Each was with either one of them or their guests during the party.

'This is her Instagram page,' Lexi explained, clicking onto the account and going through several photos.

Portia couldn't believe the coverage they had been lucky enough to receive through these photos. Megan Knight had over two million followers and most of those would see these pictures. There was one in front of the old nameplate at the entrance to the chateau driveway so people could see where she had been staying.

'These are incredible,' Portia exclaimed.

'You're not kidding there.' Charlie leant back and grinned happily at Portia behind Lexi and Remi's backs.

Comforted to see him so happy, Portia returned his smile. All the hard work to make rooms ready for Megan's stay and the effort they had all put into pulling the party together had been worthwhile.

'This is incredible,' she said. 'Thanks so much for coming here and showing these to us, Lexi. We really appreciate it.'

Lexi waved a finger in the air and beamed at each of them. 'Ah, but that's not it.'

'It isn't?' Charlie asked, staring at the screen.

'Nope.' She typed something in and then their website appeared. It did look classy, Portia thought happily. 'Look at these.'

Portia watched as Lexi scrolled down through messages, then clicked on the diary. 'They are bookings that Oliver has tentatively put into the calendar for you two to approve. Once they're done the computer will send an automatic confirmation to whoever requested it and they'll be asked to email any special requests along with their full details.'

Portia was stunned. She wasn't sure how to react as a mixture of delight and fear coursed through her. 'I can't believe it,' she whispered.

'Things have just got very real,' Charlie agreed quietly, looking from Lexi to her. 'There's no going back now.'

34

CHARLIE

Charlie slammed the edge of the spade hard into the firm ground. He had dropped Portia off at the airport for the first flight out that morning and was waiting to hear from her once she had arrived at her friend Cressida's flat in London. It hadn't mattered how often he tried to reassure himself that she would miss him and return to the chateau, for some reason he couldn't quite feel it in his heart.

He had been tempted to tell Portia he had heard her comment to Lexi. He recalled overhearing Portia admitting to being scared she might not want to return to the chateau, and even more difficult to hear was that she didn't think she knew who she was any more since coming to the island to live. He also hadn't missed the guilty look on her face when he walked back into the dining room to join them but hadn't wanted to ruin her trip to London by bringing the matter up.

Somehow, while trying his best not to repeat the mistakes his father and mother had made, he was doing exactly that. His inheritance, his run-down chateau and his struggle to fit into Portia's life in London had brought them to this and it was all his fault. If he wasn't putting so much effort into this place then maybe she wouldn't feel so unsettled.

He sighed heavily, feeling his heart break at the thought of losing her and the future he had imagined them sharing at Chateau de Caesarea. He pressed the sole of his boot onto the top of the spade and pushed hard until it sank into the soil. Portia deserved her break from the constant hard work. Just because he thought her to be as beautiful with her hair tied up and make-up free, he suspected she must miss dressing up in the fine clothes she had brought with her to the island yet not had the opportunity to wear apart from at the party. Had spending time with Megan, looking polished and relaxed, reminded her of how different her life used to be before coming here?

He hoped she didn't change her mind about wanting to live at the chateau. He shook his head to rid himself of the nagging doubt, refusing to let it torture him and lifted the spade handle again before slamming it back down into the frost-hardened earth.

He loved her so much but his mother had always insisted that if you love someone you should be prepared to let them go. He had thought it an odd thing to say growing up but now understood how difficult it was to encourage someone you love to take opportunities that might lead them away from you. He took a deep breath, needing to calm himself. Portia loved him. She would come back to him. At least he hoped so.

His phone vibrated in his jeans pocket. Hoping it was Portia, he immediately retrieved it and checked the screen. Oliver.

He answered the call. 'Hi, Oliver.'

'Sorry if I've disappointed you,' Oliver said, a smile in his voice. 'I was wondering if you might like to come to my place for a couple of drinks tonight. Lexi's out and it would be fun to catch up.'

Charlie's first instinct was to refuse the kind offer, preferring to get an early night but he reconsidered. 'Why don't you come up to the chateau? I could ask Remi to join us, if you don't mind. I'm sure he could do with a few drinks and a chilled evening.'

'Sounds good to me.'

'Great. Come whenever you like.'

He ended the call feeling slightly better. At least now he had something planned that might take his mind off his concerns about the state of his relationship. He could even ask Oliver's opinion on a few things, he thought. After all, the man knew Portia better than anyone else it seemed.

Remi was out when Oliver arrived and Charlie thought it a great opportunity to speak to him in private. He welcomed him into the dining room where he had a fire roaring in the grate and after thanking Oliver for looking after the new bookings, took a mouthful of his lager.

'Something's wrong,' Oliver said, narrowing his eyes at Charlie thoughtfully. 'I presume it's to do with Portia going away?'

Charlie shook his head. 'Not exactly, but I am worried about her. About us.'

'Go on.'

Charlie explained what he had overheard Portia saying to Lexi. 'I've felt her becoming more distant recently, mostly since the party. I mean she mostly says all the right things, but she's been a bit snappy.' He shook his head. He wasn't getting across how things were, not properly.

'You mean she's becoming more withdrawn? And then jumped at the chance to accept Cressida's invitation?'

Charlie nodded miserably. 'That's about it.' He wiped condensation from the outside of the bottle with his thumb. 'My father persuaded my mother to leave the island because it was what he needed to do.'

'When your family emigrated you mean?'

'Yes. She didn't want to go, although I have a feeling that she probably wasn't completely honest with him about the depth of her feelings. They were miserable most of the time, her becoming more withdrawn and him resentful that she wasn't happy when he had settled in well there.'

'And let me guess, you always promised yourself you wouldn't make the same mistakes?'

How did he know? Charlie looked across the table at Oliver and nodded. 'Exactly. And now I'm doing what my father did.'

Oliver stared at him silently. It was making Charlie even more anxious and he wished his friend would hurry up and say something.

'Charlie, I don't know if this is what's happening, or not, but Portia got her dysfunctional relationship tools from her own parents.'

Confused, Charlie shook his head. 'What do you mean?'

'She pretty much brought herself up. Her parents were so engrossed in their own lives, firstly with their divorce when she was about seven and then their second and third marriages. I recall my brother telling me a few things about her childhood and she's spoken to me a little over the years. I believe they both were so intent on their new lives that they forgot about including her. The poor girl spent most of her time at boarding school, or staying with friends during holidays. I recall Alastair telling me that even when she was taken away with her parents that Portia always felt like the spare wheel because both had smaller children with their new partners. So the fact that she withdraws and her initial reaction is to leave and return to a place she feels familiar with is probably understandable. The penthouse was where she found herself again after my brother's death. I think she saw it as her safe place.'

Charlie listened, feeling like Oliver had given him a hard punch in the gut. He knew his friend was trying to give him a helpful insight into Portia's mental state but all he was doing was confirming that Charlie had inadvertently been instrumental in taking her from a place where she felt safe.

'I feel dreadful doing that to her. How can I rectify what's happened between us?'

'Firstly, you haven't intentionally done anything wrong, Charlie. Secondly, don't forget Portia was the one who instigated buying the chateau. She decided to sell her flat.' Oliver took a mouthful from his bottle and thought for a moment.

'But I let her do it.'

'You *let* her?' Oliver gave him a pitying look. 'Don't think for a moment that anyone has the power to allow her to do anything. She might be vulnerable at times, like now, but she's still a formidable character.' Oliver laughed, a sad look on his face. 'As far as what to do about this situation, I wish I knew.'

'But I know she loves me. She's said it and I sense it when I'm with her.'

Oliver nodded. 'I know she does too, but I have a sneaking suspicion that could be the reason she's pulling away.'

'I don't understand.' He felt sick. This wasn't what he needed to hear right now.

'I think because she does love you so much and is frightened by it.'

'Sorry?'

Oliver stared at him for a moment. 'It feels odd saying this to you, but she was heartbroken when my brother died. I believe that even though Portia is very strong, there's still a vulnerable side to her, like there is with all of us. Maybe she can't face the thought that she might lose you if this project doesn't work out as you both hope?'

'I'd rather give this place away than lose her.'

'I know you would, Charlie, but I doubt Portia would ever let you do that. Look, don't panic. Maybe there is a way for you to both have what you want most.'

'I don't suppose you have any suggestions about how to make that happen, do you?'

'Sorry, Charlie. I wish I did.'

35

PORTIA – LONDON

Portia hoped Charlie hadn't minded when she mentioned delaying her return to Jersey but it was too good an opportunity to miss. When old friends she had met up with at Cressida's party invited her to stay on the mainland for a while longer she jumped at the chance. She loved Charlie and sensed he knew she was struggling.

She called him to reassure him she hadn't completely forgotten about the chateau. 'I hope to do some networking while I'm here. I'll tell people to look up the chateau online if they ever contemplated visiting Jersey.' He had made all the right noises, but she could tell he was disappointed regardless of his encouragement for her to take as long as she liked. 'You don't mind, do you?'

'Of course not, sweetheart. You do what you think best. I hope you're having fun though? I don't want your trip to be all about work and this place. I do remember that there's more to life than plastering and wallpapering each day.'

She sensed an undertone to his comment. Was he worried she might be reluctant to return to the island now she had had a taste of her old glamorous life in London? she wondered. Was he right to think that way? After all, she mused, if she was completely honest with herself, there had been times while she was back in London when she had wished things could be different. She closed her eyes. Charlie loved Jersey and she loved him, and at least with the chateau they were building a business together; a future for themselves.

'It's not, Charlie. I am having a good time. I have to admit it's made a nice change to sleep in a warm bedroom, although it would be far nicer with you beside me.'

'I do miss you, you know,' he said quietly. 'But I'm happy to hear you're having a lovely time.'

'I know you are, Charlie,' Portia said, before Cressida bellowed from the hallway. 'I'd better go, I've already kept her waiting for ten minutes longer than I had promised.'

'I love you, Portia,' Charlie said quietly, sounding sad.

Portia's heart ached to hear him sounding miserable. 'And I love you too, Charlie. I'll be back before you know it.'

'I know you will.'

As she pushed her feet into her stilettos Portia thought of Charlie's parting words. He might have said he knew she would be back soon, but she couldn't ignore the doubt in his voice. Was he right to be concerned? Was she kidding herself when she had sold her beautiful home thinking she could dedicate herself for months to creating a perfect place where she and Charlie could welcome and entertain guests? Would they ever be able to earn a good living running the place? Had she already given up on them?

She covered her mouth to stifle a cry.

'Portia? Is everything all right?' Cressida was frowning at her from her bedroom doorway. 'Has something happened?'

Portia cleared her throat and shook her head. 'No. I'm, er, just missing Charlie, that's all.' She stood and picked up the tiny designer bag Cressida had lent her for the evening. 'I'll be fine. We should get a move on.'

* * *

She studied the room she was standing in, listening to the friendly chatter but only half listening to what was being said all around her. It was another beautiful place. This time she was at a party being held in a fine baronial hall with antique furniture she knew had been passed down through the generations. Determined to be positive about hers and Charlie's future and unable to face her doubts at that moment, she focused on picking up some inspiration from the place to use on her return to the chateau.

It really was heavenly to be back here again. She looked down at her hands. She was enjoying being able to wear her jewellery again, her nails were immaculate and a pillar box red that went perfectly with the shift dress and high stilettos. It was a joy to wear them again after months in thick socks and work boots.

She realised she felt cleaner than she had done for the first time in weeks and had every intention of making the most of every second. She took a sip of her champagne and thought of Charlie. He was probably wearing several layers of clothes, trying to keep warm, while she was standing in this plush centrally heated luxurious place sipping champagne and eating hors d'oeuvres.

'Portia, darling!'

Distracted from her thoughts by a deep, liquid voice she recognised from somewhere, Portia looked over to see a tall, extremely handsome man homing in on her. She racked her brains trying to recall his name and how she knew him.

He stopped in front of her, kissing her on both cheeks. 'You don't remember me, do you?'

'Don't be silly, of course I do,' she fibbed. His eyes were familiar but why didn't she remember him properly. She was usually good with names and faces and it disconcerted her to be at a loss this time.

He smiled, displaying perfect white teeth. 'What's my name, then?'

She saw the twinkle of amusement in his green eyes and knew he could see straight through her lie. Portia winced. 'I wish I could tell you.'

He threw his head back and laughed. It was a deep roar of a laugh, infectious and above all, friendly. Portia joined in, surprised at how unembarrassed she was by her social faux pas.

'Go on then,' she giggled. 'Enlighten me.'

'Rory.'

Rory? No, she still had no idea. She grimaced. 'Sorry, still nothing.'

'From university.' He watched as she struggled to recall him, then shook his head. 'You won't remember me from then, though.'

'Did we attend the same uni?' What was he on about?

He drank from his glass. 'We did. But you were one of the glamorous, cool students the other girls wanted to emulate, while all the boys were secretly in love with you.'

Portia laughed. 'I doubt that very much.'

He leant his head slightly closer to her. 'I'm right.'

'So tell me why I wouldn't know you from then. Have you changed much?'

'Completely.'

She was fascinated. 'Really?' He nodded. As she studied him she thought back and it dawned on her who he was. 'I do know you,' she said aghast, picturing a shy, skinny boy who seemed so much younger than she and her friends.

He grinned, satisfied. 'You're picturing a nervous chap, always on the periphery of everything.'

'Not quite, but from what I recall you were quiet and seemed very young compared to the rest of us.'

'I was younger than most students. Now I look back I realise I should have taken a couple of years out before going to university. Given myself time to experience life, gain some confidence.'

'You must have been very clever to go earlier than the rest of us.' She recalled inviting him to join them for lunch a couple of weeks into their first term.

His amusement vanished. 'I was, but you were very kind to me, Portia. I've never forgotten how you included me when no one else did.'

She was glad he thought of her fondly. So often she worried that people took one look at her and assumed her to be a spoilt rich girl with little feeling. 'You seemed lost somehow and I hated seeing you like that.' She remembered he had left after the first year and asked him why.

'My mother died and my father couldn't cope.' He looked saddened by the memory.

'I'm sorry you had to face something so awful.'

He sighed. 'Thank you. To be honest, it was a bit of a relief to have an excuse to leave university and get out into the world.'

She took one step back and studied him. He was dressed in a bespoke suit with an expensive haircut and was clearly now in possession of a lot of confidence. 'How did things work out for you, workwise? Well, I presume.'

'Better than I could have hoped. I've got my own investment business now. I made the most of my gift for figures and studied investments. I'm now my own boss and I love it. How about you?'

'I recently moved to Jersey with my partner.' She pushed away the heavy sadness the reminder brought to her.

His eyebrows shot up. 'Jersey? I'm impressed.'

'Don't be,' she said, not wishing him to get the wrong impression. She might have always enjoyed a luxurious lifestyle but she wasn't rich enough to be allowed into the island as one of the high-wealth people who moved there. 'My partner is from the island, and it's through him that I'm able to live there as I do.'

'Sounds good. Do you work there?'

Unable to help herself, Portia smiled, wondering if he would be surprised by what she was about to tell him. 'We're renovating a chateau with another friend.'

He surreptitiously looked her up and down. 'I would never have guessed. And you're doing the work yourselves?' he asked doubtfully.

'Most of it, yes.' She was surprised at the amount of pride her answer gave her.

'I'm impressed. Maybe you'll invite me over to see the place when I'm next visiting clients on the island?' He grinned cheekily.

'If you wait until the summer you'll be able to book to stay whenever you wish.' She realised she should have thought to have business cards printed for occasions like these and made a mental note to do so as soon as she returned home.

'I might just do that.' He looked at her hand as if expecting her to hand him a card. 'Shall we swap numbers? You can then let me know when the work is done and how to book.'

Delighted to have found a potential guest for the chateau and not wishing to lose contact, Portia took his phone from him and gave him hers. Numbers saved, they swapped their phones back again.

'I look forward to hearing from you.'

'I can't wait to finish the renovations,' Portia laughed, unable to imagine that day ever arising.

That evening, back at Cressida's home, Portia was only too pleased to have changed into her pyjamas having removed her make-up and pulled her hair back, fastening it into a large clip on top of her head. She had forgotten how exhausting socialising could be and as she pushed her feet into borrowed slippers, she thought about her conversation with Rory.

She had sounded so positive when telling him about the chateau. Was it because she couldn't admit even to herself that she had reached the end of her time on the project? Or did she still have some enthusiasm for it? She loved Charlie so much, but needed to know she could cope with what life might throw at her and the one thing she doubted she could deal with was unexpected loss. What if something happened to Charlie like it had done with Alastair? Wouldn't it be better to call an end to what they had now before she got too used to their life there? Shouldn't she be in charge of her decisions rather than letting fate deal her another cruel blow, if that's what it had in mind for her? She loved him deeply, but at least now she still had connections in London. Wouldn't it be better to end things before she forgot how to live independently from Charlie?

Her mind raced until hearing Cressida call for her again, and realised her friend was waiting for her to join her for a mug of hot chocolate. Portia splashed cold water on her face and went to the living room.

She sat next to Cressida on the cushioned sofa, her feet outstretched to make the most of the heat from the log burner. She wriggled her toes to try and get some feeling back into them after standing for so long in heels at the party. It hadn't taken her feet long to get used to wearing flat footwear, she thought, amused.

'Have you enjoyed your visit?' Cressida asked, handing Portia a mug of the delicious-smelling drink she had just made.

'I did. Thank you so much for inviting me over. It's been enormous fun catching up with people again and I've loved every second.'

'Good.'

Hearing the unusual tone in her friend's voice, Portia turned to look at her. 'I sense there's something you're wanting to say.'

Cressida smiled and shook her head. 'There's no getting past you, is there?'

'I like to think not.' She waited and when Cressida turned her attention to sipping her drink, Portia became impatient. 'What's on your mind?'

Cressida made a pretence of thinking. 'Look, I know you're due to return to Jersey tomorrow afternoon, but I was wondering if you wouldn't mind staying another couple of days.'

Portia felt a pang of longing, but couldn't decide if it was because she wanted to be with Charlie again or because she wanted to extend her visit to London. She couldn't help feeling a little guilty at the thought of delaying her return yet again. Cressida had been good inviting her to stay and the temptation to spend a bit longer with her in the comfort of her beautiful, warm home was too much to refuse. Not wishing to agree too readily, Portia acted as if she was giving Cressida's request a bit of thought.

'I suppose I should ask why you want me to stay longer? Was there a particular reason or is it just that you can't bear to lose my sparkling personality just yet?' She tilted her head to one side questioningly.

Cressida laughed. 'Naturally, I'll be sorry to see you leave, but...'

Portia could see that her friend felt slightly awkward for a moment, something Cressida never seemed to be. 'Cressida? What is it?'

'I was just wondering if I was fair asking you to do this when you've told me how much work you still need to do to your chateau before opening it to the public.'

'Just tell me?'

'We've been invited out to lunch tomorrow and I thought it would be fun. That's about it, really. It would be just like old times.'

Portia didn't like to reject her friend's offer and reasoned that even if he was disappointed not to see her again tomorrow, Charlie would never expect her to turn down lunch with a friend. After all, Portia mused, when would she next be free to do something like this? 'I'll do it,' she said before she had a chance to change her mind.

Cressida beamed at her. Her delight thrilled Portia and made her feel like she still belonged in some way to her old life there. 'I'd better finish this drink quickly and go and phone Charlie though,' Portia said, aware that it was late and he might already be sleeping. 'Then I'll postpone my flight back by one day.'

'Make it two?' Cressida pleaded.

'Two? I'm not so sure I can do that.'

'Please.' Cressida pulled an appealing face making Portia laugh.

'Honestly, you always were impossible to say no to. Fine. I'll postpone my return by another two days,' she said, wagging a finger at her friend. 'But that's it. No more, otherwise Charlie will think I've changed my mind about not living in London any more.'

'Would that be so bad?' Cressida asked, a mischievous glint in her eyes. Would it? Portia wondered, struck by the thought. 'Yes,' she insisted. 'It would.'

36

CHARLIE

'Of course I don't mind you staying longer,' Charlie lied. 'You have fun and I'll see you when you get back.'

They'd chatted for a few more minutes but it was strained. Even while she told him about the party before saying good night and ending the call, Charlie sensed she was more distant from him than ever. She sounded conflicted, and he didn't blame her. Hadn't he felt the same way when they were living in London and he was trying to assure her he was happy? How the tables had turned.

He sat back against the headboard and stared at the dark screen on his mobile for a few seconds before leaning over and placing it on the tea chest. He didn't want her to feel badly about prolonging her visit to stay with her friend. If things had been the other way round he would hope she would understand his need to be somewhere that made him happy. If only that somewhere for Portia was in Jersey with him.

He understood how much she needed this break from the dust and grime of their new life and realised it had cheered him up to hear joy in her voice and see her looking relaxed as she lay in the plush bed surrounded by expensive furnishings. It only served to remind him how different she had seemed in the days leading up to receiving Cressida's invitation.

Charlie stared at the faded, peeling wallpaper on their bedroom wall. It was little wonder she was finding their new accommodation underwhelming. A thought occurred to him. If she wasn't returning for a couple of days, then he had the perfect opportunity to make some much-overdue changes to their room. Hopefully, if he gave her a taste of how their home could be, then she might feel happier there. With the dismal wallpaper and peeling paint on the shutters, never mind the freezing wooden floors, it wasn't any wonder Portia was in no rush to return, not when she could be staying in a luxurious, warm home.

His tiredness forgotten, and aware he wouldn't now be able to sleep, he got out of bed and dressed. He would make an immediate start, he decided, as he pulled on his socks. If he could remove all the wallpaper tonight and fill any holes in the wall, then it would be dry enough the following day to repaper with some of the brighter rolls they had left over from Megan's bedroom.

Feeling much happier, he went to gather the tools he needed for the job and, relighting the bedroom fire to keep out the worst of the cold, got to work.

By three in the morning his eyes felt heavy and he was ready to fall back into his bed. He surveyed his work and, satisfied he had done all he could, showered quickly and got into bed, falling asleep almost as soon as his head touched the pillow.

* * *

'Did I hear you banging about late last night?' Remi asked when Jack joined them as they were finishing their breakfast.

Jack shook rain off his hair and went to stand by the fire before noticing no one had lit it. 'This thing is cold,' he said, stating the obvious.

'Sorry, I hadn't thought to light it,' Charlie said. 'I can if you want me to though,' he added, seeing how wet Jack's coat was. He looked out of the window. 'I hadn't realised it was pouring out there again.'

'And it's set to stay this way all day according to the weather forecast,' Jack grumbled, taking off his coat and hanging it over the back of one of the dining room chairs. 'I think we should focus on working inside for the time being.'

'I agree. I have quite a few things I'd like to get done today and tomorrow, if possible.' He realised he hadn't answered Remi's question about the previous night. 'Sorry, Remi. Yes, that was me making noise last night. I'm hoping to redecorate mine and Portia's bedroom and make it a bit more appealing for when she gets back.' Charlie admitted, hoping he hadn't been too disruptive to Remi's sleep. 'Sorry for disturbing you.'

Remi gave one of his lazy shrugs. 'It did not bother me. I like to hear there is someone else in the building, it stops me listening for intruders.'

'You're hardly likely to have any of those here on the island,' Jack joked. 'Although you are a bit out of the way here,' he added thoughtfully.

'Don't wind him up, Jack,' Charlie chided. 'No one is going to come all the way up the hill then down this long drive just to try and break in to this place. Anyway, there's nothing much to steal as it is now.'

'You'd be surprised,' Jack argued. 'I've heard that builders' tools can bring in high prices.'

'In Jersey?'

Jack frowned. 'Maybe not here. I was thinking more on the mainland.'

Charlie wasn't sure what that had to do with them then. 'Right.'

Jack laughed and waved a hand in their direction. 'Ignore me. I've had little sleep over the past few nights and am probably talking nonsense.'

'That is a relief,' Remi said. 'I do not like to think of burglars coming here at night.'

'No one is going to break in to this place,' Charlie groaned. 'Now, can we please change the subject.'

'Sure,' Jack said, reaching out and pinching the last piece of buttered toast from Charlie's plate. 'No Portia today? I thought she was due back about now?'

Charlie focused on not looking as bothered as he felt about her extended trip. 'She was, but is having such a lovely time catching up with her friends that she's decided to stay on in London for a few more days.' He saw surprise register on Jack's face for a second. Jack opened his mouth before closing it without speaking.

Charlie was relieved Jack had chosen to keep his thoughts to himself. 'Let's think about what we're going to do here today?'

'Sure,' Jack replied, looking a little shame-faced.

All Charlie wanted to do was try and get as much work done as possible to make this place more welcoming for Portia's return. He would make a start by painting the woodwork in their bedroom that morning, he decided, reminding himself he still needed to sand it down. Then tomorrow he would paper the walls and wash the floor.

'I'm going to chase the boiler company today,' he said. 'It's too cold here and now it's February it's probably going to get even colder before spring arrives.' He didn't add that he wanted Portia to come back to a toasty bedroom and dining room, if at all possible.

'What would you like us to do?' Jack asked.

'Maybe focus on finishing what you can in the main kitchen?'

He looked at Remi. 'And if you could help Jack when you've finished your deliveries that would help get it finished.'

'Of course.'

'I'm going to go back to the bedroom and finish up there.' He finished eating his piece of toast. 'First though, I'm going to fetch a towel for you to dry your hair, Jack. Bella won't forgive me if you go down with pneumonia when she needs you to help with baby Maia.'

37

PORTIA

Portia took a sip from her glass of champagne as she listened to Cressida chatting about the dress and boots she had bought earlier that day. She seemed full of nervous energy and Portia wondered if her friend had always been this way or if there was something going on in her life to make her so excitable.

She loved this restaurant, not only because the food was always delicious but she loved people-watching more now that she wasn't living here any longer. She thought about how isolated it was back at the chateau with so few people around each day. It was so different to the rest of her life, apart from when she had been living with Alistair in the Highlands and had been surrounded by the hustle and bustle of a city.

Now though, she was beginning to miss the peace of chateau life. Although even that quietness was not going to last, not when they started taking in paying guests.

'Portia?'

'Sorry, I was miles away.'

'I can see that.'

She saw Cressida glance nervously towards the door and

followed her gaze. A man waved at them and began walking over to their table.

'Rory?' Portia smiled politely as he kissed her on both cheeks and then did the same to Cressida. But instead of making small talk before moving on to his own table as she expected him to, he pulled out a seat and sat at the table. She glanced at Cressida in confusion and saw that her friend didn't appear at all surprised. It also dawned on her that Cressida had been waiting for Rory to join them.

'What a perfect way to spend Valentine's Day lunch,' he said smiling at Portia and then at Cressida. 'With two beautiful women for company.'

Portia cringed. 'Valentine's Day?' She had forgotten all about it. Her second Valentine's Day with Charlie and she hadn't even contacted him?

Portia pulled her phone from her pocket and quickly sent Charlie a message wishing him happy Valentine's Day with a selfie of her blowing him a kiss. She noticed she had missed two calls from him and a message sending her his love. Bugger. Now it looked as if she was only replying to his message.

Immediately a reply pinged onto her screen.

Sorry, I hadn't realised what day it was.

Charlie wrote, immediately making Portia feel much better.

Happy Valentine's Day, sweetheart. Xx

'Are you all right?' Rory asked.

'Sorry, I just needed to do something.'

Cressida gave her a suspicious look and Portia could see her friend had noticed the kiss she had tried to surreptitiously send to Charlie. 'Is everything all right between you?'

'Yes, sure' she replied, relieved. She realised she hadn't acknowledged Rory and didn't wish to appear rude. It wasn't as if the poor man had done anything wrong. 'Sorry, Rory. Hello.'

'You don't mind me being here, do you?' he asked, locking eyes with her.

'Why should I mind?'

Cressida finally turned to her and mouthed an apology before focusing her attention back on Rory. 'I omitted to tell Portia you were joining us.'

Portia noticed Rory seemed as surprised as her to hear this.

'I hadn't meant to impose on your lunch.'

'You haven't,' Cressida insisted. 'I invited you as our guest.'

'What shall we order?' Portia asked, taking the menu a waiter was holding out for her. This was the lunch she had told Charlie she needed to delay her return for, and although she didn't expect he would mind, she still felt guilty spending time with Rory when she would have rather been with him.

She hoped Rory didn't have the wrong impression about why Cressida had asked both of them for lunch. Was this Cressida's way of getting Portia to move back to live in London? She hoped not, but knew her friend wasn't averse to putting her feelings before those of others if she wanted something badly enough. It was a stark reminder of how imperfect her life had been in London before Charlie had moved in to her flat.

It was too late to do anything now so she decided to enjoy lunch. It wasn't Rory's fault. She would have to wait to confront Cressida until they were back at her flat later.

Portia wished now that she hadn't been so easily persuaded to lengthen her stay.

The waiter took their wine and food orders and as soon as he walked away, Rory leant slightly forward. 'It's my fault. I had so much fun seeing you again the other night and contacted Cressida to ask her to persuade you to come out to lunch.'

So that's what had happened, Portia mused.

'It's true,' Cressida said sheepishly. 'I told Rory you would only come if I was here too.'

'I remember you telling me you had a boyfriend in Jersey,' Rory added, reaching out to take Portia's hand but she pulled it back gently and rearranged her napkin on her lap. 'Sorry,' he said. 'If I'd have thought this would put you in a difficult position, I wouldn't have pushed Cressida into arranging it.'

Portia had no wish for anyone to think badly of Charlie, especially when it wasn't warranted. 'Charlie would never tell me who I may or may not meet. The only reason I have an issue today is because I delayed my return to Jersey because Cressida asked me to have lunch with her,' she added pointedly.

He sighed. 'I'm sorry. I hadn't realised you'd put off going back and I can see how that might look. I assumed you were filling time while you were in London.'

'Portia,' Cressida said, her voice low as she leant over to whisper in Portia's ear. 'From what you've told me about Charlie, he isn't the jealous type, not like Alistair could be. I think you're overthinking this lunch today, don't you?'

Surprised by her friend's comment, Portia turned to look at her. Was she? She thought of Charlie and decided Cressida was probably right. Alistair had been a wonderful man in many ways, but he could be jealous at times. It had been the one contentious issue they argued about. Charlie never behaved in that way. She had been overreacting.

'I'm sorry,' she said, embarrassed. 'You're right.'

Cressida gave her a reassuring smile. 'It's fine. Anyway, as we're here now, let's make the most of it.' Desperate to change the subject, she added, 'I seem to recall you telling me about your work in finance, is it? What about your relationships, Rory? Are you seeing someone? Married?'

She could feel Cressida watching her, but instead focused on listening as Rory told her about his divorce and what a shock it had been for him to now be back on the dating scene.

All she could think about as he spoke was Charlie and how uncomplicated life was with him.

38

CHARLIE

'Am I imagining things,' Portia said, taking off her coat and hanging it up in the hallway. 'Or is it warmer in here.'

'The heating is fixed,' Remi announced cheerfully, descending the stairs to welcome her. 'Charlie was insistent to the man on the phone that he must come to fit the new boiler,' he added, passing them on his way to the kitchen.

'It was about time,' Charlie said, relieved to have managed to reach the boiler engineer immediately after he had taken a cancellation for a booking.

'Well, I'm delighted.'

He lifted her weekend bag that was heavier than his case for a two-week trip. What did she manage to fit in this thing? Taking her hand in his free one, Charlie cocked his head towards the stairs. 'Shall we go up?' he whispered. 'I've got another surprise for you.'

Portia raised her eyebrows. 'I think I might be able to imagine what that one is.'

Charlie laughed. 'That'll have to wait a while. This is something else, but I'm hoping you like it.'

'I'm intrigued.' She followed him upstairs, giving his hand a squeeze. 'It really is heavenly to be back here with you.'

He looked over his shoulder at her pretty face, hoping she meant what she said. Her cheeks and the tip of her nose were slightly pink from the cold outside and he was happy to see that she did seem glad to be back in Jersey. It was a massive relief. He had missed her even more than he had expected to and it felt comforting to hear she missed being here too.

He opened their bedroom door and placed her case just inside out of the way. 'Close your eyes,' he said, butterflies in his stomach as he waited to see what she thought of his handiwork.

She stepped in behind him. 'OK, now you can open them.' He watched as she did as he asked. Portia gazed around the room at the pretty blue and cream wallpaper, freshly painted woodwork and shutters and the curtains he had found in the attic and cleaned as best he could. He had asked Remi to light the fire while he went to collect Portia from the airport and was grateful to his friend for doing it perfectly. The room was cosy and inviting and exactly as he had hoped it would be. 'Well? What do you think?'

'Oh, Charlie, I love what you've done,' she said. He was surprised to see her eyes fill with tears but before he could comment on them, she flung her arms around his neck and kissed him. 'It's like our very own sanctuary. What a perfect surprise. Thank you.'

'I'm relieved you like it,' he admitted, his anxiety at her return vanishing. Perhaps he had been worrying unnecessarily about her feelings towards him and their life here. He desperately hoped that was the case. 'I wanted to do something to welcome you back and thought that as this was where we spend our evenings that I should start in this room.'

'It's beautiful.'

'I'm so happy you like it.'

'I love it.'

'Good.' He smiled. 'When you've changed out of your travelling clothes, I'll show you what Jack and Remi have been working on while you were away.'

'I can't wait.' She held him tightly to her. 'But first though, I thought we could spend a little time in this adorable bedroom of ours.'

He couldn't think of anything he would rather do.

* * *

Half an hour later, Charlie, happier than he had been since the party, led her into the kitchen where Jack was wiping down surfaces and Remi putting the finishing touches to the paintwork.

'Apart from blinds on the windows and—' he looked around to see what else needed to be done '—maybe a few pictures on the walls, I think we're about done in here. What do you think?'

The three men waited for her approval.

'We have an Aga?' She walked over to it, looking aghast. 'I didn't think we could afford something like this as well as the range.'

Charlie had been waiting to show her this surprise, unsure what she would make of them having two cooking areas in the kitchen. The room was certainly big enough for them and he reasoned that when they were at full guest capacity having both appliances would be useful.

'I found it online. We had to pay for it but very little compared to the cost of a new one. I think they mostly wanted the thing removed. Remi, Jack, Oliver and I collected it the day you left. I wasn't sure we would be able to have it fitted before your return but when you delayed coming home it gave me time to sort things out. Do you like it?'

'It's wonderful.' She opened one of the doors and rubbed her hands together. 'Ahh, the warmth. It feels so good now this place isn't like walking into an icehouse.'

'You're not kidding,' Jack laughed. 'It's almost been a pleasure working in here today, hasn't it, Remi?' He looked over his shoulder, waiting for a reply, and Charlie couldn't help feeling guilty that they had expected their friend to work under such low temperatures over the past few weeks.

'Very much better,' Remi agreed. 'Even nicer that you approve of our work.'

Portia laughed as she crossed the room and ran her hand along the pristine work top. 'I daren't not. I've been having fun in London while you three have been working hard back here. I'm incredibly grateful to you all for the push you've made to get so much done. In fact, I can hardly believe how much better everything seems to when I left.'

Charlie wondered if there was a spark of enthusiasm in her voice; was it happiness? He hoped it was.

'You were very tired before your trip,' Remi said quietly. 'You needed time to rest and step away from this place.'

'You're right, I was feeling rather overwhelmed by it all.'

'You're feeling more like your old self now, I hope?' Jack asked, a concerned look on his face.

'I am, thanks.' Charlie watched her look from one to the other of them and then back to stare into his eyes. 'In fact, now that I'm back I realise that I was hanging on to parts of my life that I don't need any more.'

He wasn't exactly sure what she meant but didn't care. All that mattered was that Portia seemed happy to be back.

'I think we're all very happy to have you back again. I know I certainly am.'

She smiled at him. 'I want to look at more,' she said, going to open and close several cupboards before pulling open the large American-style fridge freezer and closing it. 'I think you've done an amazing job and I can't wait to start using everything in here.' She seemed amused. 'By *I*, I naturally mean *you*, Charlie. Maybe I should have said I look forward to eating my meals in here.'

Charlie laughed. It felt wonderful to have her back home. The chateau felt more alive with Portia in it again.

'You must look at the smaller kitchen at the back,' Remi said, indicating for her to follow him into the next room. 'We have updated parts of my bakery. When it is complete I will move everything into here permanently.'

'Well, I'm certainly impressed with you all.' She smiled at each of them and Charlie could tell she was touched that they cared so much about her opinion. 'It really is good to be back with you all again.'

He was delighted to hear her say so. 'We're getting there, sweetheart. Slowly.'

'We are,' she said, taking his hand in both of hers. 'I knew we would.' She winked at him and he realised it was to reassure him.

'In fact,' Charlie said, an idea coming to him. 'I thought that if you all agreed I could cook us a celebratory meal in here tonight.' He looked at Jack. 'You could bring Bella to join us, if she wanted to?'

Jack didn't seem very sure. 'I'll give her a quick call. It's so cold out that she probably won't want to leave the cottage. But she might. Let me go and check.'

'No worries, it was just a thought.'

Portia kissed Charlie's cheek. 'I think I can speak for Remi as well as myself when I say that we'd be very happy for you to cook for us tonight.'

'We would,' Remi agreed.

Portia crossed her arms. 'I was wondering if there's any news about the jewellery you found in the walled garden?'

'Not yet.' Charlie had been so focused on his relationship that the jewellery hadn't crossed his mind for days. 'We still don't know who it belongs to, but I took it to a jeweller Lexi told me about and he's valuing it. He estimated that it is worth at least twenty thousand pounds and maybe much more.'

'That's amazing news. You must be very happy?'

'I will be if I am allowed to keep it but I still don't know if that's possible.' He wanted to sit somewhere comfortably with her. 'Why don't we go and chill for a bit in the living room while I come up with an idea for our supper. I can then pop to the shop to buy a few bits.'

'Good idea,' Portia agreed. 'We can eat at our beautiful round table.' Charlie followed her gaze to the large oak table he had found weeks before in one of the storage rooms and set by the largest kitchen window. He looked forward to the three of them eating breakfast at it each morning, and the rest of their meals when they had guests. 'Our own private space,' he agreed.

Jack took his mobile from his back pocket and left the room to make his call to Bella. Portia and Remi accompanied each other out of the room discussing which bottle of red wine they should open and Charlie watched contentedly, happy to feel that they were finally making headway with their renovations.

* * *

Leaning over the worktop with a pen in his hand, Charlie tried to decide between beef or pork for their supper when he heard Portia's ringtone. He looked around to see where it was coming from but it was too far away to be in the kitchen.

Waiting for a few seconds to see if Portia picked it up, he

realised she must not have heard it and went out to the hall, eventually finding her mobile in her coat pocket. He picked it up to take it to her, noticing the name *Rory* on the screen. Unsure what to do, he hesitated, then went to find Portia. The ringtone ended before he reached her and was replaced by a text. Instinctively his eyes were drawn to the screen and without thinking, Charlie read it and his heart dropped.

It was great fun catching up with you again over lunch yesterday. Looking forward to hearing from you and seeing you again sometime. Rory x

Who was Rory? Charlie stopped walking, staring at the screen feeling sick, then guilty to have seen the text. Not that he had been snooping, he reminded himself. Would Portia think he had? He hoped not. It wasn't something he would ever do. He tried to imagine who this bloke might be, certain she had never mentioned him before. It wasn't a name he knew either, he was sure about that. He mentioned lunch together. Yesterday. Was that why she had delayed her return home to him? Surely not. Portia wasn't the sort of woman to go behind anyone's back. She loved him, he knew that much for certain.

At least, up until now he had known that. What if he had been wrong? What if his beloved Portia wasn't as happy with him as she now professed to be?

He recalled her telling him before they had become close how she missed her life with Alistair, spending holidays with him at his family estate in the Highlands. How he was a Scottish laird who would inherit the family estate in the Highlands. Charlie could never have competed with such a man and knew that although Portia loved him, there would always be a special place in her heart for the fiancé she lost far too soon. He didn't resent her feelings for Alistair. How could he? She was far too precious for him to ever resent her having been in love before they met. But this was different. Very much so.

As much as he loved her, Charlie could never forget that he was an ordinary working man whose most glamorous occupation had been working in a hotel on the island. How could he ever realistically hope to compete with Portia's old friends, one of whom he imagined must be this Rory chap?

Hating the prospect of their happiness being shattered, but unable to stand not knowing what was going on, Charlie called out to her.

'In the living room,' she replied, sounding happy and relaxed.

The sound of her cheerful voice reminded him that they were planning an evening with their friends and he didn't want to disrupt that. He needed to find out what was going on though.

Charlie carried the phone to her. 'You've had a missed call.'

'You didn't need to bring it to me,' she said, taking the phone and looking at the screen. 'I doubt it's anything important.'

'You may as well see who it was,' Charlie said, urging her to check.

Portia stiffened as she silently stared at the screen.

Charlie sensed she was trying to work out what to do next. He wanted to know too, but at the same time dreaded hearing what she might say.

Instead of explaining away the text in her usual nonchalant way, she shocked him by looking up at him. 'It's only from Rory.' She pulled a face at Charlie. 'He was the third wheel at Cressida and my girly lunch.'

'I don't think you've ever mentioned him before.'

'Probably because he isn't important.'

Charlie bit back a retort. He could feel her irritation at his questioning of her motives and felt guilty. Then, noticing something in her eyes, realised that she was looking at him suspiciously. He desperately didn't want to continue with the conversation but couldn't help himself. 'If he's not important, then why did he just text you?'

'You've read my texts?'

'Not intentionally.'

'What's that supposed to mean?'

'It came in when I was carrying the phone to you. I just happened to see it.' Not able to look at her for a moment longer and aware his emotions were getting the better of him, he turned and left the room, closing the door behind him. Was this Rory important to her? His heart sank. He hoped not with every fibre of his being.

'And here was me happy to be back where life is less complicated,' she snapped. 'Clearly I was wrong.'

39

PORTIA

She was too upset with Charlie to want to spend any time with him.

'Why don't we go out for something to eat?' Remi suggested, probably hoping to get the two of them chatting again.

'You two go without me,' she snapped, immediately feeling bad. It wasn't Remi's fault she and Charlie had fallen out. 'Sorry, Remi, but I don't have much of an appetite.'

'Then I'm not going either,' Charlie said.

'Why not?'

'I'm not leaving you here alone at night.'

'I'm perfectly capable of taking care of myself, Charlie.' She saw him blanch. 'Or is it more that you're frightened I might start texting other men?' She saw the pained look cross his sweet face and felt mean for a second time, then reminded herself that Charlie sneaking looks at her private messages was what had brought about this argument in the first place.

'Don't be ridiculous.'

'Either way, I'm not going out.'

He glared at her. 'Then neither am I.'

Remi stood and picked up his drink. 'I think I will go to my room,' he said, looking uncomfortable.

'Please don't leave on our account,' Portia said guiltily. 'We should be the ones to leave, not you. In fact, that's exactly what I'm going to do. Charlie, you stay here and share that delicious bottle of wine with Remi. I need a couple of hours to myself.'

She suspected Charlie wanted to follow her upstairs but hoped he would stay exactly where he was.

She must have fallen asleep because she woke the following morning to find he hadn't slept in their bed. Her heart sank. It was their first proper row. They had never gone to bed without making up. She thought back to how she had felt and realised Charlie knew her well enough to realise she wasn't in the mood to make up the previous evening.

Portia lay back against the headboard and checked her phone to see if Charlie might have sent her a text. He hadn't. She re-read the message from Rory. Charlie had never been a jealous boyfriend. He had also never minded her going out alone with friends when they had been living in London and he had not seemed to mind when she extended her stay, twice. Instead, he had spent that time working hard to progress with renovations to make her happy.

She put herself in Charlie's position and tried to imagine how it would seem if he did what she had done.

Portia dropped her phone onto the duvet cover and pushed her hands through her mussed hair. She had made a right mess of things. Alarmed to think how upset Charlie must be not to sleep in their room, she realised that she had been the one to escalate their falling out. All she needed to have done the previous evening was quietly explain who Rory was and that he wasn't anyone for Charlie to worry about. She was sure Charlie would have been fine. Instead, she had over-reacted, probably because she felt a misguided guilt at having lunch with Rory.

She groaned. 'What is wrong with me lately?' Both of them were under stress and she suspected neither of them had expected the work to be so hard.

Not wishing to leave things as they were for a moment longer, she threw back the covers and went to have a shower.

Freshly washed and dressed, Portia went downstairs to look for him. When she couldn't see Charlie anywhere, she went to Remi's small bakery.

'Have you seen Charlie this morning?'

He looked a little embarrassed. 'Not yet.'

When he seemed to be avoiding catching her eye, Portia wondered if maybe he knew something and wasn't letting on because he didn't want to get involved.

'Remi, I'm sorry for what happened last night. I realise our row was my fault and want to find him to explain and apologise.'

Remi looked up from kneading dough. 'You do?'

She couldn't miss the hopeful look on his face. 'Yes. And I'm sorry too for putting you in this difficult position.'

Without thinking, she stepped forward and hugged him. 'I've been a bit of a fool lately. I promise I'll make things right and that it won't happen again.'

'I'm sure Charlie will be very happy if you make up. He was sad last night.'

'I know.' She moved away from him, eager to find Charlie and speak to him. 'Do you know where I might find him?'

'He likes working in the walled garden. He could be there.'

'Thanks, Remi.'

She pulled on her puffy coat and wrapped her thickest scarf around her neck before pulling on her hat. The snow might be almost gone but it didn't look any less cold out there.

She hurried to the walled garden, frost crunching beneath her work boots. She entered without calling to him, unsure if he would answer her call if he was hoping to be left alone. At first she didn't see him, then spotted movement in the run-down greenhouse attached to the brick wall on the other side of the garden.

Portia watched Charlie silently for a moment. He was leaning against the wall staring downwards, oblivious to her presence. He seemed utterly miserable. Not wishing him to be unhappy for a second longer than was necessary, she hurried over to the greenhouse door. As she stepped inside, Charlie looked up at her, startled to see her there. He straightened, but there was no pleasure in his expression.

'I've been looking for you,' she said, unsure what else to say now he was in front of her.

'I've been here.' He turned from her and began tidying dusty terracotta plant pots neatly on the thick wooden board fixed to the back wall.

His shoulders were hunched and she couldn't stand not to touch him for another second. Not sure what to say to make things right now she was there, she walked quietly up to him. Standing behind him, she slipped her arms around his waist and rested her head against his back. Seconds later, his hands covered hers.

'I'm sorry, Charlie,' she whispered. 'I was an ass yesterday.'

'It's fine,' he said, a catch in his voice. 'I could have reacted better.'

'Rubbish. I should have told you what happened with Rory.'

He turned to face her. 'Something happened?' The look of surprise on his face showed her he hadn't expected her to do anything untoward. He had trusted her as she knew he would. The realisation made her feel worse for causing their row.

'Not anything for you to be concerned about,' she said immediately. Without waiting for him to say anything, she explained about Cressida asking her to stay longer and Rory turning up to the lunch, then how she knew him in the first place. 'He's a nice enough guy,' she added. 'But I explained I'm in a relationship and very happy with you.'

'You are?' Relief washed over Charlie's face.

'Sorry?'

'Happy, with me?'

'You know I am,' she whispered, desperate to make things right.

He kissed her on the forehead. 'I honestly didn't mean to look at your phone, but when the message popped up, I just saw it.'

'I know. And if I'd have told you about Rory and lunch, then you wouldn't have got the wrong idea.'

Charlie hugged her tightly to him. 'I didn't really give you much chance, did I? I was too busy showing off about the work the guys and I had done here as soon as you got back, and then—'

She pictured them in bed together. 'Yes, well neither of us were interested in what happened while I was away by that point.' She wrapped her arms tighter around him.

'Let's forget all about it, shall we?'

'Please.' She stood on tiptoe and kissed him. 'Remi will be so relieved we've made up. It hasn't been easy for him.'

'Poor chap. We'd better go and tell him.' He took her hand and she let him lead her back to the house. 'Why don't we go out for that meal tonight?' Charlie suggested. 'I think Remi was disappointed when neither of us wanted to go. It'll be a great way to make it up to him. He loves his food.'

'Good idea.' The thought of spending time out socially with Charlie thrilled her.

40

CHARLIE

He gazed across the table at Portia watching her entertain Remi, Jack, Oliver, Lexi and Bella and making them laugh about how her feet had hurt when she had worn stilettos again.

'It never occurred to me they could ever feel strange in any way,' she giggled. 'I have to admit I've never been so happy to take off my shoes as I was after Cressida's party.' She grimaced. 'I've clearly spent too long wearing flats.'

'It's only been a few weeks since you last wore stilettos,' Lexi laughed.

'You two are going to have to make a point of dressing up more often then.' Bella wagged her finger at Portia, then Charlie. 'Otherwise, you'll forget how to do it.'

Portia gave a horrified groan. 'Don't say that.'

Oliver pulled a face. 'I can't see that ever happening,' he teased. 'Even when Portia and Alistair were trekking in India I gather she insisted on doing her make-up each morning.'

'Rubbish,' Lexi said, telling him off. 'Stop being mean.'

Portia shook her head. 'Oliver's right.' She grinned at Charlie.

He wasn't sure if it was because she was amused by the story or if she was checking that he hadn't taken any offence at Oliver mentioning his brother, Alistair.

Charlie gave her a reassuring smile. He didn't like to think she might worry about ever mentioning the first man she had been in love with. Her first fiancé, Charlie mused, looking at her and realising that maybe it was time to think about proposing to her. He hadn't considered proposing before, wanting to give Portia the space to keep her first proposal from Alistair special. It had been too soon in his opinion to even think about going there, until now.

The conversation moved on as Oliver shared another story about Portia. Portia leant forward and took Charlie's hand. 'You OK? You seem thoughtful.'

He gave her a reassuring smile, relieved that she seemed more settled and that they were back on track again. 'Fine, thanks. I'm enjoying the evening. It's been fun, hasn't it?'

Charlie noticed Portia trying to hide a yawn behind her hand. He checked his watch. It was only ten twenty but they had become used to rising early and going to bed earlier than both ever had done before moving into the chateau. He glanced at Bella and saw her mouth to Jack that she was ready to go and relieve her mother from babysitting duties.

'I think it's time we all went home now,' Charlie suggested to a round of agreement.

They paid and Charlie, Portia and Remi accepted Oliver's offer of a lift home. 'It's far too cold and dark for you three to walk back,' he insisted.

'I'm ready for my bed,' Lexi said. 'Oh, I forgot to mention there were a couple more bookings on the website,' she said, turning in her seat to look back at them.

'Our next job is to get an internet connection to the chateau,' he said, feeling bad that Oliver and Lexi were still looking after the site.

'Yes,' agreed Portia. 'It's about time we took that off your hands.'

Now they were getting closer to the opening Charlie made a mental note to chat with Portia and maybe Jack and Remi over the next few days to fine-tune their roles going forward. They had to ensure they didn't miss any bookings.

'Thanks, Lexi,' he said. 'I promise we're going to get more organised very soon.'

'We are,' Portia agreed. 'We've been so focused on the renovation work that we forgot some of the other aspects of the business.'

'It's fine,' Lexi said. 'I'm happy to do it. I know how busy you are and there's time enough before you start having to do everything. I just wanted you to know that people are noticing the site and obviously like what they see.'

'I'm sure Megan's social media accounts have helped to keep the interest alive,' Remi said thoughtfully.

'Yes,' Charlie agreed, impressed that Megan had been posting occasionally about her stay with them with inventive pictures and back stories to entice prospective visitors to the island. 'She's been amazing.'

'She has,' Remi said dreamily.

Charlie smiled at his friend, amused. He wondered how deep Remi's feelings went for Megan? It would be nice to see his friend in a relationship. It can't have been much fun for him living with him and Portia when he was single, especially if he did like someone.

The car slowed as they neared the entrance to the chateau driveway and Oliver turned in. Charlie gazed out of the window, waiting for the row of trees either side of the driveway to end and their chateau to come into view. He sighed inwardly as the trees parted and the first turret appeared in front of them, then the rest of the building. Moonlight reflected on the large window panes, it looked magical. He turned to Portia, happy to see her look of delight; confused when it vanished to be replaced by one of horror.

She opened her mouth and pointed. 'Look!'

Charlie snapped his head to the side to see what had upset her and spotted three, no four, men running from the house. 'What the...?'

Oliver sped up for a few seconds, slamming on the brakes as soon as the car reached the front door steps. 'Hey, come back here.' Oliver shouted as he, Charlie and Remi leapt out of the car and began chasing the intruders.

'Oi, you!' Charlie shouted, determined to catch at least one of them. He had no idea what they had been doing but wasn't about to miss the opportunity of grabbing one of them and finding out.

Charlie ran after them, surprised by Remi's speed. He wished Jack was still with them. He seemed to know everyone and might recognise at least one of the four guys they were chasing.

'Split up,' one shouted, and instantly the four men disappeared into the trees, dashing off in different directions.

Charlie saw Remi go left and Oliver follow the second one to the right, so chased the one closest to him, demanding he stop, aware there was little chance he would.

He heard a yell somewhere to his left and hoped Remi had caught the one he had been chasing. His fury increasing, Charlie forced his legs to work faster. He was catching up. Whoever these people were, they were fit. He was beginning to tire but forced himself to keep going, only just missing a low-hanging branch by millimetres. Oliver shouted something, then Charlie heard Remi's voice as he yelled something in French.

Charlie reached out and grabbed hold of the hood that had fallen back from the head of the man he was chasing.

'Got you!' he shouted victoriously.

Before he had a chance to gloat, the man tripped and sent Charlie flying forward, his shin slamming into what he presumed must be a tree stump. After a tussle, the man punched Charlie, freeing himself from his grasp, leapt up and ran off, disappearing into the trees.

'Damn.' He hadn't even managed to get a decent look at the guy's face. Charlie heard him shout something offensive as he ran off, then footsteps thundered somewhere nearby.

'Remi?'

It was Oliver's voice. Charlie couldn't miss the urgency in his tone. Something had happened.

'Where are you both?' Charlie called, hoping they were all right and wishing there was more light.

'Over here!' Oliver yelled. 'Remi's hurt.'

Forgetting the pain in his shin, Charlie hobbled as quickly as he could towards his friends' voices.

'What happened?' he asked, seeing Remi lying down and Oliver leaning over him.

'Hit his head.'

'I followed one of them and another came from somewhere and pushed me hard,' Remi explained in between groans as he held his hand to the side of his forehead. 'I hit a tree.'

Oliver went to help him up. 'We're going to have to get him inside to inspect the damage.'

'Can you walk?' Charlie asked, helping Oliver lift Remi to his feet.

'Yes.'

'Come on, mate,' Charlie said when Remi was standing slightly unsteadily. 'We'll soon get you inside. I don't know what we have by way of first aid but maybe Portia will know.'

'The girls?' Oliver said anxiously. 'I hope they're okay. I presume they went inside.'

A chill ran through Charlie. He hoped there weren't any other uninvited guests still in the chateau. 'Let's hurry. I want to check they're okay.'

41

PORTIA

Portia paced back and forth waiting for the three men to get back. 'I hope they're all right,' she said for the twentieth time as she went to peer out of the dining room window. 'They've been an awfully long time.'

'They have.' Lexi came to stand next to her. 'Look,' she pointed. 'Isn't that them?'

'Where?' Portia peered into the darkness, desperate to see them. 'It looks like one of them is hurt.'

Lexi gave an anxious groan. 'It does. It's Remi.'

'I'll get the first aid kit,' Portia said, needing to do something.

'I'll get a blanket and, um, put on the kettle to make him a hot drink.'

By the time the women were back in the dining room they could hear the guys' voices on the front steps. Portia ran to open the front door, desperate to find out what had happened.

As she opened it she saw Charlie and Oliver's serious expressions, then Remi's ashen face. 'You're bleeding,' she murmured. 'Bring him through here, we've got a few bits to clean him up.'

She noticed Charlie's trousers were torn by his right shin and his knees were muddy. He had also hurt himself, although hopefully not as badly as Remi. As they passed her she looked at Charlie. 'You all right?' she mouthed.

He nodded and gave her a reassuring smile.

'They got away,' Oliver explained angrily, as he and Charlie lowered Remi to a seat. 'One of them pushed Remi and caused him to slam into a tree.'

'Let me have a look,' Lexi said. 'I did a first aid course a couple of years ago.'

'You did?' Portia was impressed.

'Yes, I thought it best to be prepared in case any of the guests at our cottages hurt themselves and needed patching up.'

'Maybe Charlie and I should think about doing the same thing before we open this place.'

She rested a hand on Remi's shoulder to comfort him, then turned to Charlie. 'While Lexi checks Remi, I want to have a look at that leg of yours.'

Charlie grinned at her. 'Yes, Nurse Portia.' He pulled out a chair and sat stretching out his hurt leg. 'It's a bit sore but I don't think I've cut it.'

She pulled back his trouser leg, ripping the torn area until she could see the full extent of the damage and then relaxed slightly. 'No blood. But you're going to have one hell of a bruise.'

With Remi's head wound cleaned and having spoken to a duty doctor at the hospital, Portia was relieved when Remi agreed to go to the emergency department for a proper check-up the following morning. Then the five of them sat with hot drinks as they went over what had happened.

'Do you think we should call the police?' Portia asked, unnerved by the incident.

Charlie looked at Oliver who shrugged. 'We could, but I'm not sure what they can do now. You said you've checked the place and can't see any damage and as none of us managed to get a proper look at any of them I think we'd only be wasting their time.'

'I have a feeling they were youngsters taking a chance,' Charlie said. 'None of them were that well-built but all were fast and very fit. Hopefully now they've been chased by three of us they might think again about coming back.'

'I hope so,' Portia said.

'We must keep the gate closed at all times,' Remi suggested quietly.

Portia had an idea. Charlie had always wanted a dog and this could be the perfect time to get one. 'Why don't we get a dog, or maybe two? They are a wonderful deterrent. My father always said so.'

'Maybe?' Charlie smiled. 'Remi? What do you think of Portia's idea? You live here too.'

He gave one of his lazy shrugs. 'Two dogs would be good to have around.'

Portia was happy that Charlie hadn't rejected her idea and made a mental note to contact a rescue site on the island as soon as possible to see if they had two suitable dogs they might be happy to let them adopt.

The following morning Portia was woken by a knocking on the front door. She opened her eyes and saw that it was just after seven thirty. Charlie stirred next to her and not wishing to disturb him, she got up, pulled on a thick sweater and a pair of jeans and pushed her feet into her slippers before running downstairs to see who had arrived.

She pulled open the door, blinking against the cold morning air and stared in stunned silence.

'Megan?' She was surprised to see their immaculate friend standing there, a handbag in one hand and a weekend bag next to her booted feet.

'Da dah!' Megan waved at the taxi driver, then turned back to Portia. She laughed. 'Are you going to invite me in, or should I book to stay elsewhere?'

Portia stepped back apologetically. 'Sorry, I was a little taken aback to see you. Please, come in.' She watched Megan pick up her case and walk inside, still trying to process that she was there in the hallway. 'I'm sorry, were we expecting you?' she asked, hoping she hadn't forgotten Megan was coming.

'No, you weren't.' Megan undid her coat and threw it over the banister. 'I wouldn't mind a coffee though if you have one on the go.'

'Sure. Let's put these bags out of the way then you can follow me through to the kitchen.' And tell me why you're here, she thought but didn't say out loud.

When they were in the kitchen, Portia busied herself filling the kettle and taking two mugs from one of the cupboards. Then, too impatient to wait a moment longer, turned to Megan. 'It's good to see you again,' she said, wishing she had had some notice so didn't look quite as bedraggled as she suspected she did right now. 'And we're enormously grateful and impressed by your posts about the chateau.'

'Thank you. Look, I'm sorry to appear like this,' Megan said, indicating the table and chairs. 'May I?'

'Of course. Take a seat.'

'Thanks. You must be wondering why I'm here uninvited.'

Portia shook her head, hoping her surprise hadn't given Megan reason to feel unwelcome. 'I just hoped I hadn't forgotten you were coming.'

'It's nothing like that.'

Unsure why Megan wasn't looking her in the eye, Portia suspected she had missed something after all. 'Is anything wrong?'

Megan sighed. 'I may as well be straight with you.'

I wish you would, Portia thought as the kettle finished boiling. 'It's only instant coffee I'm afraid.'

'No problem.'

Portia finished making the drinks and carried both mugs to the table. 'Go on, I'm intrigued.'

'I'm here because of Remi.' Portia went to speak, but Megan continued. 'He insisted I shouldn't, but I couldn't stay away, not when he was hurt.'

Portia stared at the woman. She was clearly concerned. 'But it only happened last night. How did you know?' She took a sip of her coffee and winced when the scalding liquid burnt her lip.

'He messaged me. Said he was home too late to FaceTime.' She looked down at her hands turning the ring on her middle finger round and round. 'I'm afraid I got suspicious he might have company.' She looked up under her eyelashes and Portia noticed the hurt in her eyes. 'When I said so, he told me he'd been hurt but insisted he was fine.'

'I, um...' Portia tried to think, wishing she had been awake longer and had more of a chance to come round after such a deep sleep. A thought occurred to her. 'Are you telling me that you and Remi have been in contact all this time? That you are...' She stared at Megan, seeing she was waiting for Portia to work out what had been going on. 'You and Remi?'

'That's right,' Remi said from the doorway. 'We were keeping our relationship a secret.'

'But why?' Portia turned to him. The bruising on one side of his face had gone a dark purple, the eye swollen partially closed. She opened her mouth to speak but before she had a chance to say anything Megan leapt up and ran to him, taking his face lightly in her hands and studying it. 'I knew you were hiding how bad it was.'

Portia saw the two of them were besotted with each other. Remi's hand rose to rest against Megan's and his other hand touched her face lightly. He leant forwards slowly and kissed Megan lightly on the lips before taking her in his arms. Seemingly remembering that they weren't alone in the room, he stared at her over Megan's head. 'I am sorry I did not confide in you or Charlie.'

Feeling like she was interrupting, Portia decided they probably needed time alone. 'Hey, it's fine. Look, the kettle has just boiled. I'll leave you two to chat.'

Megan moved away from Remi. 'I'm sorry to do this to you, Portia.'

Portia didn't want Megan to feel unwelcome, especially when she thought of all the promotion she had done on their behalf. She wondered for a moment if some of that had been to please Remi and assumed it must have been.

'It's fine. I'm thrilled to see you here and I can see I'm not the only one. You're welcome at any time. I'll go and shower,' she reached up and felt her tangled hair. 'I must look a terrible mess. I'll make up your bedroom and will catch up with you later.'

'Please don't go to any trouble on my account,' Megan pleaded. 'I can make up the room if you show me where to find the linen.'

'Nonsense,' Portia argued. 'I'm happy to do it.' She looked at them and smiled. 'You two look lovely together, do you know that?'

Remi hugged Megan to him. 'I have never been happier,' he said wistfully.

'Nor have I.'

Aware that was her cue to leave, Portia did so to hurry upstairs and bring Charlie up to speed. He was not going to believe this unexpected change in their circumstances.

42

CHARLIE

March

Remi was out on his rounds with Megan accompanying him. Charlie still found it a little surreal that the two of them were in love but was happy for his friend. Remi had come out of his shell recently. Megan was a bubbly, sociable person and Remi appeared far more self-confident when she was around.

She was due to fly back to London that afternoon for a couple of weeks, but they were getting used to her visits. This was her second time back at the chateau since that surprise arrival five weeks before. She had even been a bit of help, although, Charlie thought with amusement, mostly with making cups of tea and serving sandwiches or biscuits while he, Portia, Jack and Remi did the mucky jobs.

It was almost the end of March and their opening was planned for the eighth of May, ready for their first big event the day after on Liberation Day. Charlie wasn't worried. They were slightly ahead of schedule now, thankfully, having completely finished Remi's bakery, decorated three bathrooms upstairs and one downstairs, as well as a further four bedrooms.

He was looking forward to finishing work on the library and stood back, narrowly avoiding knocking into one of the piles of numbered boxes that contained neatly packed books they had taken down from the shelves to wipe them two weeks before. He stared at the cold fireplace and pictured enjoying time in this room once it had been decorated. He looked forward to sitting in one of the two large, dark green, worn leather high-back chairs that they would put back either side of the roaring fire, a glass of whisky in one hand and a book in the other as he relaxed.

They really had worked hard to get this far, he decided, and in only a few months, too. There was still a lot more to do though with plenty more bedrooms and smaller rooms to decorate and turn into studies, or smaller snugs, for guests to use. The outbuildings that they were planning to turn into useful spaces could also wait, as could finishing the walled garden, which would take months yet, and they still needed to take down and replace the old summer house but that would have to wait until they could afford to replace it with a new one, probably next year.

After the library they would work on finishing the front garden. It was what their guests would see first, so it was vital to finish it, as was bringing the damaged pond and fountain back to its former glory. For now though, Charlie was satisfied. Well, almost. The two of them, together with help from their friends, had achieved far more than he had expected they might in the few months since they had begun their renovations on Chateau de Caesarea and at least now they should be ready for their grand opening.

He had checked the forecast that morning, relieved the weather was slightly warmer now. Water had got into one of the unused attic rooms after the most recent frost had thawed. It had worked its way down through hidden nooks and crannies in the building and ended up flooding the main living room. Their friends had rushed to their aid, helped redecorate the area and encouraged them when deliveries had then been delayed due to storms in the English channel.

He sighed contentedly. At least they had got this far with their renovations. He knew that as exhausted as he felt, Portia must be feeling just as wiped out. Reminding himself that varnishing the shelves would not be finished if he didn't stop daydreaming, Charlie picked up a screwdriver and prised open a tin of varnish. As he placed the lid onto the dust sheet, his eye was drawn to a small, tooled leather book on top of one of the boxes. He hadn't noticed it before. The leather was worn and the book looked well-used.

Intrigued, Charlie lifted it and saw it was a diary. He opened it to have a quick look inside. It had belonged to his great aunt. Surprised, but feeling a little voyeuristic reading someone's private thoughts, he went to close it when the word jewellery caught his eye. Leaning back against the book case Charlie opened the diary again, hoping to find an answer to their jewellery mystery.

I love him with all my heart,

he read,

but as much as I yearn for him to overcome his urge to gamble, I now know he has failed and is lost once more. I cannot allow him to sell my mother's jewellery, or that which he has given to me in happier times, and have little choice but to hide those treasures and other more valuable pieces and ensure I keep them safe in case we need to sell them to keep a roof over our

*heads. The thought that I daren't even write where that place is
in this, my most secret book, saddens me to my core.*

Charlie stopped reading, stunned to have come across this very page. He needed to show the book to Portia. He got to his feet and, hearing a shriek, dropped it onto the box. His heart raced at the shock in Portia's voice and all thoughts of the diary and varnishing vanished when seconds later Megan burst in through the library door.

'There you are,' she said flustered, her eyes wide.

'What is it? Is someone hurt?'

She held the door open waving for him to follow her. 'Not a person. Quickly, they need you upstairs straightaway.'

'What now?' he groaned, following her up the stairs at a run. 'I don't understand.'

'The ceiling's come down in one of the bedrooms,' she called breathlessly as she hurried ahead. 'The one on the other side of the hall to mine. The other large one.'

'It can't have done,' he said, horrified to have yet another thing go wrong.

They reached the top of the stairs and found Remi and Jack mopping water. Portia pushed past with piles of towels in her arms.

'There's been another ruddy leak.'

Charlie willed himself to remain calm, resisting the urge to walk out of the chateau and never go back. The rest of them were doing a great job clearing up and needed his help. He looked up to see the ceiling had come down, landing on the beautiful bed they had sourced second-hand and thought themselves unbelievably lucky to find. The mattress hadn't even been slept in yet and he presumed it would be ruined.

'What a mess.'

Jack shook his head. 'This is a bit of a disaster, isn't it?'

'Is this the only room that's been affected?' Charlie asked, aware that water could seep unseen into all sorts of hidden places.

Remi cocked his head to one side. 'The room next door has some damage but not as bad as this.'

He needed to think quickly. 'Has someone thought to turn off the stopcock?'

'I did,' Jack said.

'Well done. Now we need to stop this damage affecting any other rooms.' He looked at the puddle of water covering most of the floor and his heart dipped as he thought of the room directly below where they were standing. 'Has anyone checked the living room?'

Remi and Jack looked at each other before both shook their heads.

'Portia?' Charlie asked, hoping she had been in to their prime lounge area that they were all so proud of.

Portia shook her head slowly and grimaced. 'Please don't say that's been damaged, I couldn't bear it after all our hard work in there.'

Without giving himself a chance to think, Charlie ran back downstairs and opened the living room door. He glanced up, horrified to see the huge bulge where the plaster and paint they had recently spent painstaking hours redoing ballooned, ready to collapse to the floor.

He heard footsteps behind him.

'Oh no, Charlie,' Portia groaned, tears in her eyes. 'Not again.'

'That ceiling looks as if—' Jack hadn't finished his sentence when Charlie realised they had very little time to remove the pristine furniture before that too was damaged by another falling ceiling. They had six weeks before opening and everyone knew that it took six weeks at the very least for deliveries of furniture to reach the island.

'Quick,' he said running in. 'Help me get this lot out into the hallway.'

Portia called for Remi and Megan to join them and the five of them pulled and carried furniture as quickly as they could from the room.

'Just dump it anywhere in the hall for now,' Charlie instructed, manoeuvring past Remi with Jack to carry the beautiful, cushioned sofa out of the room.

They had just managed to get it safely out when there was a crack and the ceiling plaster fell. Charlie turned to see water cascading down through the rafters and closed the door behind him to protect the rescued furniture.

'Right, let's take this lot further down the hallway in case water comes out onto these tiles before we have a chance to mop everything up in there.

Once satisfied everything was safe, Charlie helped Jack to clean up the water pooling on their living room floor, while Portia, Megan and Remi continued clearing up in the bedroom above.

After several hours clearing up the two rooms, the five of them sat at the dining room table, exhausted and despondent, but freshly showered and wearing clean, dry clothes. Jack and Charlie had scraped much of the plaster from the ceilings and that had also been cleared away and Portia had cried down the phone to Oliver who immediately collected four industrial sized dehumidifiers that Charlie had sourced to dry out the rooms.

Charlie heard the front door open and Oliver and Lexi call out to them.

'In here,' he called gloomily. 'Come through.'

He watched the door open and Lexi walked in carrying two

shopping bags, followed by Oliver with another bag and seven pizza boxes. 'We thought you could do with some cheering up.'

Charlie remembered the diary. Determined to cheer Portia, Remi and Jack and divert their attention from the latest disaster, he got up to leave the room.

'Where are you going?' Portia asked. 'You've done enough today, Charlie.'

He tapped the side of his nose with a finger. 'Just you wait there. I have a surprise for you and I think you're going to like it.'

43

PORTIA

Portia swallowed another delicious mouthful of pizza while watching Charlie talking animatedly about his great aunt's diary. It was a relief to have something else to think about other than the damage and endless knockbacks that seemed to come with the renovation.

He pointed to the page where his great aunt's elegant script filled the paper. 'I can prove to the police that the jewellery is mine now,' he said, resting a hand on his chest. 'I'm so grateful I found this.'

'It is exciting,' Portia admitted, beaming at him. 'Although I feel sorry for your great aunt that she needed to hide it from the man she loved.'

'I was thinking the same thing.' He turned to Lexi and Oliver before taking a sip of the red wine the couple had also brought with them. 'Though, I've no idea how we're going to be able to open on Liberation Day now.'

Portia wondered what they should tell their guests and if they could find suitable places for them to stay at such short notice.

'We're going to have to postpone our opening.' He rubbed his face. 'I'm dreading letting the couple down and telling them we won't be able to host their birthday party after all.'

Portia understood his anxiety. 'I only hope they can find somewhere else so near to the event.' It was a nightmare.

'Hey, guys.' Oliver rested his knife and fork on his plate. 'Enough pessimism. At least now you've found out about the jewellery.'

'That is true,' Remi agreed, although Portia couldn't see how that helped their current situation.

'I suppose one positive aspect,' Charlie said thoughtfully, 'is that at least now I can have the jewellery valued and sold. I intend keeping certain pieces, of course.' Portia caught his eye and wondered why he was looking at her in such a strange way. He cleared his throat. 'The rest I will sell. I know that my great aunt would want me to put the money towards the renovations and I sense she's looking down on us, happy to see we're bringing her beloved home back to its former glory.'

Portia raised her glass. 'I agree. Good for you.'

'Finally, we have some good news.' Remi finished looking at the diary and placed it back on the table.

Charlie rested his palm on the cover and closed his eyes. 'I like being positive like Oliver, and we must remember we've had this exciting thing happen.' He sighed. 'But, that said, I still can't realistically see how we're going to be able to go ahead with the opening or party as planned, can you?'

Portia watched Oliver look from one to the other of them. He wasn't used to anything getting the better of him, but even he seemed to know when the odds were stacked too heavily against them.

'What's stopping you?' he asked, looking at each of them.

'Oliver, I would have thought that was obvious.' Portia said, seeing the look of disbelief on Charlie's face at Oliver's question. 'How can you even ask such a thing?'

'There's always a solution if you look hard enough.'

She supposed she needed to spell it out to him. 'Oliver, you know it's taken us months to do these two main reception rooms. We only have six weeks until our opening.' She sighed. 'The furniture upstairs is ruined and although we managed to save the furniture down here, we couldn't get the paintings out in time, so most of them will be ruined.' As she spoke, the enormity of what had happened hit her and she found she couldn't say anything further as her throat constricted. Charlie took her hand in his.

'It's fine,' he whispered. 'We'll come up with something.'

'I have a feeling Oliver already has,' Lexi said, adoration in her voice and something else, Portia noticed. Hope?

'I have.'

'What do you suggest?' Remi asked doubtfully.

'First of all, I want you to remember you're not alone with all this,' Oliver said.

'Go on,' Charlie said, sounding weary.

'It's simple. We use everyone's strengths to help.'

'Strengths?' Portia wondered what he was getting at but knew Oliver well enough to start feeling slightly reassured. He did have a plan, and knowing how he always played to win, suspected it was going to be a very good one. 'Go on.'

'I think it goes without saying that Lexi and I, along with other friends of yours from the boardwalk, will offer their assistance. Everyone has talents they're sure to bring when they come to help.'

'Such as?' Charlie asked, leaning forward and resting his elbows on the table.

'Jools and Marius are brilliant painters. They can help with the painting and any effects you need them to. Between all of us we'll soon have you back on track, trust me.'

Portia did. She gave him a grateful smile.

'Lexi and I aren't as good at painting but we're happy to help with that too, where we can. I'll call in a few favours and get some plasterers in here to get started on the two rooms as soon as they're dry enough to be worked on.'

'This all sounds good to me so far,' Charlie said, glancing at Portia and cheering her slightly with his smile. 'And I can call in some favours from guys I know on the island. Thanks, Oliver. Portia and I are extremely grateful to all of you for helping us through this.'

'There's no need for gratitude,' Lexi said. 'You'd do the same for us and we all know that. Alessandro will help, and I know Tony and Claire will pitch in, although Claire will probably be needed to look after baby Maia while Bella and Jack are up here, but I'm sure she'll want to visit and make pots of tea, that sort of thing. Sacha will help feed everyone, like she always does and don't forget she can help with any food needed for the party, if you need her to.'

'Betty is happy to help with anything, too' Portia added. 'She said so the other day when I bumped into her at the market.'

'You see? Everything will be fine, you just need to stay positive, work hard and trust that it'll all fall into place.'

'Not fall down, like our ceilings seem to have a habit of doing,' Charlie joked.

Portia nudged him. 'It's not a laughing matter,' she grinned. She had a sneaking suspicion Oliver wasn't just guessing that their friends were happy to help. 'Have you already been in contact with them all, Oliver?'

Oliver nodded. 'Of course. I couldn't offer their help without asking them first.' He raised an eyebrow. 'Even if Lexi was going to insist they would all do whatever was needed.'

'Well, it's true,' Lexi said. 'We all stick together when one of us from the boardwalk needs us.'

'I'm not from the boardwalk,' Remi said, an amused glint in his eyes.

'Nor me,' Portia added, aware it didn't really matter to her friends.

It occurred to her, listening to her friends, that before her visit to London she had thought she missed her old life there, but all she had been doing was hanging on to Alistair's memory. These newer friends of hers and Charlie had been there for them every step of the way since they had come to live here. A rush of love warmed her and she realised she loved Jersey life and the board-walk community and already felt a part of it.

'Oh,' Lexi added, interrupting her thoughts. 'I forgot to mention that Bella said she can source any antiques you need that she doesn't already have, like paintings, furniture, that sort of thing. Whatever it is we'll make sure you have it.'

'I think I'm going to cry,' Portia said.

'You are?'

The look of disbelief on Oliver's face made her laugh instead. 'Maybe not.'

44

CHARLIE

Opening Day

Charlie stood proudly next to Portia at the side of the living room watching their guests sing 'Happy Birthday' to their guest of honour.

'We made it after all,' he whispered, still surprised that everything had come together in time just as Oliver had insisted it would. 'You've certainly come into your own hosting this event, Portia. You must know that.'

'I suppose I do.' She smiled. 'Mind you, we couldn't have done this without Oliver's help. Although he does love the drama of having a problem to fix,' she added quietly. 'I'm glad he persuaded us to keep going though, I would have hated to let these lovely people down.'

Charlie shuddered at the thought. 'We would have ruined our reputation before we'd even begun building one if we had needed to cancel this party.'

He smiled at Alessandro waiting with Sacha for the guest whose birthday it was to make the first incision into the cake and make a wish, so that they could cut the cake into neat slices and begin handing it out.

'It was kind of Megan to agree to have her photo taken with the party guests, wasn't it?' Portia said. 'I'm not sure the couple knew who she was, but their daughter and her friends were enthusiastic enough for everyone when they spotted Megan coming down the stairs just after they arrived.'

'I don't know why people get so excited to meet celebrities.' Charlie looked over at the group of young women and their partners singing while shooting surreptitious glances in Megan's direction. It made him happy to see her standing hand in hand with Remi on the opposite side of the room. They looked very much in love and he was happy for his friend.

'So much for keeping their relationship under wraps,' Portia whispered. 'I'm sure there'll be hundreds of photos of the pair of them online after the guests start posting their photos on their social media accounts.'

'Knowing Megan, she will have thought of that.' Charlie saw Remi's feelings reciprocated in Megan's smile. She had brought so much joy to his friend's life. 'Maybe they decided this was a good way of sharing that they're a couple without her having to come out and make any sort of announcement.'

'Probably.'

Charlie looked down at the woman who meant everything to him. 'Happy?'

'Yes,' she said, giving his hand a gentle squeeze. 'You?'

'I am now we've made it this far.' He loved her without make-up, wearing her dungarees and work boots but suspected Portia was enjoying being dressed up, her hair freshly cut and a manicure done. 'You look very beautiful, but then you always do.'

She pulled a face at him. 'I don't at all.'

'No regrets?' He thought back to how difficult things had seemed for them both on occasion.

'Not now.' She sighed. 'Although there were a couple of times when I wondered what on earth I must have been thinking to suggest we do this renovation in the first place. It took me a while to realise it but now I can't imagine feeling more content than I do being here with you.'

Charlie pushed his arm against her gently. 'That makes me very happy.' He held her closer to him and lowered his voice. 'I have to admit there were times when I wondered if keeping this place was going to be the thing that broke us both.'

'Thankfully we've got through that. No regrets?'

He thought of his fears and how pushing himself too hard had almost ruined everything for them. He had learned so much in the past few months. Life lessons he clearly needed, and by the sound of things Portia felt that she had moved on from much of what troubled her. 'None.'

'I wish we could have a lie-in tomorrow morning,'

'You're not the only one.' Then, thinking of the party guests and the clearing up the two of them needed to do before their departure, and the preparation for the next group arriving in a few days, he shrugged. 'I think lie-ins are going to have to wait for a few months yet.'

'That's a shame, but I think you could be right.' She looked up into his eyes and smiled. 'I'm sure it'll be worth the wait.'

'I imagine it will.'

45

PORTIA

The following day

Portia handed the final glass to Lexi for her to dry. 'It's very good of you all to come here again now our guests have left. I couldn't believe it when Charlie told me you were all going to be here.'

Lexi dried the glass and holding it up to the light studied it before polishing it briefly and setting it down on the table next to the dozens of other clean glasses. 'We were very happy to help out. The pair of you must be exhausted after the past few months with so little rest.'

Portia dried her hands and watched Lexi hang the tea towel over the rail in front of the warm range. 'It's still very generous of you and I'm grateful.' She saw amusement flit briefly across her friend's face. 'What?'

'It's nothing.' Lexi smiled. 'I was just thinking about something Oliver said.'

Not wishing to intrude on anything private, Portia let the matter drop. 'Right, shall we go and find the others?'

They walked through to the living room and Portia realised she hadn't seen anything of Charlie for over an hour. Noticing Jack walk past the open window she asked him if he knew where Charlie might be.

'Sorry, I haven't seen him for a while,' he replied without stopping.

Was she missing something? There was a definite air of suspense. She couldn't quite put her finger on it. Portia shook her head. She was over-tired but so was everyone else after their late night and clearing up today. She rubbed her face with her hands.

'You OK?' Lexi asked coming up behind her. 'Maybe you should have a sit down somewhere?'

Portia would have loved to but didn't think it appropriate for her to take it easy when their friends were busy tidying the chateau for them. 'I'm fine, thanks.' She smiled to reassure Lexi.

Lexi opened her mouth to say something when Portia noticed Remi's van coming along the driveway. It slowed and parked at the side of the building and she assumed he must have been out doing his bread deliveries. Everyone had been such a help to her and Charlie. She would have to find a way to thank them. A lunch, or dinner, maybe?

'There you are,' Charlie said, appearing at the open living room window, as if she had been the one missing for ages. He had a wide smile on his face and seemed pretty pleased with himself.

Portia grinned back at him, happy to see him so cheerful when he must be exhausted. 'Did you want me for something?'

He tapped the side of his nose. 'I do. I need you to go with Lexi and join the rest of our friends in the secret garden.'

'What are you up to?'

He shook his head. 'You'll find out. I'll see you there in a minute.'

Portia turned and saw Lexi grinning at her. 'Do you know what this is about?'

Lexi seemed amused by something. 'Now, that would be telling.'

Portia shrugged. Her tiredness was probably getting the better of her. She supposed she would find out what he had been up to if she did as he asked. 'Come along then, let's find out what this is all about.'

Lexi linked arms with her. 'Let's go through the back of the house.'

As it was the quickest route to the secret garden, Portia was happy to agree. She didn't think her feet had ever been so sore.

They walked outside, through the gate and into the walled secret garden. Portia was surprised to see all their friends already waiting there. Some of them moved back and she saw Remi and Megan each holding what looked like a dog lead. Noticing Lexi's excited smile, Portia realised there were dogs at the end of the leads. She gasped in delight and hurried over.

They were adorable, their fluffy tails wagging enthusiastically. One was black with long skinny legs and a pug nose, the other was much smaller, sandy in colour with short legs. She wondered what mixture the little dogs could be and crouched down to stroke their heads.

'They're so cute,' she said her heart contracting when the taller one licked her hand and the little one nudged her with his nose.

'This one is Barney,' Remi said, indicating the smaller dog.

'Yes, and this one is Cello.'

'Are they ours?' she asked, hoping she was right. 'It's so typical of Charlie to surprise me like this.'

'They are,' Lexi confirmed.

Portia looked around to see if Charlie was anywhere nearby. 'Where is he?' She wanted to thank him for his perfect surprise.

'He'll be here soon.' Oliver said.

'There's a small bag attached to the taller one's collar,' Megan said, pointing at it. 'Why don't you have a peek inside?'

This day was getting more surreal by the moment, Portia thought, reaching forward to stroke the dog so that it wouldn't get a fright when she removed the small bag.

She untied the ribbon around the dog's collar and standing, pulled the top open carefully, peering inside to find a small box.

'What's this?' she laughed. 'It's not my birthday.'

She sensed movement behind her and noticed everyone's attention had shifted from her. There was a collective gasp and Portia turned to see what was going on.

Charlie was kneeling in front of her. Not exactly kneeling, she realised, her mouth dropping open – he was on *one* knee. 'Charlie? What are you—?'

His hand trembled as he reached up to take hers. It was Portia's turn to gasp. 'Is this what I think it is?' she whispered, unable to take her eyes off his.

'If you mean is this a proposal of marriage, then you'd be right.'

'Oh, Charlie...'

She followed his gaze as it dropped to the bag in her hand. 'Then this? She pulled the small box from the bag and opened it. 'It's... It's...'

'Beautiful?' Charlie suggested. 'Perfect?' He winced. 'Horrible?'

Portia's hand flew to her chest and she shook her head. 'You were right the second time. It's perfect,' she said, taking the diamond solitaire from the box and holding it in front of him, her hand shaking as she tried to stop her mind racing.

He grimaced.

'Are you in pain?'

He laughed. 'A bit. I think I'm kneeling on a stone.'

'Then get on with it and ask her the question, so you can stand up again,' Jack bellowed.

'Yes,' Portia said, unable to bear waiting a moment longer. 'Ask me, Charlie.'

He cleared his throat. 'My darling Portia, will you make me the happiest man alive and marry me?'

She bent down to him and hugged him tightly, kissing him.

'Is that a yes?' Megan asked.

Portia realised she hadn't actually answered Charlie's question. 'It is,' she said. 'Yes, Charlie, I will marry you.'

Their friends cheered and one of the dogs barked excitedly.

'Can I stand now?' Charlie groaned, before laughing and getting to his feet when she nodded. He took the ring from her and taking her hand, slipped it onto her finger.

'It fits exactly. How did you manage that?' Portia asked, turning her hand so that the sunlight caught the facets in the exquisite stone.

'Lexi helped by taking one of your rings to be measured.' He shook his head. 'Never mind that now.' He pulled her into his arms, taking her breath away as he kissed her.

She lost herself in his kiss until someone cleared their throat near to them.

'This has turned out to be a perfect day,' she said, kissing him again. 'First you buy two dogs...'

'They're adopted.' Charlie grinned. 'I have the papers in Remi's van.'

'And then you propose.' She didn't think she could ever be happier than she was at that moment. 'I know we're going to be blissfully happy, Charlie.'

She felt Charlie's lips press against hers briefly. 'I know it too.'

She had an idea. 'Ours could be the first wedding we host here at the chateau?'

'Why am I not surprised you thought of that?' he teased.

'What do you think?'

Charlie grinned. 'It's a perfect idea.'

ACKNOWLEDGMENTS

Firstly, I'd like to thank my husband Rob for feeding and walking the dogs and looking after everything else in our lives while I spend long hours blissfully lost in my fictional world.

Also my children James and Saskia, who are no longer surprised when I send them odd messages asking for character names, or checking whether bits of information might be correct that I need to use in a book.

To the wonderful team at Boldwood Books, especially Lucy Gilmour for her structural edits and brilliant suggestions that I know made this book a far better one than I had originally written. To my copy editor, Rose Fox, proofreader Gary Jukes, and editor, Rachel Faulkner-Willcocks, thank you all for your support and dedication bringing my books out into the world.

I couldn't possibly forget my best writing buddies, Christina Jones, Kelly J Clayton, Gwyn Bennett, Glynis Peters and Christie Barlow, all of them brilliant writers and inspirational to me and there in the background to make me laugh and provide inspiration whenever I need them.

And, of course to you, dear reader! Thank you for choosing to read this book, I hope you enjoyed Charlie and Portia's story.

ABOUT THE AUTHOR

Georgina Troy writes bestselling uplifting romantic escapes and sets her novels on the island of Jersey, where she was born and has lived for most of her life.

Sign up to Georgina Troy's mailing list for news, competitions and updates on future books.

Visit Georgina's website: https://deborahcarr.org/my-books/georgina-troy-books/

Follow Georgina on social media here:

facebook.com/GeorginaTroyAuthor

twitter.com/GeorginaTroy

instagram.com/ajerseywriter

bookbub.com/authors/georgina-troy

ALSO BY GEORGINA TROY

The Sunshine Island Series

Finding Love on Sunshine Island

A Secret Escape to Sunshine Island

Chasing Dreams on Sunshine Island

The Golden Sands Bay Series

Summer Sundaes at Golden Sands Bay

Love Begins at Golden Sands Bay

Winter Whimsy at Golden Sands Bay

Sunny Days at Golden Sands Bay

Snow Angels at Golden Sands Bay

Boldwood

Boldwood Books is an award-winning fiction publishing company seeking out the best stories from around the world.

Find out more at www.boldwoodbooks.com

Join our reader community for brilliant books, competitions and offers!

Follow us
@BoldwoodBooks
@TheBoldBookClub

Sign up to our weekly deals newsletter

https://bit.ly/BoldwoodBNewsletter